# Baby Grape and Huskey

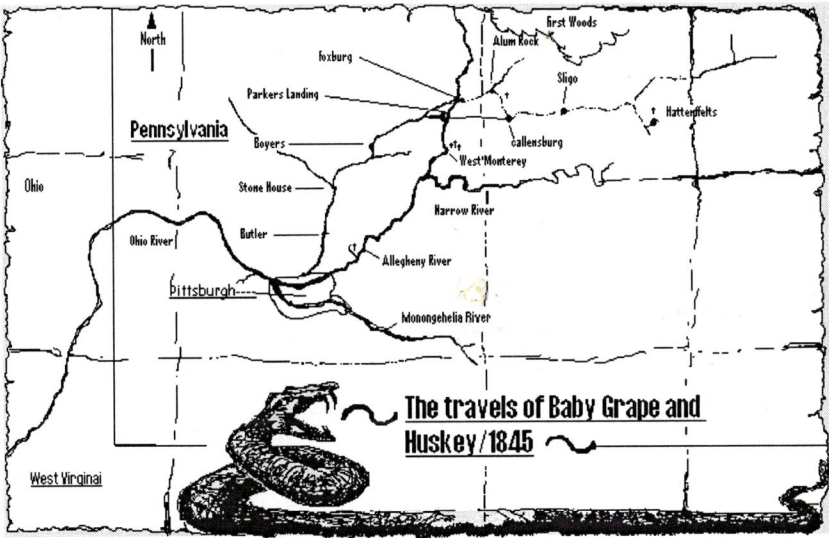

The travels of Baby Grape and Huskey/1845

Connen.
Hope you enjoy!

# Baby Grape and Huskey

## Thom Rogers

*Mill City Press*
*Minneapolis, MN*

Mill City Press, Inc.
212 3rd Avenue North, Suite 570
Minneapolis, MN 55401
612.455.2294
www.millcitypress.net

ISBN - 978-1-934937-12-9
ISBN - 1-934937-12-6
LCCN - 2008929716

Cover Illustration by Emily Zuzack
Cover Design and typeset by Sophie Chi

Printed in the United States of America

# Contents

Dedicated to: Louise W. Rogers, 1919-2008

# 1

## ~a whipping and a head start~

Toby bolted across the street through the steady rain. He ducked under an awning and wiped his forehead with the sleeve of his shirt. Carefully he edged along the building and then peered around the corner into the next street. No other boys were in sight. Nothing was there except a couple of delivery wagons, parked along the narrow streets. Their horses shook rain from their heads and pawed the pavement in agitation.

Toby ran across this street, avoiding the mud puddles, and reached the next corner. He looked down at his boots and noticed that they were still shining from yesterday's funeral.

As Toby leaned around the corner to check the next street, a hand reached around, caught him at the throat, and pulled him fully around the corner of the building. The older boy was larger than Toby and snarled in his face. "Empty your pockets!" the boy commanded. He jerked Toby several times to keep him off balance. Toby's eyes widened; he thought of the pocketknife, his father's. Before he could say anything the older boy shoved him into the wall and kneed him in the groin. Toby went down to one knee. The larger boy grabbed a handful of Toby's hair and wrenched his head back. Rain beat into his eyes and he couldn't clear them to see his tormentor.

Toby's mind raced, trying to decide what to do next. It was still early in the morning and there simply weren't enough people out yet to hear him.

Toby grimaced and whispered through his clenched teeth, "Go to hell!" The other boy pulled hard on his hair, nearly yanking it from his scalp. Toby felt the boy's hand groping at his pants pocket, fumbling for a second before he found Toby's knife. Toby struggled, but couldn't stop him. Within seconds, the thief had the knife and stepped back from Toby.

Toby wiped his eyes and looked at the thug. He realized he knew this boy, and also knew him to be a mean tormentor to other boys that worked in the area shops.

The older boy turned and trotted away. Toby was quick to his feet and started after the boy. "You filthy...give it back!" Toby shouted.The older boy looked back over his shoulder and smirked as he continued to trot along the sidewalk. He was already twenty feet ahead of Toby and broke into a run as Toby started to chase him.

As Toby closed in on the boy, he wondered what he'd do if he caught him. He knew the larger boy could beat him in a fight, and in another block he'd probably find his other buddies, all bullies. Toby figured that was the only reason he ran.

Passing the nearby wagon Toby glanced over and saw it! Lying coiled across the seat was a bullwhip.

Two strides later Toby had it in his hand, gripping the handle tightly. He let the whip uncurl and trail behind him. The older boy had seen the move and started to run for all he was worth, realizing that he might be in trouble.

Toby matched his every move. Each time the boy faked a dodge, Toby moved right up, gaining a step or two on the boy. The thief turned a corner and slipped on the wet brick street. He was nearly down, his one arm on the pavement, and his leg slid out from under him.

In one fluid movement, Toby stopped, ten feet from his target, and his arm came forward. He expertly flipped his wrist, drawing the tip of the whip down on his intended victim.

The leather of the whip's tip tore an inch by two-inch gash on the older boy's calf, just below his shorten pants. The boy grabbed his leg and howled in pain, but the sound of the drumming rain drowned out his cries. He looked up at Toby and tried to threaten him: "I'll get—!" Toby flicked the whip into the air and it found the older boy's ear and the side of his jaw. His earlobe split apart and flapped loosely. Blood burst out of the opening on his cheek. Blood was everywhere!

As the boy raised his other hand to protect his face he dropped the knife. Toby shouted, "Give it to me!" The boy tried to ignore Toby. "Give it to me NOW!" Toby shouted again. The boy slipped his trembling hand from his bleeding leg and slid the knife to Toby.

Toby bent to pick up the knife; the other boy, still defiant, said, "I'll get you someday and use that knife to…" Before he could finish the threat Toby raised the whip again, and that silenced the boy. Toby turned and walked back to the wagon without looking back. He coiled the whip and placed it neatly on the seat.

He looked down at the knife in his hand; it was wet with rain and speckled with the boy's blood. Toby rubbed it against his pants to clean it, shook off the rain water, and put it back in his pocket before he continued to the workshop. This time he didn't bother to look down any side streets or around corners.

As he trotted along the sidewalk he realized that his heart was pounding hard. He turned around several times to make sure the other boy's friends hadn't found him and decided to come after Toby. After deciding he was safe, he slowed down. As his breathing became more even he resumed his normal stride and began to whistle softly.

◊ ◊ ◊

It was only 10:30 in the morning and he was tired already. Toby thought about his first day of work and wondered if he could make the twelve hour shift that his father had done six days a week for as long as Toby could remember. Now Toby, at 14, was assigned to work as an apprentice to old Abe in the factory's workshop.

◊ ◊ ◊

Abe told Toby that they were going to finish work on this large whiskey still. It was about three feet in diameter by three feet high and had a collared opening in the top that was about sixteen inches in diameter. It had a large ball top and a lyne arm that would be used to turn grain "mash" into whiskey. Since Toby was the smallest apprentice -and the new kid in the shop, he spent the morning inside the still's pot.

It was miserable work, and Toby's ears rang from all the hammering as Abe pounded rivets into the top cap of the still. Toby's job was to hold the buck hammer against the head of each rivet as Abe peened a roundness into the head of the rivet on the outside of the pot. All the while Abe muttered to himself, something about having to finish the still *THIS* day! He seemed angry

3

and didn't say much to Toby all morning.

That was alright with Toby, because he couldn't hear much more than the ringing in his head. It was like standing inside a large bell while someone beat on it from the outside. It was fairly dark inside the pot. But then, the workshop itself wasn't well-lit. Not much light came through the grimy windows that lined Front Street. Even on a sunny day, the air outside was choked with smoke from the steel mills and other fabrication shops in the downtown Pittsburgh area. But this morning's rain further added to the darkness in the interior of the building.

Nearly all of the workers in the shops were foreigners. You could hear a dozen or more languages in the different workshops and factories across the city. The only common language seemed to be misery, and little of it communicated the strife of their lives there. Some of the men had helpers and some had their sons working with them. Even if the helpers weren't paid, they learned the trade and gained experience. Boys of all ages went to work and choked on the smoke as they wore it in their clothes, their hair, their curtains at home—and even their beds. Yet, somehow they wore their ties, their suit coats, and their dignity with a pride—but their eyes were greyed with the same dullness....

Toby used to visit his father in this workshop and marvel at the copper bathtubs, cooking ware, and some kettles large enough for Toby to sleep in. His father told him that these would be used for doing laundry, dying clothes, and preserving fruits and vegetables in the fall. Toby's father sometimes talked to him about how the copper metal was two things at once: hard and soft. It was hard on its own, but a man with a hammer and heat could shape it into different forms.

As Toby thought about his father, he suddenly realized that the hammering had stopped and people were talking. Something touched him in the darkness of the still. A hand as large as a ham reached in and pushed Toby's head down. He looked up and saw Abe looking in, touching his finger to his lips, telling Toby to be quiet.

Toby wondered what was going on. He tried to stand up but an oilskin fell in on top of him. He wondered if this was a trick. The older men often made fun of the apprentices constantly—and Toby wondered if this was a joke about to happen.

He heard someone say his name and was about to answer when he realized that several men were outside talking.

"...The boy was supposed to show up this morning, but I haven't seen him yet."

"You said he just lost his father? When was that?"

Toby listened, but his hearing was still off from all that hammering. "His father was killed last Thursday. The funeral was yesterday. But, I haven't seen the boy." Toby realized that Mr. Howard, one of the shop owners, was talking. *Doesn't Mr. Howard know that I'm inside the still?*, Toby wondered. Why was Mr. Howard lying? Then again, Toby hadn't actually *seen* Mr. Howard that morning, so it wasn't really a lie.

"Are you sure that you've got the right boy, Magistrate?" Mr. Howard asked.

The other voice answered loudly: "Yes, sir! Been at the hospital and saw the boy meself, I did! He's got terrible wounds!"

Toby realized that they were talking about the boy who had stolen his pocketknife. *That boy deserved the whippin' I gave him!*, Toby thought. Still, he didn't want to get in trouble for it. Abe had said nothing so far and Toby wondered if he would tell the Magistrate, a Court Officer, that he was inside the still. Toby shivered and gripped the buck hammer, wondering what would happen to his mother and sisters if he went to jail since he was now the sole bread winner for the family. Mr. Howard's partner, Mr. Rodgers, had visited the funeral yesterday and given Toby this job. Mr. Rodgers said he wanted to help the family since Toby's dad had worked here all these years.

The officer spoke again: "Well, sir, I have to find him. Serious problem it is with all that blood loss. And the lad's mum! Poor thing is beside herself with worry. If the kid runs, it'll be worse—far worse! The judge won't be too understanding."

Toby heard Abe clear his throat as if he was going to speak. Fear gripped Toby's throat and he felt like he might suffocate.

"That other boy," Abe said. "He'd be the Irish lad that hangs with a couple o' others nex' street over?"

"Seems so." The officer spoke haltingly, as if waiting for Abe to help explain Toby's disappearance.

"Them's a bad bunch! Bad bunch," Abe added as he spit on the floor and used his foot to drag sawdust over the spot, which made the officer step back. It also made Mr. Howard smirk.

"You'll let me know if the lad's about then." Mr. Howard and the Magistrate were walking away and their voices faded into the hammering elsewhere in the shop. Another shop-rag dropped down on Toby's shoulder. He looked up and saw Abe's hand motioning him to stay put.

It was another ten minutes before Toby looked out. Abe looked at him, his eyebrows furrowed. He tilted his head towards the shop office but said nothing. Toby pushed himself out of the opening in the top of the still and dropped onto the blocking that held the still off the floor. As he walked to the office, several of the other workers and apprentices glanced at him without missing a hammer swing.

The secretary pointed her chin towards Mr. Rodgers office, motioning Toby to enter. He walked in and saw his boss's back. Toby waited a moment and tried to decide if he should say something. Before he could make up his mind, Mr. Rodgers spoke. "…I won't turn around, in case they ask me if I've seen you. Do you understand?"

Toby cleared his throat. "Yes sir, Mr. Rodgers. I wanted to explain…" The man interrupted him.

"…I knew your father for twenty years. He helped me when I first started, even waited on paychecks when I couldn't pay him. He was a very good man—the best. I KNOW he wouldn't approve of this."

"Sir, he STOLE my dad's knife!" Toby wished Mr. Rodgers would look at him so he could see he was telling the truth.

Mr. Rodgers was quiet for a moment. Then he said, "I understand. I thought it'd be something like that. Still, it's not for me to decide! For your family's sake I'm going to help the only way I can."

Toby waited. Both of them stared out the grimy windows and watched as the rain continued pelting the window glass. Mr. Rodgers still didn't turn around. Toby held his hat in his hands, nervously sliding it in through his fingers as he waited.

Finally Mr. Rodgers sighed and said, "This night there is a delivery cart leaving here for Sligo, that's about a hundred miles—north. You'll go along to deliver that still you've been working on. It's a long ride—probably several weeks. You won't be able to go home first! You'll wait in the tool room, and early in the morning Lew will come and fetch you. Then you can go with him to deliver this whiskey still. I will pay your wages to your mother while you're gone. After you get back, things should be quieter— and healed, I hope! I think there are some clothes in the shop bin that might fit you. Take them along. It won't be so bad; Lew will—well, it won't be too bad."

Toby thought Mr. Rodgers didn't sound so sure about that. He also thought he'd heard the name Lew before when his dad had whispered to his mum sometimes. But there was no time to think about all that now.

◊ ◊ ◊

Toby lie curled under a workbench, using the clothes he'd found as a pillow. He'd been awake most of the night thinking about his mum and sisters. What they must think! *If I could just tell them what really happened*, he thought. His stomach growled, but there was nothing to eat. Eventually he drifted into an uneasy—and hungry—sleep. Not long after that Toby woke with a start when a metal door slammed open.

"Ok, killer!" a man's voice bellowed. "It's Lew! Come to sneak you outta here!"

Toby crawled out from under the bench in the direction of Lew's lantern. Again, he remembered his dad's voice telling his mum about Lew. Lew held up the lantern and Toby could see his face. He was a young man with a handsome face, even though it had several deep scars and a nose that looked like it had been broken and never mended. He wore a slouch hat and suspenders over a tight fitting blue shirt. He was smooth shaven and looked like he was going to a dance. His chest was very broad for a short man, and Toby could see the muscles through the sleeves of his shirt. His coal-black hair was oiled and his eyes were just as dramatic! They were a strange ice-blue color.

"So how ya doin' this fine morning?" bellowed Lew as he went about the shop gathering a couple of tools, a can of grease with a paintbrush in it, and a couple of pry bars. "Here." He thrust the bars into Toby's hands and Toby sank under the weight of them. He then realized how strong Lew was!

"Gotta move soon. We have to cross town and head north," Lew said. He moved in a stride that matched that of a work horse. Toby followed behind him with his borrowed clothing dragging on the dirty shop floor and the bars cutting into his hands.

They went out to a cart behind the building in a small enclosed lot where items for the shop were stored. "Ya gonna like where we're goin'. It's just too bad the trees ain't out yet," Lew said as he opened a door to the street and pulled a mule into the courtyard. "Whoa," he said to the mule. "Ya ever been north?" Lew asked Toby as he hitched up the mule to the cart. Toby didn't say anything; he just shook his head.

Lew kept talking. "Been better if'n we had the wagon, but it's been loaded and gone. But we'll make do. It's easier for Beans—or 'Bea' as I call her—to pull anyway. Hell, she don't mind bein' wit a criminal like you!" This time Lew erupted with a laugh at his own joke.

Toby guessed that he should smile at it too and gave Lew a faint grin.

"I was trying to get back my knife," Toby started to say. He wanted to tell the whole story but Lew wasn't listening and interrupted him.

"Whoa—plenty o' time for that! We got a long, long ride. Good trip though." Lew winked at him as he led the mule and cart around and lifted up the seat of the cart. He held the lantern aloft as he counted items in the toolbox. Satisfied, he looked at the shop door and made sure it was locked. He pointed at the still on the back of the wagon and said, "Get inside and don't talk. Once we're outta town and it's safe you can join me on the seat."

Toby tossed his extra clothes inside and climbed in after them. There were still hours to go until daylight, and Toby dozed inside the still, his body rocking with the movement of the cart and his side resting against the cool copper.

Toby woke up with a painful jolt to his face. He yelled and realized where he was. The cart had hit a rock in the road and thrown his head against the side of the pot. "Ow!" He rubbed his cheekbone. It started to throb and became too tender to touch.

"Quiet boy!" Lew yelled. "Pull that oilcloth on ya, and keep quiet. There's a rider comin'!" Before he pulled the oilcloth over his head Toby glanced up at the sky and noticed that it looked like early morning.

◊ ◊ ◊

# 2

## ~lies and a white bone handle~

Toby heard the rider approach. As he listened, he continued to rub his swollen cheekbone. He placed his face against the cool inside wall of the still, which helped to ease the pain.

"So, Bean, Sooo!" Toby heard Lew command the mule as the cart slowed to a stop.

"Mornin'." Lew's voice carried into the still, and Toby listened. He suddenly realized that he had to pee and squirmed a bit trying to get comfortable.

Another man's voice replied, "Morning, sir. 'Ave you seen anything of a boy along this way?"

"No boy on the road here!" Lew wasn't lying either, Toby thought. He wasn't *on* the road exactly. "Some boy get hisself lost?" Lew asked the rider.

"No, sir, got one on the run. Seems he bullwhipped a kid in town and they're pretty hot to find him. I 'eared the mother of the boy is related to someone of 'portance." Toby heard the horse scuffing its hooves near the cart. He imagined the man looking into the top of the still; he tried to quietly cover himself.

"Well, can't be of much help to you, officer." Lew's voice sounded a little disrespectful. Toby wished the man would leave. His bladder was near bursting!

"What kinda load you haulin'?" the rider asked.

"Copper kettle," Lew answered curtly.

There was a pause and the officer spoke. "Where you deliverin' to?"

"Quite a ways north." Lew replied curtly.

"Well, have a good trip, and if ya see the kid, ya watch him. He's dangerous.

9

They told us to beat him if he gives us any trouble."

Toby was furious. He wanted to stand up and tell the rider his story.

"I 'spect they'll offer a reward for him," the rider said as his horse danced in a circle.

"You reckon?" asked Lew. "Whaddya suppose it'd be?"

Toby didn't like the sound of Lew's voice at the mention of the reward; it had a little bit of interest in it that Toby thought curious.

"Dunno, but you keep an eye out." With that the rider turned and rode hard in the direction they were traveling.

Toby waited as long as his bladder could stand it and then said, "I gotta go!" He pushed himself out of the top of the still and jumped from the moving cart. He caught his balance and ran to the trees in the ditch area. Lew never slowed the cart. By the time Toby finished, Lew, Beans, and the cart—which was all he knew of this new place— were about a hundred yards away. He ran hard to catch them.

Breathlessly, he caught up and said, "Can I ride up front now?"

"Where did you get that shiner, boy?"

Toby touched his cheekbone and noticed his eye was swelling shut. "Inside, I 'spose. I hit the side of the pot when you hit on a rock or somethin'."

"You better stay hid, at least for the day. Tomorrow, we'll be quite a ways along. Doubt they'll hear of ya and your crime up north." Toby looked at Lew for a long moment and then resigned himself to riding in the tub again.

It was sometime in the afternoon when they stopped. Lew had found a low area where some water ran along the side of the road. He guided thecart to the shade of the bare trees and climbed down. He got some water in a canvas pail for the mule, then lifted the seat of the cart and pulled out a bag. He sat near the tree and opened the cloth bag. Toby was so damn hungry. It had been over a day since he'd eaten. And his muscles ached. He watched as Lew pulled bread and several yellow banana peppers from the bag. From seemingly nowhere—in one quick motion—Lew pulled out a knife and began to carve a slice of bread from the loaf.

Toby admired the knife. It had a white bone handle and the blade glinted in the morning sunlight. He watched how deftly Lew used it as he cut another piece of bread and handed it to Toby. He also speared a pepper and offered it to Toby as it hung from the end ofthe knife.

Toby knew those peppers. He'd seen some of the Italian men eating them wrapped in bread. What a lunch this was going to be! Toby imitated Lew and wrapped the pepper with the bread and hungrily took a big bite. Within seconds the bread melted away and his mouth started to burn. His lips were scorched and tears poured from his eyes. Toby dropped the sandwich and ran to the water. Lying on his stomach he pressed his face into the water and sucked it into his mouth. But the water didn't help—it couldn't cut through the oil of the peppers that clung to the inside of his mouth and lips.

He gasped for air after several drinks and heard Lew laughing. "Ya gotta get used to 'em, boy!" Tears streamed down Toby's face. He'd accidentally rubbed some of the oil of the peppers into his eyes. He sat there for several more minutes, drinking handfuls of water. Eventually he returned to Lew's side and looked. There was nothing else to eat but the peppers and bread. He looked on the ground and saw his unfinished sandwich. He picked it up and looked at Lew. He saw a smirk on Lew's face as Lew continued chewing and looking into the distance. Toby walked away and nibbled at the crust of the bread, but even that burned his mouth. He ate what he could and tossed the pepper into the woods.

After lunch Lew dozed under a tree. The day turned hot for May in Pennsylvania. Toby wasn't tired; he stood looking across the low mountains and at a hawk making a lazy circle in the sky. He was already missing his home. His mouth still burned and he wondered if he liked Lew. It seemed like a dirty trick not to tell him how hot the peppers were. His stomach hurt and it was empty except for some bread crusts and the oil of the pepper. He walked away from the area to stay hidden and let Lew sleep for awhile.

Toby sat and watched the mule munching on grass. Yesterday's events still played in his head. He could see the boy, half-sitting on the rain soaked street, holding his ear and leg, both dripping blood. Toby's father taught him to never back down and how to use a whip. Was it something he knew his son would need to know? He wondered if his mother understood what had happened. What had she heard? He wanted desperately to tell her about the fight himself to explain his side of things.

A low whistle broke his thoughts. He looked to the cart and saw Lew standing there. Toby walked to the cart as Lew was putting things away. "Guess you'd better get inside there, boy!" Lew said without looking at Toby. Come to think of it, Lew never looked at Toby. He climbed into the pot and felt the cart move as Lew climbed on.

They were off again; and the inside of the pot was stuffy and getting hot in the mid-afternoon sun. Toby could barely touch the surface without it burning. He tucked the extra clothing around him for protection. All in all, the ride was miserable. Toby crawled out once to throw up from the heat and the pepper oil and then once more to take a pee.

◊ ◊ ◊

# 3

## ~a pizzle and some bad apples~

Lew's voice woke him. He blinked several times and felt his swollen eye. "C'mon! We'll have to do some walkin'!"

Toby crawled out of the still, jumped from the cart and looked around. A trail wound up the hill in front of them. He could see that it disappeared into the woods. The road was wider now and it seemed better maintained. They walked along the trail beside the mule so that she had a lighter load to pull up the long hill.

Lew kept looking back and checking the road ahead. "Ya be ready to find a spot to hide if somebody else comes along," he said to Toby.

Toby nodded his agreement and knew that Lew had seen his head move, even though he wasn't looking at Toby. Lew seemed to see everything without turning his head.

The trail doubled back on itself several times and then ran along a ridge for quite a stretch. They could see down both sides of the leafless, wooded trail.

"Will we be eatin' soon, Mr. Lew?"

Lew snorted a laugh. "Didn't get you enuf lunch, eh?"

Toby looked at him and wondered if he was going to get any kind of an answer. "I haven't had anything else to eat since yesterday's breakfast that mum cooked."

Lew finally turned his face towards Toby with a hard look and said in sneering whisper, "I ain't your mum. We'll eat near dark. You just keep a look out for others!" Toby was astonished. Didn't Lew care that he needed to eat? Something rang in Toby's head, a memory: "…he's just damn mean-spirited." Those had been his father's words! That's the conversation he'd overheard between his mother and father. Toby looked at Lew, furious. But Lew seemed to be somewhere else, lost in thought. His eyes darted across the landscape, to a flying bird, towards the dark shadow of a fallen tree. He took in everything. Toby decided to try the same thing and to forget how hungry he was.

Not too much time passed when Lew spoke again. "Boy? You see it over there?" He jutted his jaw towards his downhill side of trail. Toby craned his neck and looked past the cart. He saw a rooftop, then another. It must be the village of Butler.

His thoughts again went to food. *Maybe there will be a tavern*, he thought. A vision of his mother's pies came to his mind and he could almost smell them.

"Get into the wood! Stay hid," Lew said out the corner of his mouth. Toby shrunk back from the cart and kept it in between him and the direction Lew was watching. He was now to the side of the road and off the crest of the hill. He was a good fifty feet from the cart and stepped behind a very large tree. Peering around the side of it, he watched as another larger cart approached. The driver seemed to be nodding as he rode, like he was half-asleep. Lew looked back and saw Toby's head peeking out. He frowned and then turned back to the other cart.

"Mornin'!" Lew yelled. The driver startled and sat up.

"You scared the pizzle outta me, mister!"

Lew sized the man up before speaking. "Ya ought to be watchin' the road for your horse's sake."

"This horse knows the road to Pittsburgh. Been travelin' it for years together!"

Lew smiled at the other man and said, "Still, I don't 'spect that horse would need your permission to break a leg, eh?"

"You're kinda a rile—'specially to a man that just woke up." The man was eyeing Lew's massive arms, sizing him up.

"Didn't mean to be that, mister." Lew laughed. Toby wondered what Lew was up to.

"What are you haulin'?" Lew asked the driver.

"Some of the apples that didn't spoil from last fall." The man wiped his nose on the back of his hand.

"That so?" Lew asked. "Could you spare some? Got me a long trip and didn't get time to prepare for it. The boss wanted this haul on the road this morning."

"That so?" The other man mimicked Lew and blew his nose on a dirty cloth. He seemed to smell an offer in the works.

"Course, Butler's not too far," Lew said. "I 'spect we—uh—I can get some supplies there. Maybe better apples." Lew hoped the other man didn't notice the slip–up, but he was busy looking at Bea, the mule.

"She is lookin' a bit hungry," the man said.

Lew quickly replied, "She's always hungry. You got tators?"

"Yep, always got them damn ol' things. Can you afford them?"

Lew started slowly. "Got a half penny…." He fumbled with his pants pocket.

"That ain't gonna get much," the man said. He pulled a plug of tobacco from his shirt and bit into it.

"Those tators gotta be soft after this winter." Lew studied the horizon.

The other man spat on the ground near Lew's cart wheel and looked at him. "They is fine, nothing wrong with 'em"

Lew held up the half-penny and saw the other man eyeing it up, his eyes opening slightly wider. "This get us a dozen tators?" Lew asked. "And a dozen soft apples?"

The other man drew a long breath and slowly nodded. "Just so," he said and added, "Only 'cause I care for your scrawny mule!"

They both smiled. The man stepped down from the wagon and Lew handed him the coin. They went to the rear of the cart and the man pulled open a bag. Several apples rolled onto the deck of the wagon. Even from where Toby was hiding he could tell that the apples looked bad. But he was so hungry his mouth started to water.

Lew snorted. "Ain't interested in them! You tryin' to poison my mule?"

The other man smiled and clenched the coin in his hand, "Deal's a deal!" he said, backing away.

In half a heartbeat Lew had the man by the throat and whipped out his bone-handled knife. The other man's eyes were wide with fear. "Ya probably ought to just take the whole bag," he said in a shaky voice.

Lew didn't move. His eyes bore into the other man's. He waited. "Ta-take a bag of tators, too!" the man stuttered.

Without ever taking his eyes off of the man's face, Lew released him and pulled two bags from the wagon. "You better get along," Lew said with a snarl.

"Yeah, I'll do just that." The man hopped to the side of his wagon and onto a spoke of the wheel, then up into the seat. "Eee-upp!" The horse jerked forward but the cart didn't move. The driver realized that the wooden brake handle was locked. He kicked it loose and the wagon leapt forward.

Before long the wagon disappeared south, down the long path towards Pittsburgh. Lew mounted his own cart, and without a whistle to Toby had the mule moving and continued on. Lew never looked back to see if Toby was there. By the time Toby caught up with him, Lew had eaten four apples. Toby trotted alongside the cart and looked at Lew. Lew kept his eyes on the road and finally asked, "You gonna walk or ride, boy?"

Toby looked longingly at the bags of apples and potatoes in the front of the cart, but it was clear that Lew wasn't going to give him any. He hopped onto the back of the cart. "Where we headin' next, Mr. Lew?" he asked.

"Next stop, after Butler, is the Ole Stone House, boy. It's a tavern-stagecoach stop. Now quit your yappin' and get in that still!"

Toby climbed into the pot and settled into his little nest of clothing. An apple dropped into the pot after him. It was a sad apple, and even in the near darkness of the still pot Toby could see the black spots and could feel its softened skin. He ate it anyway, and its mush was a dry paste in his mouth. He didn't have as much of an appetite as he'd had earlier. He'd seen the whole trading episode and figured the other man hadn't gotten one tenth of what the two bags were worth. Another apple fell into the pot. It was worse than the first.

"You gettin' full yet, boy?" Lew laughed through a mouthful of apples.

Toby wondered if the mule had eaten anything at all today.

◊ ◊ ◊

# 4

## ~a cold tator and a dark town~

"Take a peek, boy, but stay hidden," Lew said. Toby raised himself to the opening at the top of the still and then slowly pushed his head out. The sun had brightened, and through the trees Toby could see the town of Butler at the foot of the hill. It looked to be another two miles away. He thought he could see people moving along the streets. He looked behind the cart and checked the road. No other travelers were there, so he stood to his full height. He folded his arms on the rounded lip of the still's collar and imagined himself as someone important entering the town as part of a parade.

"Will we be there soon, Mr. Lew?" Toby asked excitedly.

"I will. You're gonna stay hid, and keep an eye on the cart—and Bea."

Toby stared at the back of Lew's head. He chewed on the inside of his cheek and wanted to argue, but he thought better.

Bean's footing was unsteady as she went down the hill and the cart pushed her forward. Lew pulled hard on the reins and held her back. Occasionally, one of her hooves slipped forward and the cart jolted her ahead.

They wound along the path for another hour and then found themselves at the bottom of the hill, facing a bridge that crossed a small stream into town. Lew guided the cart into a small clearing to the right of the bridge's entrance. They were no more than fifty feet from the water's edge below.

"Stay Put!" Lew ordered. Toby could hear the rustle of the cart's harnessing and Bea moving around as Lew untied her from the cart. Lew took out a potato and some apples and cut them up for the mule.

"Listen to me, boy. You're gonna stay here and mind Bea. Get some sleep, but *keep an eye on things*!" Lew's voice was commanding. "Stay outta sight, and don't talk to anybody! At 'bout midnight, you hitch Bea back up an' get your ass on this road, understand?"

Toby spoke hesitantly. "Yes."

"Get yourself straight through the town, and watch for the sign that says 'North.' Got that?"

"Yes, Mr. Lew." Toby chewed on the inside of his cheek.

"When you get past town—past the last house—you wait for me. I should be there ahead of you anyway."

There was some noise from the front of the cart as Lew dug through the box under the seat. "You understand all I tol' ya?"

"Yes sir, midnight on the north road."

"An' stay hid!" With that order Lew walked away and Toby could hear the leaves crunching under his feet.

Toby slunk into the still's tub again and settled in. When he felt that Lew was a good distance away, he crawled out of the still. He found the bag of apples first, but he was full of apples. He took two and offered them to Bea, who accepted them greedily. "I'm gonna watch out for you, Bea," he said. "And myself!" he added sourly, looking to the bridge and beyond. He pulled two potatoes from the other bag, one for him and one for the mule. They shared the food and waited for nightfall as Toby kept one eye on both directions of the road.

Sounds drifted from the town and on occasion Toby could hear music, shouts, and greetings from a building he assumed was a tavern. Toby was full. His stomach was happy and Bea seemed fine. Things would be fine, he mused, except it was getting cold! He thought of the clothes in the still. He climbed up onto the cart and back into the still, which he was beginning to think of as his new home. He felt for the woolen coat and pulled it on, thankful that it was heavy and warm! Again he stood up and looked around. Some stars shone through the bare trees and the lights of the town twinkled in the distance.

Suddenly Toby noticed a rider coming from the south! There was still enough light from the late dusk for the rider to make his way towards the town. But it was dark enough that Toby's campsite off the side of the road remained hidden. The rider passed without noticing Toby, the cart, or Beans.

Toby watched the road until it was completely dark and then settled down for the night. He drifted into a sleep but then woke from a horrible dream.

There was a child's face dripping blood, and Toby had a bloody whip in his hands. Toby started to cry in the dream. Hot tears slid from his cheeks, but he felt cold. When Toby shook awake from the dream, he immediately grabbed his pants pocket and felt the pocketknife. He gasped and drew deep breaths as he realized where he was and how he'd gotten here.

Toby looked up at the sky and the moon. Some fog had settled along the creek banks. It was probably less than fifty degrees by now and Toby reckoned by sunup it would be cold, probably in the upper thirties. He figured he still had another couple of hours before he had to ride out to meet Lew. *But why not wait on the north side of town? After all, it might be warmer*, Toby thought. *Sure! Get away from this damp fog!*

After some struggle in the dark, Toby hitched up the mule and backed her onto the roadway again. He looked inside of the seat bench and found Lew's hat. He pulled it onto his head to keep him warm, but had to keep pushing it back as it fell over his eyes.

He mounted the cart and snapped the reins along Bean's back. She moved forward obediently. Bean's pace was slow and she walked quietly. The wooden planks of the bridge creaked a little as they crossed it. The road on the other side was paved with small stones and they made a crinkling sound under the steel rims of the cart's wheels.

Toby passed a house, a couple of buildings, and then a livery stable. Inside a horse stirred and then fluttered its nostrils. Silently, Bea and Toby made their way up a small hill, passing numerous houses and storefronts. Most of them were darkened and lifeless.

*It's a nice place!*, Toby thought, his eyes darting from building to building. Light still shone through the windows of some buildings, and he could see nicely down the street where the night's fog hadn't risen this far above the creek. Several side streets disappeared into darkness on either side, where only the lights in the windows were visible.

They crested the hill and he saw a large building in the center of town. It looked official and was too tall for Toby to see the top of it. At first Toby thought it must be a church or a town hall. Then he saw a lamp-lit sign and realized that it was a police station! He quickly pulled down his head until the hat's brim touched the up-turned collar of the coat. He steered Bea ahead quickly.

As they drove on, Toby wondered how he'd ever find the sign that said "North" on such a dark night. The buildings along the street had turned mostly into houses and they were darkened now. Soon he'd reached what he thought was the last of the houses and still hadn't seen any signs. Several of the houses were large brick ones and Toby could make out their nice white fences. At the last house, a dog began barking and followed them along the fence. A low light shone from the open window and a voice spoke to quiet the dog's barking.

They went on a bit until Toby thought it was safe to pull off the road. He jumped down and paced around, stomping his feet and waving his arms to keep warm. He watched the moon advance to its apex in the night sky and then start a descent to the top of the hill that faced him to the north. Toby's night vision was good and he kept his eyes peeled for any sign of Lew or others. He continued to pace to keep warm. Every so often he'd stop to pet Bea's head and keep her company. After awhile he thought of his mother and sisters again, wondering what they were doing. Were they awake, worrying about him? Had Mr. Rodgers talked to his mum? He paced some more.

Toby knew it was long after midnight by now. He was beginning to worry that he'd gone the wrong way and was in the wrong place. *Lew's gonna be mad!,* Toby thought. He feared Lew. There was something vicious and cold in the way he'd forced that man with the apples earlier today. Lew might even be accused of stealing from him. The more Toby considered it, the more it seemed like theft.

Eventually Toby was so tired that he rested his head on Bea's shoulder and dozed a little bit. He swerved as his body relaxed and woke as he caught himself from falling down. Boy was it cold now! Toby looked at Bea, standing there as quietly as ever. He wondered if she was cold and ran his bare fingers along her back. Her coat was still thick from the winter and Toby figured she was alright.

Toby heard a hushed whistle come from somewhere in the dark behind him. Toby jumped a little and then asked softly, "Lew?"

"Yeah, it's me." Lew's voice sounded weak. He coughed. "Where the hell you at, boy?" Another cough broke the silence, followed by a moan.

"Lew?" Toby whispered again. "I'm over here."

Toby heard another cough, this one much closer to him. Lew approached the back of the cart and struggled up onto the back of it. With another cough and a groan, he told Toby to drive them up the hill.

Toby frowned and wondered what was going on. What was wrong with Lew? He took Bea by the halter and led her along the steep road.

Toby saw a bunch of square-shaped objects in a patch of clearing ahead of him and tried to figure out what they were. They looked like boxes, but not quite. Suddenly it hit Toby: a graveyard! *Damn!,* Toby thought with a shiver and hurried his steps. They continued on, but Toby kept glancing over his shoulder. He whistled to distract himself—and to ward off evil spirits.

It took them nearly an hour to make it up the winding path. By the time they got to the top, the sky was just starting to show some light, but the road was still mostly dark. Toby guided Bea to a small area off to the right of the road and tied her to a nearby tree. He went back and looked at Lew. He hadn't moved or made a sound during the ride. Toby was afraid Lew was dead, but he could hear his rattled breath, so he decided to let him sleep. Silently he pulled two more potatoes and two apples from the bags.

He gave one of each to Bea after removing her bridle. The mule ate heartily and nuzzled at the apple Toby was finishing. Toby smiled and gave the core to her. He patted her neck and together they waited for sunup. Once the sun appeared the air warmed quickly, and Toby felt a little better towards the coming day.

He checked on Lew every so often and had to re-cover him with the oilcloth a few times. Lew hadn't moved an inch from when he'd first fallen into the wagon. Every now and then Lew let out a cough or a grunt, startling Toby.

◊ ◊ ◊

# 5

## ~hot potato and a bloody lump~

By 10:00 in the morning, Toby and Bea had driven north several miles. They passed through pastures and along fenced areas containing various livestock. The area was mainly cleared farmland and was beautiful. Toby couldn't believe the crystal clear skies. He was used to the smoke and fumes from the factories, the crowded streets full of people, all contributing to the bustle of the city.

Along the way they passed several very large wagons, each with two drivers and four horses. Both wagons were hauling coal dug from mines to the north. Each time they passed, the other drivers waved or nodded, but didn't stop to talk. This suited Toby anyway. They didn't seem too concerned about him or his load, and Bea and Toby were doing fine maneuvering the sometimes narrow, heavily-rutted roads.

It was warming up and Toby removed his coat. He checked on Lew several more times. He still hadn't moved and just rocked back and forth with the motion of the cart. Toby could see about a half mile ahead down the long slope of the road. There he saw another wagon just crossing a small bridge over a little creek. It had stopped and the drivers were watering the horses. Toby slowed Bea and tried to judge their timing so that the others would be moving again by the time he and Bea reached the bridge. He didn't fancy a conversation with anyone until he'd talked to Lew again, or at least until Lew was able to talk for them both. On the other side of the creek Toby saw another long hill and knew he'd have to walk with Bea to lighten her load. He gave a reproachable glance to Lew and thought that he should be walking, too.

The other wagon started to move, coming towards Toby's cart quickly.

Toby watched the horses struggle upward towards him. The drivers repeatedly cracked a whip over their heads and yelled at them. Toby wondered why the drivers were so harsh. The horses seemed to know exactly what to do without the drivers' prodding.

Toby realized that this wagon wasn't giving up any part of the roadway; it was coming straight at Bea and the cart. Toby watched in confusion, thinking, *Why don't they give road?* The other cart continued on and Toby eased Bea to the edge of the road, which was still soft from the winter's freezing and thawing. He felt the wheel of the cart pulling them into the mud.

One of the drivers cracked his whip loudly as they rode past, which startled Bea. With a surge of nervous energy she tugged the cart onto the road on her own, without Toby's encouragement. Toby swiveled his head to see the other drivers' heads turned towards him. They were laughing! One craned his head and looked at the covered lump that was Lew. He seemed to study it a bit longer than Toby would have liked, and then he waved at Toby, still laughing.

Toby imagined what would have happened if that wagon had upset his cart. Bea could have gone over with it, along with Lew and the load. Toby knew he couldn't lift the copper still pot on his own, and Lew was still of no use.

*Those men were certainly mean-spirited*, Toby thought. He remembered his father's expression again and thought of Lew. Toby turned his attention back to the job at hand. They were just reaching the creek and he pulled up before it. He decided to give his legs a stretch and crawled down from the cart.

He walked up to Bea and patted her neck. She seemed unconcerned about the wagon of mean-spirited men, but did seem to be eyeing up the water. Toby fetched the canvas bucket and went to the stream. The others had muddied the water so hewalked about twenty feet upstream to find some clean water.

Bea drank the entire bucket quickly. Toby thought he'd let her settle that drink before he got her another. He walked to the back of the cart and looked at Lew. He must have finally moved because his arm was holding his ribs. Toby stepped forward and said in a soft voice, "Mr. Lew?" He waited and asked again. "Mr. Lew?"

He stepped closer and pulled aside the oilskin. Lew was covered with blood! It was all over the chest of his shirt, his arm, and dried to his hands.

"Mr. LEW!" Toby's voice quivered. "Are you hurt?" He put his hand on Lew's muscled arm and pushed at it gently. There was no response. "Mr. Lew?" He pushed him harder.

A few seconds later Lew moaned and rolled his head to the other side. Toby then saw the handle of Lew's knife. It was covered with blood, too! Toby stepped back and stared with his mouth hanging open. He looked up and down the road hoping for someone to come along and help.

Toby tried to revive Lew again. "Mr. Lew? Can you hear me?" Toby thought he heard a slight whisper, but then Lew was silent. That's when Toby saw the blood on the side of Lew's head. Toby checked Lew all over and found nothing else hurt except for the cut on his head.

Toby hopped on the cart and into the still. He grabbed a shirt and went back to Lew. Tenderly, he lifted Lew's head and placed the shirt under it as a pillow. Then Toby pulled a small piece of cloth from the seat-box and soaked it in the bucket of water. He applied this to Lew's head. Lew sighed and moaned. He was alive, but Toby wasn't sure what else he could do for him at the moment. After another bucket of water to Bea, Toby led her along the road towards the top of the next hill. *But then what?*, Toby wondered. He kept glancing back to the cart and its passenger.

They topped the hill and looked at the road ahead. The view didn't change much. It was just another hollow and a hill beyond. More patches of cleared trees, stumps, and a field waiting for the spring planting.

Toby saw no one as they continued north. It was early afternoon now and he figured Bea could use a rest and some food, so he watched for a spot to pull over again. When he found a good place to rest, Toby used the flint and steel to start a small fire. He put two potatoes on a stick and plunged it into the soft ground near the heat of the flames.

Bea ate some apples and some grain Toby had found in the wagon-seat storage box. He tended the fire and turned the potatoes, trying to even the charring. He was very hungry for meat, but that would have to wait, as potatoes would have to do for now.

About half an hour later he sampled the potatoes. They were fantastic! But oh! For some pepper and salt! Toby brushed off some of the charred black from the skin and ate that, also. He used his father's pocketknife as his eating utensil.

As he ate, Toby became more concerned about Lew and wondered if they might reach a homesite near the road before nightfall. He could stop and ask for help; maybe they'd know what to do. Then Toby thought: *What if Lew was also in trouble?* It looked like he'd been in a fight. Toby thought that maybe someone had jumped Lew and he got the head wound in self-defense. Then again, Toby knew that Lew had started trouble with the applecart driver. He decided that maybe it was a bad idea to get too near anybody at all! He decided to wait and see if Lew would be able to talk soon. He paced up and down for awhile and then decided to move on.

Toby and Bea made another six miles that afternoon. At dusk, Toby started eyeing up the nearby woods for a place to park. A lane-like opening in the woods appeared to be the best spot to pull into. The lane didn't look used enough to lead to a homestead. Toby edged the cart over and found a suitable site to stop for the night. Some large sandstone rocks projected up from the ground and some large trees were close by—good cover from the light breeze that would turn cold later.

Toby unhooked the harness from the cart and Bea and then hobbled her with a short rope. Then he built another small fire. It was dark now and this time he decided to roast an apple.

Lew remained still—too still. Toby was afraid that he would not be able to rouse him. He wanted to give him some food or water, but he knew not to give water to someone who was out cold. He took the large handkerchief from Lew's pocket and dampened it with water from the jug behind the seat.

He dabbed it to Lew's forehead, and Lew moved his head away from the cold cloth. Toby took Lew's hand and wiped the blood from it. The little light from the fire wasn't enough to see very clearly, but Toby thought he got it all.

Soon, Toby had Lew covered with everything he could find, including the coat Toby had brought with him. Toby figured he could sit by the fire to stay warm, but he couldn't carry Lew to the fire!

The night passed very slowly. Toby woke a number of times. He dreamed that Bea was gone! But he woke and was relieved to see her not too far away. In another dream, Toby imagined that he and Lew were now on a sheriff's "wanted" poster. This time he woke up trembling—from the dream or the cold, he wasn't sure which. Either way, he moved closer to the fire.

He imagined his sisters and his mother in their house, sitting by the fire. Toby was homesick and tired. The trip so far wasn't that bad, but he felt he should be home with his family so soon after losing his father. He hugged his knees to his chest and stared into the fire, falling asleep again.

Twice more he woke and checked on Lew, put more wood on the fire and petted Bea. He stared at Bea for awhile. She was so content. Toby realized that Bea expected nothing. She just took whatever came along. She probably didn't expect or want it to be warmer. To her, things simply were the way they were. The long hills were what they were. Nothing else existed to Bea except the moment she was in. Toby thought that must be rather nice. Or was it? Would people be happier if they were the same way? He wanted to think more about it but his eyes were heavy with sleep and dried out from the fire. He blinked a few times and fell into another fitful sleep.

Toby woke in the morning's early light and went to relieve himself behind a tree. As he stood there he looked over at the rear of the wagon and saw Lew crumpled on the ground in a heap. Toby quickly buttoned his pants and ran to Lew.

He stopped and said, "Mr. Lew?" No answer. He knelt down and felt his arm. It was cold! Toby's heart leapt. "Mr. Lew?" He shook Lew's arm and spoke louder, "Mr. Lew!?" He noticed a foul smell and realized that Lew had wet his pants. He also smelled of vomit. Toby looked on the cart and saw his coat covered with the foul-smelling bloody slime. The vomit had also run across the cart's bed and into the burlap sacks with the potatoes and apples!

Toby pulled the oilskin from the cart and covered Lew. The shirt he'd used as a pillow seemed ok, so Toby pulled it on and rolled up the sleeves. He walked back to the fire and kicked at the now cold, charred wood. There were still some hot coals beneath the ashes. Toby looked to the sky and wondered why it was still not getting brighter. He realized that it was going to rain. Toby wondered how he was going to get Lew back onto the cart and how to keep himself and Lew dry and warm.

◊ ◊ ◊

# 6

## ~a painful smell~

There wasn't much water left in the jug; maybe just enough to water Bea. There definitely wasn't enough to clean up some apples to eat, wash the puke from the cart, clean up Lew again, and have some left over for Toby to drink.

Toby was disgusted. He kicked again at the dead fire wood and looked at Bea. As always, she was fine. Nothing seemed amiss to her. Toby remembered that he'd been thinking about this when he fell asleep last night. He felt a surge of confidence that he didn't understand. He led Bea back to the cart. "You seem to just take what's there," he said to her. "You don't seem to mind it at all, do ya?" He patted head and began hooking her to the harness of the cart.

Toby stood over Lew and tried to think of how to get the big man onto the cart. He wanted to kick him and get him to move on his own. Instead, he stooped down and pulled on Lew's arm.

He stunk! As Toby tried to wake Lew, a very large, cold raindrop hit him on the shoulder. It went through his shirt and chilled him instantly. *Damn it!*, Toby thought.

But the tug on Lew's arm got a response. Lew moaned and curled up some more. "Lew!" Toby shouted, "Come on, get up! It's going to rain. Get up!" Toby tugged on his arm again.

Toby pulled Lew into a sitting position and held him there. Lew moaned in pain and coughed. The rain started falling harder and seemed to help revive Lew. Toby let go of Lew's arms and he wobbled for a second before catching himself and sitting up. Lew put his hand to his head.

"It hurts! MY JESUS! It hurts!" Lew started speaking in Italian, mumbling words Toby didn't understand. Lew still had one hand on his head and the other arm was holding his ribs, but he stayed sitting. As the rain fell on them, Toby took Lew's arm away from his head and helped him to stand.

Toby wasn't going to worry about the condition of the wagon right now. He just wanted Lew on it! Lew was still babbling in Italian. He pulled at Toby's shirt and said "Boy-Yas!" With Toby's help he crawled back onto the cart. It was wet from the rain, but Lew didn't seem to care. Toby covered him again with the oilcloth and then tucked it around him to keep the water out. Lew grabbed Toby's arm firmly and said, "Get us to Boy-Yas." With that he fell backward into another sound sleep.

Toby guided Bea back onto the lane. The rain was cold, and it wasn't yet 8:00 in the morning. Toby repeated to himself what Lew had said: "Boy-Yas." Toby didn't understand. Was that more Italian? What the hell was Boy-Yas?

Toby just sat and let Bea do her thing. She plodded along and they turned north on the road again. *Boy-Yas.* Toby kept repeating the phrase to himself. He was soaked and shivering. He kept his head down with his eyes on the road ahead; he tipped the hat to keep the rain off the back of his neck.

Toby was so lost in thought and misery that he didn't even hear the other wagon approach until the other driver called out. "Yo, driver! Whoa, horses. Ho! Whoa!"

The driver stopped beside the cart. Toby looked at him blankly. At this point he didn't care what was going on. He just waited for the other driver to speak.

"That's some shiner you got yourself, boy," he said. Toby had completely forgotten about his black eye. He simply looked at the man and said nothing. He shivered.

"Hey, boy, you all right? You look like you could use a hand." The man was still smiling, but had a concerned look on his face.

"Jus' cold," Toby managed to say though clenched, chattering teeth.

"Boy, you mor'n just cold." The driver tied off his reins and dismounted. He approached the cart, looking first at Bea, then at the cart, and lastly at the load on the back of the cart.

"Don'tcha got some rain cover, boy?"

Toby just shook his head and looked at his feet. He felt the rain running into the tops of his father's boots. His socks were now wet and his feet were getting cold.

"How far are you going?" the man asked him.

"Just a bit north," Toby lied.

"You ain't gonna get too far like that." The man had sincere concern in his voice. "We live just a little back some—it's the way you're heading. You could stop and get dry and warm. I've probably got some oilcloth.... Could get you some to cover up with."

Toby still couldn't answer him. He shivered and his teeth chattered again. He nodded at the man.

"You jus' keep going. I'll get to a place to turn this wagon and then I'll catch up with you, boy!" The man shouted through the drizzle. With that he mounted his wagon, gave Toby another concerned look, and flipped the reins. "Not mor'n a mile, boy. Straight on. Get that mule movin'!"

Toby nodded and shivered some more.

After the man's wagon passed Toby, he followed the other man to a small farm where the man dismounted his wagon and stood holding the door to the barn open. Toby guided Bea into the barn and dropped the reins. He felt the man lift him from the cart's seat, but he was too tired and cold to notice much else.

◊ ◊ ◊

# 7

## ~hot stew and missing Lew~

Toby's head fell forward and he woke with a start. His eyes moved around the room. He blinked to clear them and began to remember what had happened and how he got here. He first noticed the woman standing in the small room. Next he saw the man that had stopped to help him in the rain.

"He's awake! Are ya coming back to life, son?"

Toby's voice cracked when he replied: "Uh….Yes. Yes, sir!" Toby realized that he was inside the man's house and that the lady must be his wife. He looked across the sparsely furnished room. It was clean and warm. He nodded to the woman and sat up straighter in the chair.

He realized that he was wrapped in a blanket and sitting at their table. Then he saw his clothes hanging on the back of a wooden chair near a pot-bellied stove that was heating the room.

Toby slowly realized he would have to think of a story to tell them, when the man asked, "You sure you're ok?"

Toby nodded. He thought of Bea and Lew. What of Lew? He must still be in the barn. He asked the man, "Is my mule alright, sir?"

"Fine, fine," he said in a hushed tone. "We were a bit more concerned about you!"

Toby ran his hand through his damp hair and nodded. "I'm good, sir. But, we—uh—I need to get on."

The woman interrupted him. "You'll eat first! Your mule has been wiped down and fed. Now it's your turn." She moved to the stove and carried a pot to the table. It was filled with hot stew and smelled terrific! Toby's eyes shifted to the man's face and he nodded.

"Eat up, son. You can get on with your trip shortly." The man sat next to him at the table and studied Toby's black eye. Toby kept his eyes on the stew. It was even better than his mother's cooking! "The misses is the best cook around," the man said. "Course, we don't have many neighbors!" He laughed and she swatted him with the towel she'd used to carry the pot.

Toby liked them; they were kind. "I can't pay you for the food, and I can't stay to help work it off," he said quietly. "I have to get the cart up the road and meet a man that's going to direct me on." He didn't like lying to them—especially when they were so nice. He looked at the man and wondered if he believed him. Something in the man's face told him that his story wasn't working. He spooned more food into his mouth as the woman set a plate with homemade bread and butter on the table.

Toby's eyes widened. Stew *and* hot bread! He tried to hide his worry about his companions in the barn.

As Toby ate, the man said, "I'm thinkin' the rain is over—for today, anyway. You're at least dry when you set out again. I just want to ask you: Why weren't you usin' that oilskin over yourself to keep dry with?"

Toby didn't understand the implication of the man's question at first. When it dawned on him what the man was saying he panicked. He wondered what had happened to Lew. Why had the man not said something about him? Surely he'd seen Lew on the back of the cart if he'd seen the oilcloth. Toby tried to imagine what had happened. Had Lew fallen off the wagon? And if he did, was he still alive? Toby couldn't say anything.

When he looked at the man and woman they were exchanging looks and glancing at Toby, as if waiting for an answer. What was the question again? The oilcloth! "I was suppos' to keep the crate covered," Toby said. The man nodded and looked away. He lit a pipe of tobacco and leaned back into his chair. His wife had a worried look on her face and kept looking at her husband.

He puffed on his pipe and waited. Toby guessed he was waiting for some more information when Toby started to feel angry. He certainly owed them for helping, but he didn't owe them any more than that! He pushed the plate away and smiled at the man's wife. "I can only thank you VERY much for the food, ma'am. You are a great cook—just like your husband says. But I have to leave."

Toby pulled on his clothes and walked to the barn. He spied Beans and the cart, but no Lew. His eyes traveled along the line of woods and back to the barn again. Still no Lew!

The man had harnessed Bea and they were backing out of the barn when Toby arrived. "Sir, where is the next village to the north? Or where can I find the Ole Stone House? It's a tavern-stagecoach stop…."

"It's not far," the man said with a smile. "I was headin' back from there when I ran into you. It's about two miles further than where I found you."

"Two miles?" Toby was now in the seat of the cart and held the reins. "I gotta get there soon!"

The man nodded and stepped back. Toby said, "I certainly owe you and your wife. Thanks again." Toby trailed off and just nodded respectfully.

The man nodded at Toby and said, "You'd better git. It'll be dark in several hours, but you should be there in plenty o' time."

Toby studied the barn once more. He was looking for Lew and still couldn't figure out where he had gone. He turned and looked to the back of the cart and saw the oilcloth that had covered Lew rolled up and tied to the crate. He couldn't think of anything else to do, so he waved to the woman on the porch and nodded again to the man as he drove Bea away.

Toby felt strong. He was dry, fed, and rested. Bea seemed to know the way out the lane, so Toby just let her go on her own. As he scanned the woods on both sides of the road, he watched for a movement—any movement! Surely if Lew was there he'd see them leaving. He worried that Lew would be angry since he'd missed out on the meal, and he was probably wet and cold. That's if he wasn't lying dead somewhere! They were well out of sight of the small farm house when Toby stopped the cart. What was he to do? He didn't like or trust Lew, but they were supposed to deliver the cart's load together! He couldn't take it on by himself; he didn't have directions and he had no experience. Isn't that what all adults would say?

Toby waited for twenty minutes, pacing up and down, still looking at the woods behind him. Then he heard a soft whistle and turned quickly. It was Lew! He loped up the lane and leaned against the cart. Toby started to walk towards Lew to help him, but Lew waved him off as he approached. Gasping for his breath, and holding his sides, Lew grimaced as he levered himself onto the cart, rolled over, and pulled the oilskin over himself.

Toby was relieved not to have to talk to him and happy that Lew didn't yell at him. He climbed into the seat and they continued. Toby studied the road's landmarks. He hoped to come back here and repay the couple's kindness, maybe on their return trip.

◊ ◊ ◊

# 8

## ~money "helpers" and furtive activities~

Toby watched the road closely as they worked their way further north. Another coal wagon approached; this time the men were courteous and nodded as they passed. They rode in a larger cart, and a boy no older than Toby looked glumly at him. His face was grimy and he looked gaunt. Toby looked at both the men and saw that they looked exhausted, too. Their horses leaned into the harnesses and seemed mechanical and lifeless, as well. Toby knew nothing of the mining process or of their lives. He had seen men like them in Pittsburgh, unloading the coal with shovels. They also seemed to be tired people. Just lifeless! He puzzled over the whole picture in his mind when he heard Lew's voice.

"You get to the tavern. Leave me covered up in the back here," Lew said. "Get some bread. Some cheese. And meat! I put a Liberty on the floor. Can you see it?" Lew coughed again.

"Yes, Mr. Lew, it's here." Toby had only seen a Liberty once before when his mother gave one to the undertaker. It was a lot of money. Toby figured Lew probably got it from Mr. Howard or Mr. Rodgers. Toby wondered how much more they'd given Lew for the trip.

"You buy Bea three days of grain, too," Lew said, still coughing. "Ya hear me, boy?"

"Yes, Mr. Lew."

"Three days worth of—" a retching cough erupted from Lew's mouth, "—food for each of us. Be as quick as you can!"

"Yes, sir."

"Smart-arsed-kid," Lew mumbled as he curled up and coughed again.

Toby could see the tavern along with several horses tied to a rail in front of the porch. Another coal wagon was parked outside near a grassy area where the horses chewed at anything green. The tavern was a large building made of field stone. As Toby approached he heard voices shouting and laughing inside. He even heard a young girl's squealing giggle.

A dog lying on the porch watched as Toby pulled the cart near the grassy area to let Bea graze. Toby jumped from the cart and went to the door of the tavern. Inside, it was warm and stuffy from a burning cast iron stove. Everyone in the room turned to look at him, and several men continued staring as he walked tentatively to the counter.

The counter served as a bar and as a place to purchase items from the shelves. Toby looked around, avoiding the eyes boring into him when the man behind the counter approached.

He spoke in a raspy voice: "Get you sumpin', boy?" He wasn't mean, but wasn't overly friendly either. Toby couldn't quite get used to everybody calling him "boy." There was a kind of insult to it, and he wondered how old he would have to be before people stopped saying it. He pointed to the hard loaves of bread on the shelf.

"Uh, yes sir, two loaves of bread. Some cheese, too." Toby tried to sound confident, but felt small and scared. "Do you have grain for a mule? Sir?"

A man sitting at the counter erupted in laughter. "Same grain that's in the bread 'ur gettin'!" Other men laughed at the joke. Toby smiled, thinking that it couldn't hurt to humor them. They were drinking and he thought it safer to play along.

"Uh...some dried meat, too," Toby added. He ignored the continued staring.

"Mule meat!" another man's voice added laughingly.

"Mind dem P's and Q's over there!" The man behind the counter yelled. "This young man's spending money!"

"P's and Q's?" Toby asked quietly to himself. He'd never heard that phrase before. The tavern owner looked at him as he scooped cornmeal from a barrel and put it in a cloth sack. "P's and Q's: Pints and quarts," he said, making a motion with his hand like tipping a drink to his mouth. He smiled at Toby. Toby smiled back.

Then Toby saw the young girl he'd heard laughing earlier. She came to the counter and bent forward to get something from underneath it. She wore an off-the-shoulder blouse and Toby got quite a view of her bare chest. He blinked several times and gulped. She smiled at him as she stood up and he blushed. Then in a loud voice she said, "You guys better not make this one mad. He's got quite a shiner from his last fight!" She laughed and turned away. Some of the men laughed loudly as they tried to get a glimpse of Toby's eye. The last he saw of the girl was as she turned to him at the doorway, smiled, winked, and then disappeared into another room.

When he looked up, the tavern keeper was waiting for another order from Toby. "That's all, sir," Toby said as he tried to remember if there was anything else Lew had told him to get. It didn't seem so.

Toby put the Liberty on the counter. When he saw it, the man's eyes widened. "I'll have to get change," he said and went into the same room the girl had gone into.

When he returned he gave Toby several coins and some paper bills. Toby wasn't sure how much he'd spent or how much change he was due, but he acted as if it were correct. He thanked the man and lifted the two heavy bags.

"Need help with that?" one man asked.

Toby hefted the bags and shook his head. Before he could say thank you, the man added: "Not with the bags! With the MONEY, fool!" There was a roar of laughter from the others. Toby walked out the door and could still hear them laughing.

He was putting the bags onto the cart's floor when he heard a voice behind him. "You stayin' for the night?"

It was the girl. She was smiling—and waiting for an answer.

"Uh, no. We're going north—right now!"

The girl was playing with the lace on the front of her blouse; her fingers drifted over her skin just above the blouse's neck line. She made Toby nervous.

A cough! The girl turned her head sharply. She looked terrified when she realized that someone else was in the back of the cart. She turned and walked away quickly without looking back.

"Get movin', boy. Before you lose my money!" Lew whispered harshly.

Toby didn't quite understand what had just happened or why the girl was so scared. He just hurriedly did as Lew told him.

Five minutes passed as Toby let Bea pull the cart. Lew's voice whispered again: "Anybody around us?"

Toby glanced around and to the rear, back down the road. "No, sir."

"Then take the next path to the right."

"That won't be north!"

"Just do as I say. Ya kinda told that girl where we were headed, and now we have to take a longer path. Another day's journey. Hard path, too."

Toby didn't understand why Lew cared if the girl knew where they were going, but again he did as he was told. He found the path just about dusk. A short way along it he pulled over to makecamp for the night. He unharnessed the mule, put out feed for her, made a fire, and cooked some of the corn meal with water in a pot.

All the while, Lew sat with his back to the cart wheel and watched Toby. His eyes never blinked and his gaze troubled Toby.

When the gruel was ready, Toby sliced some meat and bread and handed the food to Lew. By the time Toby got some bread and meat for himself, he looked at the pot and saw that Lew had eaten all the gruel!

Anger rose up in Toby's chest. He clenched his jaw and went to a log by the fire where he sat by himself. He chewed at the bread and the dried meat, and again realized that the mule was "just there." She really wasn't concerned with anything. She calmly accepted what was. Toby relaxed a little and drew a slow breath. He chewed some more bread. Again he promised himself to follow her lead. He decided that he wasn't going to get disturbed about anything that happened. No, he would just accept situations as they came along.

Toby sat at the fire for awhile and began to doze off. When he woke, the fire was nearly out and Bea was sleeping, her head hanging close to the ground. Toby was cold, so he went to the wagon and looked for his coat. Lew was using it as a blanket! Toby thought he could use the oilcloth as a cover, but Lew was lying on top of it.

With nothing to cover up with, Toby mounted the cart and climbed into the still pot. At least he'd be protected from the wind in there.

At about midnight, Toby woke and had to pee. He crawled up, out of the still and dropped to the ground. He went outside of the campsite and relieved himself. When he returned he went to the fire and added some more wood. There was probably enough to last until morning. Once he warmed himself he went back to the cart and climbed up. Looking to the rear of the cart, he saw that Lew was gone!

Toby looked to the woods, thinking that maybe Lew had gone to relieve himself, too. Toby decided to crawl back into the still when the idea struck him: Get the coat! He pulled it on; it was still warm, so Lew hadn't been gone long.

Toby put the oilcloth over the top of the still to keep in the heat. He curled up inside the pot and drifted back to sleep, wondering where Lew had gone. It was the last question of the day.

◊ ◊ ◊

# 9

## ~from a station to a farm~

Toby woke, cold and hungry, which was getting to be the usual start of the day. He looked up and noticed that the oilcloth was gone. He could just make out the greyness of the early morning sky.

As he looked out of the top of the still the first thing he noticed was Lew standing near the refreshed fire. Flames were licking at the logs and Lew stood with his back to the cart. As Toby climbed out of the pot and jumped from the cart, he saw that the oilcloth was lying on the seat and had been cut. He walked to the fire and said, "Morning, Mr. Lew." He rubbed his hands together at the fire and looked up at Lew. He saw strips of the oilcloth wrapped around Lew's chest.

Lew's eyes never left the fire. "Mornin'. You sleep well, boy?"

"Uh, sort of." Toby squatted down to warm his face near the fire.

"'Sort of?'"

"I was worried when you weren't here, that you were sick again." Toby didn't look up at Lew as he stared at the fire's flames and felt its warmth. There was a lengthy pause, interrupted only by the call of a grouse somewhere in the woods.

Lew finally spoke: "Jus' felt like an early mornin' walk. Jus' somethin' I do." There was another long pause while Toby thought this over. Lew said an early morning walk, but it was nearer to midnight when Toby noticed he was gone. Toby thought that was odd, but decided not to mention it.

"You think you cracked a rib?" Toby asked, nodding his head towards the homemade oilcloth bandages.

"Sure feels like it. I think one is broken." Lew pointed to a rib with his thumb.

"Can I fix some food?" Toby looked at Lew but the man's face was expressionless.

"I 'spect you ought to get something done, but make it quick and get the mule hooked up. We've got a hard, fast ride to make."

"How far do we have to go?"

"'Bout another sixty, maybe seventy miles. We ain't halfway yet!" Lew's anger surfaced and he added: "Enuf damn questions. Get fed and feed that mule! I need some sleep." Lew seemed alert and full of energy, but Toby thought maybe he needed the rest for his sore ribs. Toby hurried with the morning's pre-start chores. The sky was still grey and looked like it would stay that way all day.

Several hours later Toby had walked most of the several miles they had traveled. He and Bea seemed like-minded in their purpose, as neither wanted to be reminded of the cart or its passenger.

It warmed up during the morning's trip and was just right for travel. Toby watched the trail ahead for anything that may cause them a problem. He feared a hole or rock that could cripple the mule. And knowing Lew, Toby would have to pull the cart!

It was close to midday when the first of the coal wagons began to appear. As the third wagon drove by a man called to Toby: "That mule kick you in the eye, boy?" The man with him laughed heartily.

The wagons passed them in about half hour intervals now. Toby would usually walk Bea to the side of the road and let them pass. The other drivers seemed to appreciate the gesture and nodded to Toby.

Toby took a moment as one wagon passed and walked into the woods. He relieved himself and stood looking across the rolling hills ahead. As he finished his business, he buttoned up his trousers and went back to the wagon. Lew was in the seat and said, "Hand me up the reins." Lew deftly backed Bea onto the road and used the tail of the reins to swat her backside. The motion angered Toby. He started to say something when Lew shot him a glance. The cart was moving quickly so Toby swung up onto the back of it. He wondered if Lew would have left him here if he'd stayed in the woods a minute longer. Toby clenched his jaw and sat on the crate that held the rest of the still's lyne arm.

Considering that Bea hadn't gotten her midday rest and grain, Toby spoke up. "Don't you think Bea needs a rest? Mr. Lew, she's had a hard pull on that last hill."

"She's fine! We don't have that much further. And I don't want to sleep outside tonight! If you think she's tired, why don't you jus' walk and give her some rest *that* way!"

Toby didn't reply but hopped off the cart and walked behind. He leaned into it as he walked, helping Bea. Another coal wagon approached. Toby noticed that Lew kept his head down and barely glanced at the passing drivers.

Toby thought it was curious that Lew was still worried about the incident in Pittsburgh. He didn't think that the police would be looking for them this far from the city. *Or maybe Lew just doesn't like people very much*, Toby thought. Lew was looking pretty rough. He hadn't combed his hair like he did in the city and he hadn't shaved. His coal-black stubble dulled the features of his face.

On the next horizon Toby saw smoke! *It's from a chimney*, he thought as he looked up the steep hill they were about to climb.

"Better get to pushin', boy. Give this mule-friend o' yours a hand." Lew slapped the reins on Bea's back again. "Ya-up, mule!"

Toby pushed hard. It helped to burn off the anger he felt at the way Lew treated him and Bea. He felt Bea struggling and he pushed harder to help her.

They topped the hill and turned left onto a larger road. A hand-painted sign reading *Annandale Station* was nailed to a tree. Below that was another sign that read *Boyers –2*. Lew sat up straighter and jiggled the reins again. Now that they were on the level road Bea didn't seem to have much trouble. The road had a fine stone covering and was well packed by the heavy wagons.

They passed a number of wooden-sided shacks along the road. One shack had a sign over the window that read *Trades and Supplies*. Another building had a sign that read *Dry Goods and Livery*. Both signs looked worn and hand scrawled and in need of fresh paint. A toothless woman in a plain dress stood in a doorway smoking a corn-cob pipe. Toby grinned and nodded a greeting to her, but she scowled back at him.

The road ahead disappeared and Toby realized they were about to give back the climb they had just made up the hill. Toby decided to help Bea and hold back the cart as best as he could. The hill seemed twice as long—and twice as steep!—going down as it had going up.

They descended for the better part of half an hour. A few dozen houses sat at the bottom, many with stick fences surrounding small yards. They contained the usual chickens, rabbit cages, barking or sleeping dogs, and kids. Toby waved at two small children in ragged clothes; they just looked at him with those sullen glares he'd seen from the wagon drivers.

The late afternoon sun disappeared into shadow as they passed the houses and wound their way along a brushy stream bed. Houses here were more spread out and sat on larger plots of land. Some of them had small gardens along with extra livestock and larger outbuildings. Many of them were in poor condition, but it almost seemed that they were built that way. Some were nicely kept though, and many had small stone gardens with a cross in the ground. Toby wondered if they buried their family members in their front yards.

Clothing hung from ropes tied between trees and billowed lazily in the late afternoon sun. A woman hung a carpet over a porch railing and beat it with a small coal shovel. Black dust drifted into the light breeze. Lew turned the cart down a lane that was barely visible and Toby turned to look back at the woman. She'd stopped beating the carpet and was shading her eyes from the late day sun. She studied the cart but quickly looked away when she realized Toby was looking back at her.

Lew drove the cart down the hidden lane, through some dense trees. Toby tried to memorize the surroundings. He wanted to ask Lew where they were but couldn't think of how—without angering him!

He didn't like not knowing where he was, without some idea of the roads around him. It wasn't like being in the city, where streets had names and were labeled with signs. Lew steered the cart towards a house about a half mile into the forest. It was a little larger than most of the others they'd passed, and in better shape. There were several other buildings on the property. Dogs erupted from beneath the porch, barking and running wildly, opening the distance between each. They trotted towards Bea and she glanced at each of them. Lew yelled at the dogs to settle, and Toby was surprised to see that they instantly responded to his voice.

One dog continued to approach and began wagging its tail, but Bea kept her wary watch. Bea was cautious, watching each of the dogs fan out in a circle around them, and Lew guided the cart to a spot near the porch. Toby saw a man's head appear from behind the barn door. At the same time, the porch's outer door, which was covered with a burlap material, opened.

"It's Lew!" shouted a woman. She bounded down the porch's two stone steps and crossed the ten feet to the cart's edge. "Lew! Lew! It's so good to see you! Didn't expect you till the summer. What's going on?" She turned as she saw Toby sliding off the crate-seat on the back of the cart and gave Lew a quizzical look, tugging the shock of hair away from her face.

Lew jumped from the cart and said, "C'mere, Maria!" He hugged her in what Toby thought was a rather undignified manner.

"Lew!" The man from the barn had just arrived. "Lew!" The man looked just like Lew, only a little older. Toby thought it must be Lew's brother.

Lew looked up, laughed, and said, "Lucca!" The men hugged and grinned. They stepped back to size each other up and then clasped their hands onto each other's backs and hugged again.

All three began to talk at once in Italian. Toby didn't understand anything after that except when Lew told him in English to take Bea to the barn. The three kept talking without another word to Toby. Without as much as an introduction or acknowledgement, the woman looked back at Toby, then turned again and followed Lew and the other man into the house.

◊ ◊ ◊

# 10

~a basket case and bad dreams~

Toby spent the next half hour or so tending to Bea. By the time he unharnessed her, rubbed her down, and fed her some grain he'd found in the barn, it was well past suppertime. He was hoping for a hot, home cooked meal, but had a feeling that wasn't going to happen. So he pulled out the bread, cheese, and dried meat from beneath the cart seat and cut into each with his pocketknife. As he munched on his cold supper he looked around the barn. The two bags of puke-soaked apples and potatoes were still on the cart, and he thought to clean them off at the first chance he got. Bea ate the feed that he'd given her and some of the corn he'd gathered off the floor of the barn. There were no other animals in the barn and Toby figured they must be kept elsewhere. But there were barrels along one wall and the faint smell of something spoiled. Toby thought it must be the smell that barns get in winter from being damp.

He took the canvas bucket and went to the water trough that was just outside. He hung the bucket on a post in front of Bea so that she could drink. When Toby thought she'd had enough, he got another bucketful of water and splashed it on the back of the cart to rinse it again. He doubted the smell of puke would go away any time soon.

Toby also washed the oilcloth and draped it on a stall divider to dry. He thought about washing off his coat, but wondered if he might need it tonight. Surely, they had an extra place to sleep in the house, he thought. But considering the welcome he'd received so far, he wondered if they would even feed him.

He heard a noise behind him and turned to see a girl standing there looking at him. She seemed to be a couple of years older than Toby and was just a little taller. Her hair was light brown, unlike everyone else in the house; they all had jet black hair. She had a wide jaw and the same sullen look in her eyes that the people along the road had had. She stood with her head down andher shoulders hunched.

"They tol' me to fetch this to you." She held forward a basket. Toby took a few steps towards her. She still hadn't offered a smile, so Toby did. "Thanks!" he said and took the basket. He waited for a return smile, but got none.

Inside the basket was a biscuit broken in half and smeared with apple butter. There was also a yellow pepper, but Toby decided that he'd pass on *THAT* one! He took the biscuit and offered half to the girl, but she shook her head and stepped back.

Toby bit into the biscuit. It tasted great! The girl waited for Toby to finish so she could take the basket back to the house. As Toby ate, she occupied her time looking at Bea.

Toby was full after eating the biscuit and sucked the apple butter from his thumb and wrist. "You their daughter?" Toby asked.

She shook her head.

"Well, who's Lucca? Is he Lew's brother?" he asked. The girl nodded. "And Maria is Lucca's wife?" Again, she simply nodded and kept her sad eyes on Bea.

"That's Bea! She's a good mule," Toby said. "She's pulled us here from Pittsburgh. You ever been there?" Again, the girl just shook her head. Toby wondered what it would take to get her to speak.

The girl stepped to Bea and patted her nose. She seemed to be easy with animals. As she studied Bea from one end to the other, Toby noticed that the mule stood with one leg slightly off the ground so it wasn't bearing any weight. Her leg, at the fetlock, was curled under, and the girl bent to look at it more closely. Clucking her tongue to sooth the mule, she lifted the foot and inspected the hoof. "It's bruised! See?" she said in a soft voice. Still holding the mule's foot, she pointed to a can on the wall shelf. "Hand that over to me," she said. Toby's eyes followed the direction of her arm. He pulled down a tin can and gave it to her. She scooped her fingers into the white, waxy goop and rubbed it on Bea's hoof.

The mule moved her foot around as the girl applied the medicine. Again, the girl clucked her tongue several times. "You got any cloth to wrap it in?" she asked Toby. Toby thought a moment and remembered the oilcloth. He pulled out his pocketknife and cut a patch from it. As she wrapped Bea's hoof in it, the girl said, "It'll be fine…in the morning."

Without any further word, she gathered up the basket and started for the door. She paused for a moment and turned back to Toby. She tilted her head towards the house and pointed at Toby's face as she asked, "He give you that?" Toby was confused for a moment and then remembered his black eye and touched his cheek.

"Naw. Hit it on the inside of the still." He jerked his thumb towards the cart.

She turned to look at the large, round copper pot. She looked back at Toby and then turned to go.

"Wait, what's your name?" Toby asked.

The girl paused for a few seconds with her back still to Toby. "…Gina," she finally said over her shoulder and then walked out the door. Toby watched as she walked back to the house and thought he saw her put the hot pepper in her dress pocket. "What an odd girl," he said to Bea.

Toby realized that he was probably going to spend the night in the barn. Why else would they have sent food out to him? As it got dark he heard loud voices from the house all mixed together in laughing and singing. He'd heard Lew say the word "grappa" to the other man when they first arrived at the house. Toby had heard some Italian workmen say "grappa" before they headed to the tavern after work. He knew it was some kind of alcohol, and he was sure that the adults in the house were drinking tonight.

Toby nested himself into a pile of straw and used it to cover himself up. He slept awhile until a noise woke him up. He raised his head up to listen for the sound again. It was pitch dark, but he could see a light from the house.

Again he heard the noise from the house, but he couldn't make out what it was. Toby rose and went to the doorway to listen. He didn't hear anything else. He had to pee, so he stepped around the side of the barn, walking gingerly in the dark. As he made nature's call he heard the sound of a girl crying! He wondered if it was Gina. He didn't like to think of her crying, but didn't know what else he could do. He knew he'd get in trouble if he went to the adults in the house, so he just stayed put. He didn't know who else was in the house, and he knew it would be his hide if he went in there. Some families just dealt with their own—and NO ONE ELSE dare interfere. It was just that: a family law!

Toby had another fitful night's sleep. Dreams came and went, mixing up the events of the last several days. In his dream he saw a coal wagon go by carrying several bodies and Gina riding on Bea. And then he dreamt that the cart and its load were gone!

Toby woke again and thought he'd heard another scream that wasn't part of his dream. Bea and the cart were still there beside him. There was nothing to do but roll over in the straw and go back to sleep.

◊ ◊ ◊

# 11

## ~pork bellies and "his pig"~

Toby was summoned early the following morning. It was after dawn; he'd been up a short time, had watered and fed Bea, made the trip to the outhouse, and was back in the barn.

Maria called his name from the porch of the house. Toby waved to her and walked from the barn to the house. When he stepped inside he smelled hot food. "Got your face and hands clean?" Maria asked as she busied herself over the stove.

"Yes, ma'am," Toby said. As he waited for Maria to respond, Gina entered the room. Toby started to say good morning when he noticed that something wrong: Gina's face was swollen and red. She didn't look at him and carried some bread to the table. Toby waited for Gina to say something, but she didn't, and she didn't look in his direction.

"Sit and eat. You're going to be real busy today—both of you! Better earn some keep!" Maria said as she wrestled some pork belly slices into a skillet. The green meat sizzled in the pan and Toby spied a plate of scrambled eggs nearby.

His mouth began to water and he swallowed hard. His stomach woke and began to hurt. Toby moved to the table and sat in the chair he guessed was his. Gina sat across the table and kept her eyes lowered. Toby saw a cut on her swollen lip and a bruise on her jaw. His eyes implored her to look at him, but she spread some butter on the bread and handed him a slice. When she did finally look up she shook her head and gave him a stern look not to say anything.

The bread was fresh and Toby relished each bite. The crust was nice and chewy and the soft center melted in his mouth. But Toby knew that he'd be hungry in a couple of hours without any meat in his stomach.

Maria set a few broken, over-fried eggs and two tin cups of milk on the table. Toby glanced past her at the fried pork slices, but she ignored his interest in the other food. "Eat!" Her voice was not mean, just forceful. Toby and Gina ate without a word between them. He began to wonder why Maria didn't talk to him either; he thought she'd want to know about his family or the trip at least.

When Maria was back at the stove, Toby looked longingly at the last piece of bread on the plate, but Gina put it into her dress pocket. She gave Toby a pointed look, which Toby hoped meant that she would share the bread later.

Maria returned to the table and poured some weak coffee on top of the last of the milk in Toby's cup and said, "There, that ought to keep you till noon. Gina will show you what you're going to be doing this morning." She turned to Gina and said, "Get those grape vines fertilized. Take the 'barrow' and take the barn scrapings to them. One bucket per vine! Now get on, both of ya."

Toby followed Gina to the barn and she pointed to the wheelbarrow that leaned against the barn wall. She grabbed a pitchfork and a shovel for them to begin with and walked around the corner of the building to a large pile of smelly manure. Gina was wearing a pair of shoes with high-tops, but they were hardly meant for work in this area. Toby looked down at his boots and was thankful for them as he stepped into the mushy slop near the pile.

Gina held out both tools and Toby selected the shovel. He pushed it into the pile of sloppy manure and lifted the load into the hull of the wheelbarrow, which was simply a wooden box with gaps between the boards. The manure's "juices" ran out and splashed back onto the ground. Gina dug the pitchfork into the drier part of the pile and didn't suffer the same problem. *Experience counts even here*, Toby thought.

Toby looked back at the house before asking in a whisper, "What happened to your lip and cheek?"

"Shh! Don't talk! I'll tell you in the field." Gina kept her head down and her eyes on her work.

Once the wheelbarrow was full, they struggled up the hillside with it to the grape vines. Thankfully, they weren't far from the barn. Each vine had recently been trimmed back and was about six feet long. They were planted in neat rows about six feet apart and each tied to a spindly post.

Gina took the shovel and turned some soil at the base of the vine. She motioned for Toby to use the pitchfork and put some manure at the base of the plant. Gina twisted the shovel and mixed the soil and manure together. They moved to the next, then the next. By the fifth plant the wheelbarrow was empty. Without looking up, Gina said, "You fetch another load and I'll turn dirt at the other plants."

Toby nodded and returned with the fork to the pile. He loaded the wheelbarrow and struggled with the next load back to where she stood. They continued on like this for two hours and had only completed one row. There were four more to go. Each trip was further from the barn and took longer to get the manure to the plants.

At mid-morning Gina went to the house for a pitcher, which she filled with water from the well. They paused for a few minutes and took long drinks, passing the pitcher between them. Maria interrupted their rest by barking orders at them. Gina returned the pitcher and came back to Toby.

He felt the skin on his arms and neck burning from the sun. Gina's skin seemed to soak up the sun without turning the same red color his did. Her arms were thin, but muscled in thin strips under the skin. Her nails were broken and blackened, and there were small cuts on her hands.

They labored till after noon. Lew and Lucca appeared on the front porch. From the corner of his eye, Toby saw the men watching him and Gina. After awhile they left the porch and walked along a gorge at the edge of the wooded area behind the house. A wooden building stood near the spring running down the hillside towards the back of the barn. Toby thought of how clever it was to have the water flow near the buildings. It saved them all from having to carry it to the animals. He didn't realize that a stone channel had been buried towards the house and carried water to the cistern that they used for fresh water in the house.

Lucca was walking in an imaginary square, his arms delineating intersecting lines. Lew stood nearby and nodded at the path Lucca made. Toby and Gina worked along another row, and she still hadn't spoken a word to him. Toby heard wood being chopped and saw Lew and Lucca driving sticks into the ground. He realized that the men were laying out a spot for another shed. They would squat and sight levels to the spring and then drive another stake into the ground. There was a lot of loud laughing and Italian spoken.

Toby was getting angry with Gina's silence. Finally he tossed the pitchfork onto the wheelbarrow and squatted to pretend to tie his boot. "What happened?" he whispered. Gina glanced at the men first and then whispered back to Toby: "He's a pig! Just a filthy pig!" Her eyes filled with tears. He could see the emotional pain she had just talking about it. "One day I'll kill him!" she sputtered. She thrust the shovel into the ground and turned away from Toby, her shoulders shaking with silent sobs. He stood and waited. Toby thought about putting his arm around her to comfort her, like he'd done when his sisters had cried at home, but he didn't dare. He knew that if Lew and Lucca saw them they'd be in trouble and would be separated. A few seconds later Gina recovered, and a look of grim determination replaced her tears. Toby thought that she was stronger and braver than the girls he'd known in the city.

Maria called out to Toby and Gina. She pointed at them and then to the barn.

"C'mon," Gina said in a husky, broken voice. Toby followed her with the wheelbarrow. As they neared the barn, Maria set a basket on the wood chopping block. "You'll eat out here; I don't want that manure stinking up my house!" She took one look at Gina and asked rudely, "Have you been crying?"

"No, ma'am. Just overheated from the work and the sun!" Gina said in a low voice.

Maria watched her closely and then said, "Good thing. You got it good here, girl! Don'tcha be forgettin' that. Ya hear?"

"Yes ma'am."

Gina raised her eyes as Maria turned and walked to the house; halfway there, she changed direction and went to where Lucca and Lew were working.

"She's his pig!" Gina said, jutting her chin towards the group of adults. With that she turned and went to the rain barrel to wash her hands and face. She cupped her hands and poured water down her back and around her neck. When she finished she said, "Go and wash. I'll wait." Toby did just that and felt a lot better after he cleaned up. As he sat down on an un-split log, Gina uncovered the basket and they looked at the food.

There were several scraps of the cooked pork slices and some fried potatoes, both now cold, along with two small pieces of irregularly shaped bread. Toby suspected that these were the leftovers from the men's breakfasts. Gina pushed the basket towards him and let him take what he wanted first.

They ate in silence. Finally, Gina asked, "When did Lew say you were going to ride on?"

Toby thought for a moment and said, "...don't know. He doesn't say much....and I don't think he said that at all." He looked over to the area where the men had been working, but they had gone to the house to eat. "I figured he jus' wanted to spend some time with his kinfolk," he added.

◊ ◊ ◊

# 12

## ~kittens and whip practice~

Gina considered Toby's statement while she ate. "Not likely," she said in a conspiratorial voice. I think Lew's here for awhile." She glanced up at the vineyard, trying to make it seem that they weren't talking, in case Maria or the men were watching them from the house. She turned her back to Toby and added, "I think Lew's here for awhile, as I said...."

Toby thought about it and finally said, "Can't be. We got to haul that still another forty, maybe fifty miles! The man we work for said it had to be there by the end of next week. And besides, Lew told me we got some big river to cross. And we ain't crossed one yet."

Toby looked around as they continued the conversation. "My boss is countin' on us to deliver that still. He's a good man, my boss. He's taking care of my mum and sisters while I'm away.... My dad died a couple of weeks ago." Toby's voice trailed off and he felt for the pocketknife. The idea of not going forward disturbed him. "Anyway, we've gotta deliver that load. It's only right!"

Their conversation was interrupted when two men riding large draft horses came up the lane. The multitude of dogs barked and ran to greet the visitors. Toby and Gina studied the approaching men and nodded as they passed. The younger man eyed Gina and rode directly towards Lew and Lucca, who were now standing on the porch. The visitors slid from the backs of their horses and all four men stood talking.

Lucca seemed to point out the new building location to them. It wasn't long though, before Lucca and one of the men were arguing. Their voices grew louder and Toby could hear them all speaking Italian. Gina listened and Toby watched her. "You understand them?" Toby asked.

"Shh!" Gina said without moving. She giggled. Then she shook her head. "The pig is at it again."

"What are they sayin'?"

"Quick, get moving. We better get back to work."

Toby followed her to the back of the barn and asked again: "What was going on?"

"Lucca's trying to cheat the men. I knew that the one man owed some money to Lucca from last fall. And now he wants the men to do more than they owe for. Fill the 'barra!" Gina seemed to be hard in thought as she filled her half of the "barra." It was near sunset when they finished the last of the grape vine tending. They walked back to the barn and took buckets of water to splash on the tools and wheelbarrow to clean off the manure. "Never leave anything dirty," Gina said. "Lucca will beat ya if ya do." She walked away as Toby finished with the tools and then he rinsed off his boots.

Toby was inside the barn, using a curry comb to brush out some of the dying winter hair in Bea's coat when he turned and saw Lew standing in the doorway.

"Hi, Mr. Lew." Toby wasn't sure if that was the right thing to say. Lew just grunted at Toby and stepped in to look at the cart and its load. He stretched out an arm and lined himself up with the still. He slid his finger along his arm and onto his chest. Then he stretched his arms along the wooden crate and did much the same. Toby watched, trying to seem busy with the mule. It was as if Lew was measuring the still. When Lew looked up he caught Toby looking at him. His stare defied Toby to ask anything and he started to walk back to the door. "Mr. Lew?" Toby said. "Will we be traveling on soon? I was thinking about home and my family."

"You don't worry 'bout that! We leave when we leave! *I* tell *you* when!" Lew jerked his thumb at his chest and repeated himself: "*I* tell *you* when. You keep quiet and do your work. *I* tell *you*." He turned and left the barn.

When Lew was out of earshot, Toby repeated what he'd said, imitating Lew's voice and motions: "*I* tell *you*! *I* tell *you*!" He went back to Bea. As he calmed down, he realized how Bea was still unaffected by things. Toby wished he could be like that, but he wasn't sure that was the answer to things as they were starting to happen.

Toby finished with the mule and paced along the barn wall where the tack hung, still muttering "*I* tell *you!*" He found a short bull whip and absentmindedly took it from the wall. He flipped it out and studied its length. It was about eight feet long. Shorter than the twelve foot one his father and he had used. He snapped it several times and liked the shorter whip! But he noticed that Bea didn't like the sound and flurry of it at all!

He walked a short distance to the other end of the building and cracked it again. A fly sat on the wooden stanchion. With a flick of Toby's wrist and the new whip, the fly was a smear on the wood. He tried again to hit the same spot and was only an inch or so off. After several more snaps he had the length just right. The whip felt good in Toby's hand and he continued to pick spots to aim at. In one snap he sent a corn kernel on the floor flying ten feet. *Not bad*, Toby thought. He turned around and backhanded a shot at a post, nailing it perfectly. He continued playing with the whip until his arm, which was already sore from the day's work, ached. Finally he rolled up the whip and put it back on the tack wall.

It was getting late and he waited for his food. He sat on the same stump where he'd eaten the midday meal and looked at the house. He could hear all four men talking and laughing inside, evidently no longer arguing. He wondered where Gina was and if she would bring him food. Toby waited and waited, getting hungrier and more frustrated. Maybe he should go to the house, he thought. *What the hell?!* He'd worked all day and they owed him some food!

He set out for the house but wasn't ten feet from the barn door when he heard someone whisper his name. It was Gina. "I brought you some food, but don't let them know!" She quickly ducked into the barn.

She was hiding something in the front of her dress with the skirt gathered in her hands, exposing her legs up to her mid-thighs. Toby gasped when he saw them: Her legs were so white! They weren't anything like the deep brown of the skin on her arms and neck. He followed her inside, looking back at the house over his shoulder. Gina handed him a piece of cheese, a hard biscuit, and a piece of salted beef. "They won't miss it!" she said ruefully. "They're drinkin' the grappa. Come on." She went to a ladder nailed to the wall and climbed to the loft. Toby got to the ladder just as she stepped onto the loft. Again he saw her naked legs!

Blinking several times, he tossed the food up to her and climbed the ladder. He joined her against the outside wall. She stopped and whispered and then clucked her tongue. A cat meowed and poked its head out from beneath a box. She offered it a piece of cheese, using the food to coax the cat to her. "Look behind the box," she said softly. Toby looked and saw kittens. He smiled and watched as the small cats wobbled around looking for the softness and warmth of their mother.

He and Gina ate and watched the kittens nurse from their mother when the cat returned to the nesting area. The mother cat licked each of her babies, knocking them over. Gina told Toby that the cat did this so the kittens would struggle and build up strength.

Toby watched Gina brush the biscuit crumbs from her chest, knocking them into her lap. He didn't understand why he seemed to be watching her more closely than before. But he noticed some shape under her loose clothes that he hadn't seen earlier in the day. What was wrong with him? He didn't think much of girls, especially with four of them at home! Come to think of it, Toby realized he was sort of glad to be away from his sisters for awhile.

Gina picked up the larger pieces of leftover biscuit from her lap and ate them. It seemed like she was still hungry, and yet, she'd given all her cheese to the cat! There was a whistle from the house and Gina stiffened. "I've gotta go! Go to the door and show yourself. I'll go to the outhouse."

Toby crawled down from the loft and went out the barn door. He wondered how Gina was going to get to the outhouse. A moment later he heard the outside toilet door   shut and Gina answering Lucca's call.

◊ ◊ ◊

# 13

## ~bye-bye "Boy-Yas" by midnight~

Toby hung a lantern on the side of the cart and lifted the seat. He rummaged through the toolbox and came across an oilskin packet tucked along the side of the box. Inside was a crude map. Toby studied it for a moment and realized that it was the trip-map for the delivery! It showed the town of Butler, the Stone House Tavern, Annandale Station, and then a line showing the roadway to another town called Parsonsville. The roadway continued on to another village, but it wasn't Boyers! Toby recalled their travels so far and realized that they weren't on the map. He understood that Lew wanted to visit his family, but he wondered where they were. He looked at the map again and saw a town called Parker's Landing. The two parallel lines crossed at Parker's Landing. *That must be the river*, Toby thought. Across a gap in the drawing, the scrawled path continued to another town. It was Callensburg; the next was Sligo.

"Sligo," Toby repeated several times out loud. "That's where Mr. Rodgers said we're headed," he said to himself. The place had a strange name and it sounded even stranger as he repeated it for the third time. If the map was to scale, Toby realized that the trip was only halfway done. And then they'd have to make the long trip home! Again, Toby started to think of his mother and the girls.

He folded the map and started to put it back into the pouch when it jammed. He pulled it out and looked inside. There was something else there. He tipped over the pouch and out came money—and a lot of it! Toby counted it: Nearly twelve dollars. That was more than his father would make in a month. So why had Lew skimped on food for them and grain for Bea at the Tavern? There was plenty of money to feed all three of them very well for the entire trip—both ways!

Toby replaced the money and the map. He tapped the pouch on his hand and looked towards the house. He wondered it Lew was going to keep the money for himself. "We'll see, we'll see," he murmured, placing the pouch back into the toolbox and closing the lid.

Toby reckoned it was about 8:00 and he was tired. He stopped his pacing to pet Bea and then went to prepare a sleeping spot in the hay pile. He got comfortable and stared out of a window opening in the wall. He'd seen the half moon rising in the sky when he was outside earlier. It was bright enough that he could see the lane, the house, and the vineyard. Within a few minutes he drifted off to sleep.

"Toby! Toby!" He woke up to Gina shaking him. "Wake up! We have to go!"

"What?" Toby was still shaking off the sleep. "…I don't understand, what are you…?"

"We HAVE to go, NOW! He isn't going to deliver the still!" Toby started to interrupt her when she continued: "Listen! I overheard them talking. They plan to use it! HERE! They're going to keep it and make more grappa! They don't know I understand Italian! And they were drunk. They were talking about the new building and how they'd put the still in it. They laughed about how disappointed the still's owners were going to be."

Toby was awake now and looked at Gina in earnest. Suddenly everything made sense.

"Hurry, we can't waste *any* time leaving. Can you get the mule hooked up? Take this!" She pushed a thin blanket into his chest and then paused. "I have something else to get—I'll be right back! Get everything we need into the cart!"

Toby got up and got to work; it was all too clear to him now. Lew *was* going to keep the money! He was probably leaving—chucking his wife in Pittsburgh and the job with Howard and Rodgers Company. As Toby hurried with the harness and the cart, his mind raced with other questions. What had Lew planned to do with *him*? Surely Lew didn't think that Toby would just stay here and work, did he?! Or that Toby wouldn't go back home and tell what had happened? As Toby eliminated possibilities, another answer smacked him with enough force to give him another black eye: *Maybe Lew had planned to kill Toby!*

Anger and fear made Toby move even faster. *I've got the map, plenty of money,* and *the still,* Toby thought. "That cheating bastard!" he said under his breath. He jerked at Bea's harness and she let out a small noise. He caught himself and stopped to pat her. "Easy, girl. Easy."

He studied the cart's contents: What else would they need? Toby looked across the dark barn and thought hard. *What had been uncomfortable on the ride so far?* He thought of being inside the hard, cramped still. He gathered several armloads of hay and pushed it into the top of the still. What else? His mind raced. Another cover! Something to keep rain off them! He looked around but couldn't find anything that would work.

Toby pushed the door open and was preparing to back Bea out when Gina returned. She was carrying a large, heavy bundle. He looked at her and whispered, "If you steal anything, we could go to jail!"

"If they catch us, we WON'T be going to jail!" She lifted the sack of goods onto the cart. Toby knew she was right. He got Bea out of the barn and took one last look inside. He went to the far wall and took down the whip.

Quietly, Toby took Bea by the bridle and led her away. In the moonlight, he could see Gina looking over her shoulder towards the darkened house.

At the end of the lane, Toby asked her, "Do you know the way to Parsonsville?"

"I was there a couple of years ago. I remember the way. There are a few roads that the coal wagons use to take coal to the blacksmith's there."

"Which one would be used the least?" Toby asked as they hurried down the same road that he'd first seen on his way in.

"They all split off the road from the Station's Road," Gina said.

Toby's heart sunk at this news. It meant that they had to climb that steep hill; if Lew followed them on horseback, he could make it far quicker than they could. "Isn't there a flatter road? Somewhere they might not consider looking for us?"

They were at the end of the road to the farm now and passing through the village of Boyers. Several dogs barked as they drove by. Toby flipped the reins and Bea quickened her pace. Toby's eyes had finally adjusted to the moonlight and he felt safe with Bea's course.

He turned to Gina and waited for an answer.

"Well!?" he finally asked.

"Yeah, at the bottom of the hill; it's a logging road. It's kinda rough, but it would save us hours. And I don't think they'd think we'd use it! Yeah, it's perfect!"

Gina watched closely for a trail opening into the woods. "Here!" she said and Toby guided Bea off of the main road. They left behind the small village. It was darker here in the woods, but Bea seemed to have no trouble following the path.

Now that they could talk without being heard Toby asked Gina to repeat the conversation she'd heard earlier in the evening. Even a second time through, Toby still didn't want to think of Lew and Lucca having such evil plans.

When he told Gina this, she laughed scornfully and said, "Lew was an Indian fighter. It changed him. At least, that's what Maria said. There are Indian scalps hanging up on the wall in the back room of the house! He's a killer. No, he's a *mean* killer. I heard Lucca telling some men one night that Lew was supposed to escort twenty Indians to a fort, but they never arrived. Lew had killed them all!"

Toby shuddered. His thoughts ran wild. He had traveled alone with Lew all that time. He felt lucky to be alive. Suddenly Toby thought back to Lew's disappearances. What had he been doing?

Gina told Toby about other times that Lew had been to the farm: the fights with men who came to buy grappa and how Lew had beaten one man so badly that they had to deliver him home in a wagon.

Toby interrupted her and asked, "Is that how you got the bruise and the cut lip?"

Gina clenched her jaw and turned her face away from him "Yes," she said quietly, nodding her head.

"But why? What happened?" Toby asked.

"I'm tired," Gina said. "Can I sleep? It's about two hours to reach the 'Hill Yard Mine.' Just go straight through." With that, she turned in the seat and raised her leg to climb over it. Toby turned to look at her and got another glimpse of her bare legs. She climbed back to the still and he heard the hay inside rustle as she curled up inside.

So much ran through Toby's mind. He kept going over all the things that Gina had told him and recounting everything that he and Lew had been through since leaving Pittsburgh. Now that some of the shock had worn off, there wasn't much that Toby couldn't believe about Lew.

◊ ◊ ◊

# 14

## ~rotten eggs and a seedless grape~

The next several hours passed without much incident. He thought they should have been to the next village by now, but Toby figured that girls weren't good at travel or distances! *Well, maybe we'll make better time in the daylight,* Toby thought. As usual, Bea just plodded along and didn't seem to care that it was nighttime, where they were, or where they were heading.

Toby smelled Hilliard's Mine before he could see it. Actually, he could smell the "boney"—the sulfured rock that often comes with coal mining. It smelled like rotten eggs. Miners picked the rock out of the coal by hand and tossed into piles that smoldered when left in the air for too long. Sometimes they buried the boney in the mine tailing or threw it into a creek to keep the air off it. But that usually turned the water to acid and killed the fish and wildlife.

He heard a sound behind him and realized that Gina was now standing up in the still, her body from the waist up poking out of the top of the pot. She rubbed her arms to keep off the cold and then said, "It's ahead, a good road to the left. It takes us to Parsonsville. We'll get there by sunup."

"Gina? Do you think that Lew or Lucca would use the logging road to get ahead of us?"

She thought for a moment then replied, "Hmm…I guess they could, if they thought we were going on with the delivery. But, why wouldn't they think you weren't going home—back to Pittsburgh? Do you think Lew would think you knew the way to deliver this?" She tapped her fingers on the side of the still and it made a ringing noise.

"I don't know what he thinks of me. I reckon he might figure me to be a mama's boy and head home."

Gina ruffled Toby's hair and asked with a laugh: "*Are* you a mama's boy?"

Toby pulled his head away from her hand and forcefully barked, "No!"

Gina laughed and dropped her hand to his shoulder. "No, I don't think you're a mama's boy, either. And I don't think you're a 'Baby Grape' like Lew called you."

"*Baby WHAT?*" Toby asked, turning to look at her.

She looked around the landscape and the road ahead with a majestic air. "Yup. Lew said you were a 'Baby Grape'—because you have no seeds!" She gave a hearty laugh at her own joke.

Toby fumed. "Yeah, well, Lew's a bastard! And a killer! *And* a thief!"

Gina's voice turned serious as she said, "Yes, he is! Always remember that! ...BABY GRAPE!" With that she dropped back into the still pot. A moment passed and Toby heard another giggle coming from inside the still.

"Baby Grape!" Toby muttered and clenched the whip that he'd kept on his lap --during the trip. *No seeds! I'll show him! This baby grape bites!,* he thought and flipped the reins. *Baby Grape!* The name kept surfacing. He was so mad that it seemed like even Bea turned and smiled at the joke. Maybe lack of sleep had dulled Toby's sense of humor, but as he considered things, a sense of humor was going to get this job done. He had no idea of what was ahead, and if he did, would he do what he was supposed to do?

Toby stewed for awhile more, but in the end he was more tired than angry. Sunrise came and found Toby's head bobbing up and down with the cart's motion. He woke with a start to the sound of horses' hooves thundering towards the cart.

◊ ◊ ◊

# 15

## ~better food and a fast follower~

The rider passed the cart without slowing down. As his fear subsided and his breathing returned to normal, Toby figured that the man was probably late for work and was hurrying to get there. But boy! Toby was wide awake now!

He realized that Bea had been going all night and must be tired. He steered her off the side of the road. He gave her some water, but she didn't seem too thirsty. He also gave her some grain and then let her eat a few apples from his hand.

"I'll get you better food at the first chance, Bea," he said softly.

"And what about me?" Gina asked. "Will you feed me better, too? I'm real hungry! It's hard work, ya know—sleeping through the night with you two making all that noise!" Gina laughed as she climbed out of the still, her dress riding up her legs. There was simply no graceful way to get out of the pot, and Toby was just a little glad about that!

"Tell me what's up ahead," he asked Gina's back as she walked into the wooded area. She disappeared behind a tree. When she reappeared several minutes later she said, "Parsonsville," as if he had just asked the question.

It was early in the morning and few people would be in the center of town at this hour. Still, Gina suggested that they disguise themselves, just to be safe. They covered the whiskey still in the back of the cart and Toby hid underneath the oilcloth. Gina pulled on a pair of men's pants that she'd brought in the bundle and used a short piece of rope as a belt. Then she covered her head with a hat that Lew had left in the toolbox and put on Toby's coat.

They turned the cart onto what looked like the main street and saw several shops along it, including a dry goods store, a blacksmith's shop, and a feed store. A drug and general merchandise store stood at the end of the street. Toby peeked out from underneath the oilcloth and saw a sign with arrows on it. They pointed the way to places he hadn't seen on the map: North Hope and Eau Claire.

Toby had given Gina a dollar and put one in his own pocket. After tying Bea to a post, she headed to the general store with a mental list of supplies while Toby slipped from under the cloth and went to the feed store. He carried two small sacks of feed back to the cart and waited nearby for Gina. He was nearly tired of waiting for her when she showed up. She tossed several wrapped bags onto the cart, untied Bea, and climbed up into the driver's seat. Toby started to walk over towards the cart but saw Gina shake her head "no" at him. She guided Bea between two buildings and then onto a second street that ran parallel to Main Street. Toby followed the cart from a distance. It was better if they weren't seen together.

At the edge of town Gina turned the cart down the hill and waited for Toby after the crest. He caught the handle on the cart's seat and climbed up beside her. She flipped the reins and Bea went forward. After two miles they tuned into a field entrance and followed a wood line. Once they were out of sight of the road they stopped to eat.

Toby was thrilled to see that Gina had bought fresh bread, eggs, and smoked ham! He started a fire and they had hot food in no time. They were both hungry and ate in silence. The morning sun warmed the air. Toby's belly was full and he fell asleep in a patch of sunlight. Bea dozed, too.

Gina woke Toby. She'd already hooked Bea up to the cart and put out the fire. "I think you can walk with me, to give some Bea some relief," she said. "We'll stop early this evening and give her a longer night to rest."

Toby nodded. It seemed like a good plan, but he resented that Gina had made all the decisions without him. Still, he couldn't find any fault with the plan, so he just grunted his agreement.

The land here rolled along gently and the travel along the road was some of the easiest of the trip so far. Toby could see ahead for long distances. He studied the horizon for awhile, thinking about how beautiful it was here, and how different it was from the smoky city he was used to. Then something made him look back over his shoulder and he saw a man on a horse, traveling fast on their tail.

◊ ◊ ◊

# 16

## ~murderous news and a she in wolf's clothes~

"Gina, look!" Toby said. She looked back at the rider. He sure seemed to be in a hurry. "You'd better get under the cover," Gina said.

Toby snapped his head towards Gina. He started to get angry with her. Here she was telling him what to do again. She saw the look on his face and before he could protest she added: "Wait! Listen to me! I was the only one seen on the cart in town. So we don't want the story to change if Lew comes asking around. Besides, you talk funny. Folks recognize your city talk. C'mon! Quick!" She pointed to the back of the cart and then stuffed a few stray hairs up under her hat.

Toby lifted the cover and rolled onto the deck of the cart. He covered himself and listened as the rider approached.

"You there! Cart ahead! Hold up!" Toby heard the rider yell to them. A moment later the horse's hooves stomped to a prancing circle at the side of the cart.

"Boy, you keep a watch out!" the rider said. "I carry news of a man who killt a young girl at a tavern, and they think he's the one that killt another man in Butler.... Think he's riding up this way. He's supposed to be on a cart...." The man paused and Toby's heart skipped a beat. "...well, he's supposed to be on a cart like you got, boy!"

Toby thought the man was talking to him; maybe he'd seen Toby get on the back of the cart. He was about to uncover himself and sit up when Gina answered. It was her voice, but a lot deeper than normal: "I thank you. I'll sure keep my eyes open. He sounds like a mean one! I got my whip here to keep me safe." Underneath the oilcloth, Toby smiled.

He could hear the rider's horse still dancing about; it wanted to run. The rider continued: "You might need mor'n a whip. And yeah, I'd say he sounds like a mean one!"

"You takin' the news to where?" Gina asked in the same deep voice.

"On to Farmington, an' over to Parker's Landing," the rider said.

"How far is the Landin'?" Gina asked. "Oh, and how's the road that way?" Toby was impressed with her cunning. He listened for the reply.

"Oh, 'bout six miles to Farmington. An' maybe a dozen more to the Landing. I gotta go. The road's pretty fair—you'll make good time." Toby heard the rider spur his horse on and call back to Gina: "Take care, boy!"

"Thanks, mister!" Gina yelled back. The cart began to move again but Toby stayed hidden.

A minute or two later Gina said, "It's ok, Toby." He rolled out from underneath the oilcloth, jumped down to the ground, and trotted to the front of the cart. He bounded up onto the seat beside her.

"That was a pretty good job you done there—*boy*!" Toby said, laughing.

Gina gave him a good-natured sharp elbow in the ribs. Then her face turned serious. "I *told* you that Lew's a killer!" she said.

Toby thought back to Lew's disappearances and how he'd came back hurt and bleeding. Everything seemed to fit: Lew had killed those people! Toby and Gina talked about it until they exhausted the subject twice over and had nothing left to think on.

Toby mentioned that the sign he'd seen in Parsonsville didn't match the road they were on. "It didn't mention Farmington; just some place called Eau Clair," he said.

Gina laughed and told him that the name had changed but that the people hadn't. "They're just slow to accept the town's new name," she said. "It'll probably stay that way for a long time—till the old ones die. It's just the way people are!"

Toby looked at Gina, still dressed like a boy. She'd been hardened by work on the farm and was a little thin, so her face looked more boyish than other girls Toby knew. He compared Gina to his sisters back home, who were better fed and not sun-parched. He realized that Gina might even be pretty if her face was softened a little. He kept these thoughts to himself. His dad had always said, "It's best not to tell a woman too much." Toby figured this was good advice.

Gina handed Toby the reins and he watched the road—both ahead and behind! The afternoon passed slowly, and they took turns whistling tunes to each other. They each knew a few church songs that the other didn't.

Finally they saw Eau Claire up ahead on top of a large ridge. They could see the church's steeple and some other rooftops. The town was larger than Parsonsville, which meant more people to see Toby and Gina. There were bound to be people here who knew Lucca and who would tell him about the two fugitives for a free jug of grappa.

"We'll wait till dark," Gina said. "And then maybe get through town. We just need to watch for signs."

"That's tough in the dark!" Toby said. He wanted to be the one calling the shots, but Gina seemed to be one step ahead of him every time. Once again, he couldn't find any fault with her plan, so he just agreed to it. They pulled off the side of the road and hid the cart until well after dark.

By midnight they had made it through Eau Claire and several miles past the town. Nothing had happened along the way and they stopped in a patch of woods along a path that left the main road to Parker's Landing.

They were far enough off the road that a fire wouldn't be noticed, so Toby built a small blaze. As the light grew, he gathered more wood, carrying a torch made from a handful of the dry hay inside the still.

"Let's sleep late. We'll give Bea some extra rest—she deserves it!" Toby said to Gina. He acted like this was his idea, even though Gina had said the same thing earlier in the day. But she just nodded. "I 'spect it's gonna get cold by morning. I want to cover Bea so she won't be so stiff later on." Toby was thinking out loud and Gina seemed lost in her own thoughts. She was still wearing the men's clothing from earlier, and Toby figured she kept them on to be warm.

"We won't have but one blanket to share," Toby said. "But if we both slept in the still we'd be warm. Kinda cramped, I guess. But warm."

"Okay," Gina replied.

Toby stood up and offered her a hand. She took it, rocked up off of the log-seat, and followed him into the still. It was a little awkward, but they seemed to melt together to fit the tight quarters. They curled up together and soon fell asleep.

Toby woke near dawn. He wanted more sleep but had urgent business with the first tree he could find. He realized that his hand was on Gina's chest. Through her coat he could feel the softness of her breast. He quickly lifted his hand and tried to stand. His legs were stiff and he wobbled a little.

Gina stirred but slept on. Toby pushed aside the oilcloth and climbed out. After answering nature's call, he went to the fire and pushed at the still glowing logs. The fire began to burn again. He decided to get some breakfast cooking so they could eat and be on their way when Gina woke up.

As he gathered up the food, Toby saw Bea's ears perk up. He listened and heard the sound of a wagon approaching. He wanted to warn Gina but there was no time! Toby realized that the wagon was coming up from the lane that they'd turned into. It must be the property's owner. The wagon came into sight and Toby could see two people riding on it. The dim early light made it hard to see the passengers clearly, but Toby could see the outline of someone holding a rifle!

◊ ◊ ◊

# 17

## ~a story and something to put right~

"Good morning, sir!" Toby said loudly, hoping that Gina might wake and think to be quiet.

There was no reply as the wagon approached. Toby shuffled from one foot to another and decided to try again.

"Good morning!" The wagon stopped and the men looked at him without saying a word. They eyed up Toby and surveyed the campsite.

The driver finally said, "You trespassin', boy. This is our land." He spoke in a quiet, menacing voice.

Toby thought quickly and said, "We're real sorry. Um, I'm sorry!" He tried to correct the slip-up, as he didn't want the men to know about Gina.

The passenger lifted the rifle and began to scan the woods behind Toby. The driver's eyes never left Toby's face.

"Who's wif ya, boy?" the driver asked.

Toby quickly answered, "My uncle. He went into the woods just before first light—wanted to find us some meat for a meal." Toby looked at the driver and then to the passenger to see if they believed him. He waited for a response.

The passenger was still turning in the seat, searching the woods. Evidently, the idea of a hunter in the woods—who could have them in his gun's sight—didn't rest easy with either of them.

Toby realized that he was in a position to bargain and added: "We jus' needed to rest our mule and sleep off the ride. Soon as we eat we'll be going on to the Landing." Toby gave the men a smile, thinking it might help.

It seemed to work. The passenger nudged the older driver with his elbow. Nothing happened for a moment. Then the driver grunted and tossed the reins.

The horses started to move. The driver looked sternly at Toby and snarled, "I don't like trespassers—*or* poachers! Best be gone soon as ya eat!"

"We will. Yes, sir. We'll be gone real soon—a quick meal, too…Sir."

They pulled away and Toby sighed. He realized that the men had reason to be upset with him. After all, it *was* their land, and he and Gina *were* trespassing. Toby was grateful that nothing worse had happened. When the other wagon was out of sight he called to Gina.

She lifted the oilcloth from the still and slowly raised her head. Looking around and seeing that the coast was clear, she hopped out and ran into the woods. She was laughing when she returned. "I nearly wet myself!" she said. "I got pretty scared for a minute. You did great!" she exclaimed. She squeezed his arm and he nearly wet *himself.*

They prepared a good meal and ate by the fire. Toby thought about the men on the wagon and said, "They sure seemed unfriendly—almost scared like. You shoulda seen the man with the gun. Boy he sure was nervous!" Toby imitated him looking around into the woods. They laughed and kept whipping their heads around, pretending to look for "Uncle."

They got back on the road and were surprised to see other travelers passing them in both directions now. They passed several men on horseback as well as a wagon of timbers pulled by large draft horses. A man who looked like a preacher stopped his buggy to talk to them and asked lots of questions. "Too many!"Gina said as she nudged Toby in the ribs and nodded ahead. Toby wasn't interested in leaving too much information about them along the trail, either. He looked up and down the road. Lucca and Lew could be anywhere; they needed to move on. It was probably a little rude to the preacher, but they begged off and made to leave. The preacher was still asking questions as they pulled away.

"Where do you suppose they are?" Toby spoke his thoughts aloud.

Gina shuddered and shook her head. "I don't know but I wish I did," she said, her head still moving back and forth. After several minutes she added, "Maybe even ahead of us…but probably behind. Oh! I don't know! But, he's not going to get me and take me back! I'll kill them both!" She paused and then continued her rant. "If I have to go back there I'll burn down the house when they're all asleep. Just like they did to us!" Gina burst into tears and cried loudly. Even Bea turned her head at the noise.

Toby didn't say a word; he waited for her to calm down some. She continued to cry for a full five minutes, pounding her fist on her thigh a few times. After that she gathered herself, began to control her breathing, and straightened up. For awhile she gazed at the landscape and said nothing.

Toby watched the road ahead and guided Bea along—not that she needed the help; but it helped the time pass.

"I wanna tell you," Gina said softly. She sniffed and drew a large breath. "Me dad—sorry!" Her voice caught and Toby thought she was going to cry again. "My dad died in a mine accident. My mum and I, and my sisters and lil' brother were left on our own. We did odd jobs for money: cleaning, farm work, canning, laundry. We worked from sunup to dark but there wasn't ever much money. We didn't have a lot of food and not much for clothes or other stuff...

"We were in a field one day, digging up potatoes. It was in the fall and it was cold and windy. My little brother was sick, but he dug the best he could." She sobbed again. "And then he started coughin' and coughin' and he couldn't stop!" She looked up at Toby with tears streaming down her face now. "Then he was coughin' up this—this slime. It hung from his mouth to the ground—and he *still* coughed up more!" She pounded her fist against her leg again. "Me momma held him, and tried to let him cough up the mess. He coughed for 'nother spell and then he just collapsed!" Giant tears rolled down her cheeks. "He was dead before my momma could get him to the house. He was five years old! We buried him in the woods behind our house—beside me father... my father.... Momma changed after that. She didn't laugh anymore. And she didn't work anymore. My sisters and I kept working, but we got most of our food from some neighbors who were kind to us."

Gina was calmer now; she paused to wipe her nose on her sleeve. She sniffled a little and brushed at her pant legs. When she was ready, she continued: "Not too long later, Lew and Lucca showed up and demanded money from me momma. Lucca kept sayin' that father owed him money and he was going to take it! It was quite a fight between 'em—screamin' and shoutin'! Then Lew said he was taking me to work off the debt! Momma didn't know what else to do. I just remember her and my sisters standing at the door as Lucca pulled me onto his lap and we rode away."

Gina cleared her throat and her voice changed; it sounded more far away.

"I went to stay with Maria, Lucca, and Lew. They treated me terribly! Lew would laugh while Lucca beat me. Then later Lew started to beat me, too. But HE couldn't quit! Lucca had to pull him off me a couple of times. Lucca is mean, but Lew is crazy-mean!"

Gina pressed her eyes into the palms of her hands and put her elbows on her knees. She stayed like that for a few minutes. Finally she lifted her head and looked into the sky. Toby looked at her and saw that her tears had dried. She turned to him and continued.

"Onenight Lew disappeared right after dinner. He took a bottle of grappa and left the farm." She held Toby's gaze as she continued with the story. "The next morning, I was gathering eggs in the barn when some men rode into the farm. They hollered as they rode up, but I couldn't make out what they said. When they left, I walked back to the house with the eggs and Maria took me inside. I asked what the men wanted but nobody would look at me. Lucca left the house and went to the barn. Maria gave me breakfast with a lot of extras." Again Gina looked hard at Toby.

"Maria then told me that momma's house had burned down and that…that she and my sisters had died…." Gina sniffed again, drew her sleeve across her nose, and stared across the field beside the cart. "Lucca came to the house, and later he carried a bundle to the barn. I was crying, but I heard the horse gallop away. Lucca came back to the house and that was the last time I'd seen Lew—until you both showed up! Stop the cart."

Gina left the cart and walked into the field. She didn't move for several moments. Toby saw her looking into the sky. Then she crossed herself and returned to the cart.

She looked at Toby and smiled sheepishly. "Thanks for listening," she said. "There's a lot more, but you've had enough for one day—or longer!" she added with a little laugh.

Toby just looked at her, too stunned to say anything. He clucked his tongue at Bea and they started to move again. Toby thought it was best to mimic the mule and remain quiet. Inside, his mind was racing and his stomach ached at the thought of everything Gina had told him. Every so often he glanced over at her to see if she was alright. Once she smiled at him and gave his arm a little squeeze. She seemed to be lightened of a terrible burden now that she'd told him part of her story.

Toby's hatred for Lucca, Lew, and Maria was stronger than ever. He imagined the cruelty that they, collectively, had inflicted on this girl. He chewed on the inside of his cheek and promised himself that he'd somehow make things right in this whole mess for Gina.

◊ ◊ ◊

# 17.5

## ~a cold wet dream~

After they stopped for a late afternoon rest and ate a light meal, they continued on to the next village. They didn't need any supplies except a lantern to replace the one they accidentally left hanging in a tree where they'd trespassed the night before. Toby circumvented the town with the cart while Gina walked in and purchased a lantern and a bottle of lamp oil.

After traveling down and then up another very long, steep hill, they'd made the first mile towards Parker's Landing. *Ten more miles to go*, thought Toby. Since it was already close to dark and felt like a cold night coming on, they decided to find a good place to camp and get an early start in the morning. Toby kept his eyes open for a secluded spot to camp away from the road. Surely, Lucca and Lew would be looking for them by now. And if they thought that Toby and Gina were headed for the Landing, then they might be traveling this road, too. The possibilities were getting slimmer and Toby didn't like the slimming chances of their escape.

Toby tried to think of ways that he and Gina could escape from Lew and Lucca if necessary. But he had no idea of what was ahead and not a clue about what he might have to do. He looked at Gina and thought of telling her about his fears, but she smiled at him and he decided to leave it till another time.

They passed a section of very large pine trees; Gina called them hemlocks. The huge trees were spaced well apart. It would be easy for the cart to pass between them as they looked for a place to camp out of site of the road. They could build a fire and cut some of the branches to help hide the firelight. *Even use some to make a soft bed!*, Toby thought, remembering his own soft bed at home. He longed for his mother's voice, her cooking, and even for the teasing of his sisters. He wondered what his own life would be like if they had died in a fire like Gina's family had. He shuddered.

Gina saw him and asked him if he was cold. He shrugged. She patted his arm and smiled. "I'll keep you warm, lil' grape!" He shoved her away, and she giggled.

"Here. Take the reins," Toby said as they turned off of the road. He got down from the cart and followed along behind it, kicking fallen leaves over the tracks that the mule and cart left. He doubted that anybody would see the marks in the late day sunlight, but why take any chances? "Find a good campsite," he said. "I want to look around." He turned to leave the cart but stopped and grabbed the whip to take with him. He walked a short ways from one side of the trail to the other. He didn't find anything of any importance except some large rocks with a spring of clear water pouring from them. The smell of the pine trees and the dampness of the area were kind of nice. He thought it would be agreat place to build a house. He wandered along and circled the area, eventually finding Gina and a very nice place to camp.

She had already unhooked Bea and was filling the lantern with oil. Toby used the flint and the piece of steel to get some sparks into the hay that he took from the inside of the still. A small fire started quickly and Toby added twigs and wood to it.

Gina took some rope and tied it between two trees near the fire. She hung the blanket, coat, and some clothing across it. When everything was dry and warm, she gathered the pieces and quickly pushed them into the still. She reasoned that the cloth would stay warm in there, and so would they while they slept! The wind was increasing and they had to watch the fire closely. Several times it blew into the pine needles and they quickly stomped it out. When the wind got too severe, they put out the fire and sat in the falling darkness. They looked at the clouds racing across the dark sky. Even though they could only see a small patch of sky through the tall pines, it was clear that the sky was filling up with a solid covering of black clouds.

As usual, Bea remained calm and unconcerned with what was going on around her. She dealt with the wind by turning her rear into it to shelter her head. The lantern hung nearby and its flame flickered when the wind gusted. As the wind picked up and whipped through the hemlock trees, their limbs swayed and rasped against each other. The wind started to make an eerie howling noise through the trees. It was still early in the evening and should still be light out, but the woods were nearly dark! Toby was dismayed. They would have to get inside the still and wait out the coming storm.

He stood looking at Bea and wondered if it would be best to hobble her rather than tie her to a tree. Before he could decide what to do he heard the rain coming! It started beating on the tops of the trees, which kept the water from reaching the ground right away. But it quickly penetrated the limbs and dripped onto Toby, Gina, and Bea.

Gina and Toby checked the site again, took the lantern and went to the still. Inside they pulled the oilskin over the opening and sat on the warmed clothing and blanket.

Even through the oilskin they could see the lightning as it lit up the sky. A huge clap of thunder made a deafening crack and Gina grabbed Toby's arm. He turned off the lamp and stood up to put it outside the still. "Can't we keep it on?" she pleaded.

"No, it'll kill us if we keep it in here tonight," Toby replied. He wasn't sure why that was true, but it was something his father had taught him about lanterns. He thought that it was common sense and that Gina should have known it, too.

They sat in the dark of the still. More lightning flashed, followed by thunderous noise. Before long they were wrapped in the blanket, the clothing, and each other. Toby held Gina and felt her jerk every time the lightning flashed. He could smell her hair and the scent of sweat. He liked the feeling of holding her and the warmth she gave him.

The storm raged on for several hours without ever letting up much. Sitting in a whiskey still on the back of a mule cart in the middle of a vicious storm was stressful. Eventually, exhausted from the tension, Toby and Gina fell asleep. The rain on the outside of the still was deafening and they were both fitful. Toby kept waking up thinking about the story of Gina's family

Sometime during the night, Gina was in the midst of a dream: She felt the man's hairy arm against her throat; she moaned and cried softly. If she made a sound he would hit her repeatedly. She felt a hand on her hip slid to her leg. She couldn't do this again! She WOULDN'T do this again! She began to slap at the man! She hit him, she tried to get away, but she was pinned. There was no room to get away. She screamed and started punching. Then she stood up. Her knee hit him—hard—in what she guessed was his face. Gina shouted incoherently and struggled to get out of the top of the still. She got tangled in the oilcloth and pushed at the sides of the still. Finally she grabbed hold of the opening and pulled herself out. She fell onto the crate and scraped her shin. Still tangled in the oilcloth, she tumbled to the ground. The pine needles made a soft landing spot. Gina jumped to her feet.

Toby had followed her out of the still and onto the ground. He grabbed her by the arms and shouted, "Gina! What's wrong? What's wrong?!?" By now she was fully awake, but still dazed. Her arms hung limply at her sides and she didn't answer Toby.

The rain was still coming down hard. "Gina, what happened?" Toby asked. When she didn't answer, he gathered her against him and picked up the oilcloth. He half tugged and half pushed her onto the cart deck and motioned for her to get inside the still. She climbed in silently and Toby followed her. He pulled the oilskin over the top. They were out of the rain now but soaking wet.

Gina's body shook and shivered with cold. "We need to get rid of these wet clothes," Toby said. Still, Gina didn't speak or make a move. Toby realized that she would stay like that all night if he didn't do something. He tugged at her shirt; she seemed to come to and looked at Toby. He said, "Gina, you have to get out of these wet clothes or we're going to freeze to death. Do you understand?"

She nodded and started pulling off her clothes. She handed them to Toby and he pushed the heavy clothing out of the top of the still. Each piece landed on the cart deck with a flop. Toby pulled off his own wet clothes and threw them out, as well. It was warm inside the still, but Gina was still shivering. Toby pulled the blanket around them and listened as Gina caught her breath. She seemed calmer now and her trembling subsided to a light shiver.

Toby felt strange as her wet skin lay against his. He'd seen his sisters bathing in the kitchen, but he'd never touched the warm flesh of a girl before. He was too scared to move. He realized that his face hurt from where she'd kneed him. Gina fell asleep and Toby sat there without moving until dawn. He was still trying to sort out the stories she'd told him earlier....

◊ ◊ ◊

# 18

## ~wet gruel and a copped squat~

Toby looked up and saw dim sunlight through the oilskin. His bladder hurt and he needed to get out and relieve himself. He slipped his arm from under Gina's neck and stood up. She stirred but kept sleeping. He pulled aside the cover and pushed himself up and out of the still opening. The sun was warm. He quietly stepped onto the deck of the cart and lightly jumped onto the ground. Bea saw him and started pawing the ground.

"I know, I know...." he whispered to her as he hurried behind a tree. He sighed in relief as he drained his bladder. He looked about and thought of how a rain like last night's always swept Pittsburgh clean. The sky would be clear and the air would smell so fresh—for awhile. The streets would be clean, the soot gone, and the grass would lose its greyish tint. Here he smelled the pine trees and fresh country air. Birds were chirping and he thought he saw a deer moving far off in the woods.

He walked over to Bea and patted her head. She nodded her head, chiding him for the night before. "I know. I know. Wasn't *my* fault!" he whispered to her. She nuzzled his hand and kept turning her ears to sounds in the woods.

Toby hung their wet clothes on the line that Gina had strung up the night before. He retrieved the flint and looked for some dry wood. It took several attempts to get things going, but the dead hemlock finally caught and crackled into a warm fire. Toby held his pants near the flames. He figured they'd take awhile to dry out, so he hung them up again and stood by the fire until he warmed up.

Gina was still sleeping, so Toby decided to feed Bea. The canvas bucket was full of wet grain and water. He poured it into the cooking pot and sat it next to the fire. Then he filled the bucket with dry grain and gave it to Bea. She munched on the food and looked around, her ears cocking forward and back, still listening to sounds in the woods.

Toby stood near the cart and picked up the whip. He remembered the routine his father had showed him and decided to practice it. He walked a short distance from the cart and looked back at the fire. Satisfied that it was ok, he pushed aside some pine needles with his foot. He did that twice more until he'd made a triangle-shaped clearing on the ground. He stepped from one point to the next, each time turning to face the center of the triangle. He drew back the whip and snapped it in the air. With each snap he stepped to another corner of the triangle. He snapped the whip both forward and backward. As he turned each time he created a six-pointed star with the whip cracking at each point.

After twenty times around, his form was perfect. He selected targets and snapped the whip at them: small tips of a hemlock bough; a spot on the ground; an imaginary target elsewhere. He was sweating now and his breath came in quick gasps, but he could feel that he was getting stronger and more powerful with the whip. He stopped and stood quietly for a moment and then looked at the cart. Gina was standing inside the still, naked from the waist up, watching him. He cleared his throat in embarrassment.

"You're really good with that whip," she said as she pushed herself up and out of the still. He stared at her body as she moved and then realized that he was naked, too. He quickly turned around and said, "Thanks!" He wished she hadn't seen him this way, but it was too late for that!

She walked away into the woods, surveying the campsite as she went. He stood rooted to the spot, watching her walk away from him. When she disappeared behind a tree Toby went to the fire and turned his pants on the line. They were nearly dry. He decided to pull them on before Gina came back.

He tested the gruel he'd made from the grain and water. It was hot and tasty, even though some kind of flavoring would have helped a lot. He rummaged inside the bags and tried to think of something that would help with the flavor.

Gina had bought an onion! Toby peeled off several of the outside layers and cut them into small pieces with his pocketknife. He dropped them into the pot and used a stick to stir them into the gruel.

Toby looked up and realized that Gina still wasn't back yet. Puzzled, he looked to the woods and began to wonder where she'd gone. He was about to call out for her when he decided not to. He was afraid of giving away their hidden campsite. The smoke from the fire was bad enough, and he didn't want to take a chance of any loud noises.

He started to walk in the direction she'd gone and then decided to take the whip with him. He grabbed it from the cart's seat and walked into the woods. It wasn't long until he saw her. She seemed to be squatting down with her head leaning on her forearms and her arms resting on her knees. She wasn't moving. Toby hesitated to approach her like that. He didn't want to embarrass her while she was doing her business. But he had a feeling that something was wrong.

He stepped towards her and gave a soft whistle. She didn't move. "What's going on?" he asked out loud. She didn't respond. He stepped closer to her and whistled again. He could now see that her knees were purplish red from squatting for a long time. He went closer. "Gina?" he said.

She turned her head ever so slowly. Her eyes were wide with fear, and she shifted them slowly to look back down at the ground on her other side. Toby immediately sensed the danger and circled the squatting girl. Then he saw it: a copperhead rattlesnake, probably four feet long, coiled and ready to strike!

Toby walked slowly, glancing around to make sure there weren't others. He drew the attention of the snake away from Gina and its head pivoted with Toby's movement. Toby was at the whip's length from the snake and safely away from Gina. If he cut the snake with the whip, would she be able to move away quickly? He doubted it. Her legs would be too stiff. Could he draw the snake further away and give Gina time to roll away? He knew the snake wouldn't move from that coiled position until it felt safe. Toby didn't want to take a chance of missing the snake and put her in further danger!

He shook the whip out behind him and made sure it was ready to strike. Gina turned her head in his direction and stared at him with wide eyes. "Gina," Toby said in a soft voice, "I think I can hit him if you can toss yourself aside. Blink if you think you can!" Toby waited for her response. Gina just stared at him. He thought maybe she was too afraid to blink, so he reversed the question to double check. "Then if you *can't* move away, blink!" She blinked. "Are you sure?" Toby asked. "Because I don't think he's going to go away. So you're gonna have to do whatever you can to get away. Ok? Blink if you understand." Gina paused for a second and then blinked again.

"I'll count to three and then whip it," Toby said. "One...two...three!" The whip sailed through the air and cracked the snake squarely on its head. It rolled into a coil and writhed in pain, its head split wide open.

Gina put a hand on the ground and pushed herself to roll away. She was about five feet from the snake when she rolled again and then bounced to her feet. Toby cracked the whip again and again! The snake twitched a few more times but was obviously contracting in its death convulsions.

Toby ran to Gina and they backed away, watching the snake. Gina was shaking so hard she couldn't talk. Retreating to the campfire, they watched for anything that could even resemble a snake. Gina ran ahead and pulled her clothes from the line above the fire. She hopped around, pulling them on. Toby walked back slowly, tightly gripping the whip as he studied the ground. By the time he got back to the campsite, Gina was dressed and sat huddled up on the cart seat hugging herself.

He walked to her and offered her a hand. She slapped it away and trembled.

"There's food," he said. He pointed to the pot near the fire and waited for a response. She shook her head and wrapped her arms around herself more tightly, trembling slightly. Toby knew that she wouldn't step on to the ground the rest of the day. He lifted the pot from the fire and carried it to the cart so she could eat there.

He packed everything away, folded the dry clothes, and moved the still damp ones closer to the fire. Gina became interested in the food once the smell of the gruel reached her. Soon she was eating quickly and Toby thought that she might eat his portion as well. He decided to eat a bit himself before it was all gone.

After Toby ate, he packed up the rest of the clothes, put out the fire, and hooked Bea up to the cart. She was as serene and unaffected as ever. She tugged at the cart and turned it back towards the road. Toby asked Gina if she could take the reins. She nodded and took them from him. He walked ahead to look up and down the road. The lane was open enough to see a good distance in both directions, and Toby was relieved not to see anyone ahead or behind them. He returned to the cart and steered the mule out onto the road. Toby mounted the cart and clucked his tongue. Bea started to walk, but Toby wanted to move quickly and got her into a trot. After just a few miles they saw a large house in the distance.

◊ ◊ ◊

# 19

~choices on a one way trip~

They rode in silence. Toby figured Gina was embarrassed about her nightmare and being naked and then the snake. He glanced at her several times, but she seemed to be content to bask in the sunlight; she radiated a peace and calm that Toby hadn't seen in her before. She didn't seem upset anymore, so he left her to her own thoughts.

Toby watched the road in both directions as they approached the house. He noticed that it was very large, especially compared to others he'd seen in this area. A big porch wrapped around it. Locust trees with long, skinny, twisted trunks surrounded the house, which sat at a fork in the road. A large stone in the fork had the names of two towns painted on it in white paint. One arrow pointed to the left and towards *Foxburg*. Below that another arrow pointed to the right towards *Parker's Landing*.

Toby guided the cart up to the sign and stopped. A young boy standing in the yard waved to them. Toby waved back and watched the house as the boy approached the cart.

"Mornin'!" the boy said in a squeaky voice. He was filthy, like all the kids Toby had seen on this trip.

"Good mornin' to you," Toby said. "You live in that fine house?"

"Yes sir, my family and my grandma, too!" The boy squinted at them. "Hey, you're the man that they was askin' 'bout!"

Toby glanced at Gina and then turned to the boy again. "How's that, boy?"

Toby enjoyed using the phrase on someone else for a change.

"Two men came ridin' by yesterday, asked about a boy with a black eye!"

The boy pointed to Toby's eye.

Gina quickly asked, "Which way did *they* go?"

The boy pointed right in the direction of Parker's Landing and smiled. "They was nice men—gave me a haf-penny!"

"And they asked about us? What did they want to know?" Gina asked, not letting Toby get a word in.

"I don't know, they was talkin' to my daddy. All they said to me was to look for a boy with a black eye. I can go and ask my daddy 'bout the rest!" With that the boy turned and ran towards the house.

"That settles that!" Toby said and wheeled Bea around to the road to the left. "I don't know where this is going to take us, but it ain't followin' them!" Toby got Bea trotting quickly away from the house and Gina watched over her shoulder for the boy's daddy to come out. But they were out of view of the house before she saw anyone. The road towards Foxburg was easy, and they traveled down a long, winding road that sloped gently. They both knew that Lucca and Lew would scour the countryside to find them, but Gina pointed out that they couldn't be gone from the farm too long. "I think they'll turn back in another day or two," she said thoughtfully.

Toby studied her face and furrowed his brow. He thought about what she said and wished it were true. But he considered the load that he and Gina were hauling and its value to somebody like Lucca or Lew. No, he didn't share her opinion, but he didn't tell her so.

After passing a couple of farms that sat back from the road at the end of long lanes, they came to a creek. It had a wooden bridge that overlooked a small gorge bounded on both sides by huge rocks. The hemlock trees were large here and nearly blocked out the sky. It was dark on both sides of the road, and the road itself came to an extremely steep path that dropped nearly straight down the hill. Toby and Gina looked at each other and then back down the path. Toby got off and walked ahead to study the roadway. Large tree roots crisscrossed the road and Toby thought of Bea losing her footing. Gina got off the cart, too, but was warily looking at the ground for snakes.

Toby walked back to Gina and shook his head. "It's a bad one! We would lose the cart *and* the load if something happened," he said. "But I remember a street on a steep hill in Pittsburgh. Some men tied a large rock to a wagon to slow it down." He peered over the hillside "I'm thinkin' that a log might work.

If we can get it to drag behind the cart, it might keep the cart from pushing Bea down too fast." Gina listened somberly.

"We could cut one, maybe six feet long, and tie it to the back of the cart. If it gets hung up on somethin' I can use a bar and pry it loose."

Gina shrugged in agreement. Toby took the axe and looked into the woods in each direction. He didn't see anything suitable there so he climbed the steep bank and started into the woods. "Toby...do you have the whip?" Gina called to him.

He smiled and pointed to the seat on the cart. "Naw, I left it for you!" He smiled and held up the axe. "I got this!" Gina drew a deep breath and walked back to the cart. She stood by Bea and heard Toby's axe chopping at a log not too far away. She patted Bea's neck and watched the ground around her.

Soon Toby jumped down from the bank. "I need the rope. Get Bea unhitched. She'll have to pull it from the woods." Toby took the rope and reentered the woods. In a couple of minutes, he returned, paying out the rope until he reached the cart path.

Gina guided Bea in a circle towards the rope. Toby tied the rope to Bea's harness and told Gina how to handle her. He took a longer bar from the work box and went back to the log. "Go ahead!" he called.

Gina led Bea forward and the log fell from the bank onto the roadway. She led the mule back to the cart and hooked her up. Toby fastened the log to the cart's axle. They started down the hill *very slowly*. It took nearly half an hour to go just two hundred yards down the steep slope. Gina coaxed Bea ahead gently. Several times the stubs on the log got stuck on a root and Toby had to pry it loose.

Bea could actually lean into the harness and barely had to pull—and the cart would advance. Several times the road came close to the stream that wound along the side of the trail. The water dropped ten feet in places, making a thunderous rushing noise that drowned out their voices as they shouted commands to keep the cart and Bea steady. They stopped twice along the way and drank the fresh stream water. Toby and Gina were both amazed at the size of the boulders along the stream. Some were larger than a room of a house and most were moss covered.

In four hours they were nearly three-fourths of the way to the bottom. Through the trees they caught glimpses of the river below. It was cold here: The trees shaded the path and the cool air of the woods slid down the hillside and settled in the valley. They continued the process of moving slowly, carefully dragging the log, and prying it loose from time to time until they made it to the bottom of the hill where the path intersected with another road. Across the river there was a small dock and a crude pier made of river stone. Away from the dock area and up against the hillside were some cabins and shacks that looked empty.

"That must be Foxburg!" Toby said. He was relieved to be done with that horrible hill and glad to still be alive! He untied the log and rolled it to the side of the road, then sat down on it to rest. Gina sat on the crate in the cart and looked across the river. She saw a road winding up the hill on the other side of the river. "Toby, do you think we could *cross* here!?" she asked. He looked over and thought on it.

Several flat boats that looked like barges floated in the river below them. One was loaded with lumber and another with bags and barrels. Toby pondered the question for awhile, but he didn't have any answers. He hoped a local might come by so they could ask him, but none did.

"Well, we could sit here for days, hoping for someone to come along," he said out loud. He noticed Gina looking at a path that led along the river; it went north—away from the direction of Parker's Landing. There was a shack in the distance, on their side of the river.

"We could ask up there!" Gina said.

"That's the best idea so far. And I don't figure we'd get across tonight, anyway." Toby was still scanning the docking area for any sign of activity. "I guess we should be safe from our…uh…followers, for awhile."

As they made their way towards the shack they saw a small boat tied up at the river's edge. Smoke curled from the shack's chimney. Toby noticed that the door was open, and inside, a shadowed figure was watching them.

◊ ◊ ◊

# 20

## ~the lady of the mansion~

They wound along the pathway towards the shack, which stood on a low-lying strip of land between the path and the river's edge. The afternoon sun would soon disappear over the large hill they'd just descended, and Toby imagined that the temperature would drop quickly.

It was exciting for Gina as she was excited to see the river and commented on its immense size; all she'd ever seen before were the small streams and creeks where she lived. She smiled and seemed happy as they made their way closer to the shack.

The grounds around the shack were picked clean, and short, green grass grew in colorful contrast to the river, which was muddy brown from yesterday's rain. A few goats grazed near the shack. One of them stood on top of a rock the size of Toby and Gina's cart and looked down on them. Other goats stood around munching on the grass and any living plant within reach. A small goat balanced on its back legs to reach some leaves on a branch that the others had missed. The ravenous appetite of these creatures gave the grounds surrounding the shack a manicured look.

Gina giggled and pointed at some of the young goats who were playing. They bleated as they pranced and butted each other. They seemed mildly interested in the cart, but more so in Bea. A couple of the older goats walked towards the cart and separated to approach it from different directions. Toby didn't particularly like the situation, so he pulled up short and got off the cart. He handed the reins to Gina and told her to wait.

He took the whip and walked towards the shack. "Ho!" He called, keeping one eye on the shack and the other on the goats. "HO!" he called again. A figure stood inside the doorway, out of the fading sunlight so Toby couldn'tsee it clearly.

Two goats began to approach him. Toby wasn't sure if they were just curious or trying to protect their young, so he walked slowly. He was now closer to the shack than the cart and decided to run for the house if the goats decided to get nasty. They had short, pointed horns that could cause a bad leg injury if they charged at him. Toby was now within conversation distance and couldn't understand why the person inside the shack wouldn't respond. He stopped and looked back at Gina. She shrugged her shoulders to show that she was just as confused as he was.

Toby let the whip end drop and trailed it along behind him. He thought to snap it a couple of times to see if the goats would back off, but they didn't. In fact, the whip just seemed to excite them more. One goat bleated and the other snorted. They moved closer to him.

"Eeeeeyut!" a voice yelled from the shack. One goat turned and trotted towards the sound. The other stood with its yellow eyes fixed on Toby.

"Eeeeeyut!" Toby was sure it was a woman's voice. He didn't want to look too long and take his eyes off the last goat. Six of the other goats had gone to the porch now, but the one still glared at Toby.

Toby stepped towards the porch and said, "Can ya call this one over? Ma'am?"

"He'd probably wouldn't mind, if ya was-zin' carryin' that snake!" the woman's voice responded.

"It's a *whip*!" Toby said in voice, louder than he needed to.

The woman laughed and said, "Yeah, but he don't know that, does he? Maybe you can tell him! They like to kill snakes." Again she laughed and called the goat. Toby slowly wound up the whip and tucked it in the back waistband of his trousers. The goat lost interest immediately.

"Can I come over an' talk for a moment?" Toby asked respectfully.

"Sure. Whatcha got to talk to me about?" The woman stepped into the last of the sunlight and looked towards Gina and the cart.

"We need a place to camp. And I...I wondered if I could maybe work off a trade with you."

"What kinda trade?" She looked him up and down and added, "You may as well call in your mule and missus."

Toby waved to Gina and she drove Bea into the yard towards the shack. Toby looked around. Except for the shack and an outhouse, there were no other outbuildings. Toby noticed that the shack was built on stilts and that it was closed in around the bottom. He guessed that's where the goats were penned—if they were penned at all.

Toby looked more closely at the woman and saw that she was pretty and fairly young, probably just in her late twenties. Her dress was clean and so were her hands. He walked closer, still keeping his eyes on the bigger goat.

The woman didn't seem threatened by him, and he was thankful. "Ma'am, we was campin' last night and Gina," he nodded at her, "had a time with a rattlesnake this morning. She ain't quite over it. I was thinkin' that if you could put her up this night, well, maybe I could do some work for you—for trade?"

By then Gina and the cart were twenty feet away. The woman studied Gina for a moment, smiled, and said, "You both come inside and we'll talk there. Just keep that damn whip put away! Let junior get himself calmed." She nodded towards the goat. Toby went to the cart and laid the whip on the seat and offered a hand to Gina. She looked at his hand, gave him a puzzled look, and then jumped from the cart herself. Toby was a little insulted, but he walked her to the porch and kept between her and the goat.

The woman had watched the little exchange. When they were on the porch she introduced herself. "I'm, well, I'm the lady of this mansion!" She laughed as she swept her arm towards the shack; Gina caught the humor and smiled. "My name is Ella, Ella Jane Mack, to be formal! And you would be?" She offered her hand to Gina.

Gina flushed and smiled again. "Gina," she said. Then so as not to have to give a last name she quickly pointed to Toby and said, "And he's Toby. We've traveled several days, and—"

Ella interrupted, "—AND you two come in and we'll have some hot tea. Toby, unhitch your mule and let her graze....The goats won't bother her. Then come in and wash up—you need it!" Gina and Ella both laughed at this and walked inside.

Toby, again feeling a little insulted, turned Bea loose. She looked at the goats and then buried her face in the sweet grass. He took his whip and put it in the box under the seat. While he had the lid up he noticed the paper wrapping from the food that Gina had purchased. He looked inside and saw a plug of tobacco. *Why would she have this?*, he wondered. He took it and slid it into his pocket next to his knife. He'd ask Gina about it later.

Toby reached the steps to the shack's porch and listened to the women's voices coming from inside. "Indians! You bet! They are the best customers!" Both laughed. "Of course there are the river-men. They're always comin' 'round; I swear they'd be happy with a goat!" Again both of them laughed. Toby didn't know what they were talking about and he was happy just to sit on the steps and watch the river. A baby goat approached and he petted it. It smelled bad, but he didn't care. It snuffled at his pants pocket and took a bite! It had tried for the tobacco but gotten a piece of his thigh instead! Toby yelped and smacked the goat. He quickly stood up and retreated up another step. When he turned, both of the women were at the doorway, smiling. Gina struggled to keep from bursting into a laugh as Toby rubbed his thigh. He stood and stormed off. "I'm going down to the river!" He'd had enough of the goats, the trip, and women at the moment.

"Mind the snakes!" Ella's voice called to him.

Without missing a step Toby swung towards the cart and grabbed the whip. He tucked it in his pants and went to where a rowboat was tied. It was up in the high water. He could tell that it would normally be on dry ground, but the muddy water had risen with the last storm. He pulled on the rope and when the boat was near, he stepped in. It was a flat-bottomed john boat. He'd often seen them in Pittsburgh. It could travel, loaded, in just inches of water. It was probably sixteen feet long and could carry four people comfortably. He sat in the middle seat and placed his hands on the oars, which were still in the oar locks. He imagined traveling the river in such a boat: *It'd be nice to have all the gear stored and just float along—no hill climbing, no Lew and Lucca chasing us. No sleeping inside a damn copper still! All the water you wanted to drink and bathe in. Laying in the open boat at night and staring at the stars....*

Toby was still lost in the fantasy when the sun disappeared and the mosquitoes appeared. They began biting him before he realized it. By the time he was out of the boat and jogging to the house he'd given up quite a bit of blood.

Smoke was coming from the shack now, much heavier than when they'd arrived. He smelled food cooking! He went inside and looked around. The women were busy at a long counter along the side of the cabin, where there were windows overlooking the river. A table with two chairs and a barrel sat along the other wall, and a wood stove warmed the cabin. To his left, another door led into a darkened room, which Toby figured was a bedroom.

Ella said over her shoulder, "Get the kettle and pour us some hot water in the cups, Tob'. I've got some mushrooms that I'll fry for us. And of course there's always goat cheese!" Toby bristled at being called "Tob" and being given more orders. But he kept quiet and poured water into the cups. Gina put a spoonful of dried tea leaves into each and smiled at Toby. He was still angry and just looked away.

Ella put a heavy, black iron frying pan on the stove and stood looking at the river as she waited for it to heat up. Gina looked at Toby and furrowed her eyebrows. She waited for him to offer a response, but he just ignored her and watched Ella. She moved near the doorway and lit something that looked like a bundle of straw.

The smoke wafted up and hung along the ceiling.

"It'll keep the mosquitoes from coming inside," Ella explained. "Now get in that room and use the wash water to clean yourself."

Another command! Toby didn't like this! But he thought a wash would be nice, so he walked into the small, dimly-lit room. There was another chair, a bench with shelves below, and a made-up bed covered with a nice quilt. Near it sat a small table with a heavy, metal washbasin on top. Toby washed his hands and face with the water inside. He looked into the wavy-glass mirror and brushed his fingers through his hair. He thought his face had changed somehow, but he quickly dismissed the thought. The black eye had faded a little, but the yellowish tint was still there. His stomach rumbled.

He heard the women talking again, but they spoke in low voices and he couldn't understand them. His sisters did that too, and it was maddening. Toby returned to the table and sat on the barrel. He decided that might be the only manners he would extend if they kept bossing him around *and* whispering!

Ella and Gina brought the food to the table and realized that Toby was feeling grumpy. At first the conversation was a little stiff. Both women noticed Toby's mood and decided to play up to him. Then Ella started talking about life on the river. "Now Ernie, my husband—I call him that even though we was never 'church married'—he built this cabin. He works the river from Foxburg downriver to Parker's Landing. He has barges and hauls lumber, coal, feed—

whatever comes along, really. All down river to Parker's Landing, then further on to Pittsburgh at the end of the season. He makes real good money and all the men he deals with like him."

Ella laughed a lot as she talked. "You seem really happy here," Gina said.

"Oh, this place makes me that way," Ella replied. "But I don't like going back to Pittsburgh in the fall!"

Toby thought this was odd, but didn't make any comment – ( but he did resurvey the room for something he'd missed).

Ella continued: "Yes, Ernie and I close up the cabin and travel downriver to Pittsburgh, where we live in the winter months."

Toby was very interested in this and asked where they live in the city. When she told him the street, he announced that his mother was only blocks away. He realized that her house was in a nice area of the city. They talked about Pittsburgh for quite awhile and Gina sat quietly, listening intently. She was fascinated by the tales of city life and the places and things that Toby and Ella described.

As Ella talked, they ate mushrooms with some fried eggs and goat cheese. Toby was thrilled to have a tasty home cooked meal. They finished the food and sat around awhile longer, enjoying the warmth from the stove and talking some more.

Toby and Gina yawned at the same time. They were both exhausted from the trip down that treacherous hill earlier in the day. Ella saw them yawn and said, "Follow me." She went out to the porch and around the corner of the shack towards the river. Here the porch turned into a room covered with a gauzy material to keep out the bugs! Inside was a bed large enough for two people to stretch out on. "We *love* sleeping out here during the summer nights and listening to the river and the wild critters," Ella said. "But you young'ins can stand this cold night better than we can, so we'll sleep inside tonight. Ernie'll be home after you're asleep." She stepped back and said, "Goodnight" before going back inside.

Toby decided to check on Bea and get the other blanket from the cart. He also wanted to give Gina time to get ready for bed. Toby took his time, making sure Bea was ok and checking the cart. He delayed as long as he could and then returned to the porch-room. The door squeaked softly as he pushed it open. He closed it behind him and sat on the edge of the bed.

Toby could hear Gina breathing softly as he untied his boots. He undressed and pulled back the covers. As he crawled into bed, his bare leg brushed up against hers. She moved her leg away and rolled closer to her edge of the bed. Toby rolled over too, facing away from her. Within minutes the day's events melted away. Toby drifted asleep listening to the river flowing near the house.

◊ ◊ ◊

# 21

## ~a Lucca look-a-like~

Toby woke the next morning in an empty bed. Lying there, he slowly recognized the porch-room and realized where he was. He felt the warm sunlight and listened to the sounds coming through the cloth covering of the outdoor room.

As he sat up and put his feet on the floor, he realized that his clothes were missing. Everything was gone! except his whip and boots! "What the—?" Toby muttered. He was about to yell for Gina when he heard her voice coming from the river. He looked at the bank below the shack and saw Ella and Gina chatting away—and washing clothes. His clothes!

His anger subsided. Their clothes *were* dirty; they'd worn them for a lot of miles. *Even with the other night's rain*, Toby thought, *they were gettin' gamey.* He sat back on the bed, leaned against the wall of the shack, and thought about getting some breakfast. He figured he could wrap the blanket around him and head to the kitchen. He glanced in the yard and saw that Bea had her face buried in the grass, eating away. All seemed well on the river.

Toby heard Ella and Gina laughing and smiled to himself. He imagined that Ella didn't get much chance to spend time with other women, and she seemed to get on well with Gina. He decided to leave it at that. Suddenly he thought of his pocketknife and panicked at the thought of it getting lost in the river. He grabbed his boot and something rattled inside. He turned it over and out came his pocketknife and the plug of tobacco. He turned the tobacco over in his hand and thought that even it might taste good about now!

He raised the plug and smelled it. It smelled good so he bit off a chunk. He wasn't sure what he was supposed to do with it, so he began to chew it, like he'd seen others do.

He sat with his back against the wall, watching the river, the women, and the clear sky. It wasn't long before he felt the juices of the tobacco filling his mouth. He didn't have any place to spit out the juice so he swallowed it. That was his first mistake; the second was to repeat it a few more times!

Not even five minutes later Toby jumped up from the bed, still naked, and ran outside. He hung over the porch railing and threw up again and again. The women heard the retching, and Gina ran to the porch. She saw Toby staggering and trying to open the door to the porch-room. He coughed and kept wiping his mouth. His eyes were watering. He fell onto the bed face down, clutching his still-convulsing stomach. Gina sat down beside him and started to rub his back. She asked him what had happened three times before he answered her. With his face still buried in the pillow, he held up the remaining plug of tobacco. She took it from him and patted his shoulder, saying, "My poor little grape!" Toby swung his arm at her, but Gina dodged it and backed away to the door. He moaned again and fell asleep before he had a chance to hear the women laughing down by the river.

When he woke later in the morning, his pants, shirt, and socks were lying on the bed, dry and folded. He sat up slowly, blinking at the bright sunlight. The vomiting had left nothing in his stomach and he was extremely hungry.

"Gina?" he called in a soft voice.

"Coming!" Gina's head appeared at the doorway to the porch-room. "How are you feeling, Tob'?"

Toby nodded to her. He looked at his clean clothes and sheepishly said, "Thank you."

Gina smiled and gave a small curtsy. She added, "Got some *good* food for you to try. Ella showed me some ways to make things I think you'll like. So hurry and get dressed."

Dressed, his face washed, and seated on the barrel at the table again, Toby watched as Gina made her way around the room. She set several plates of food in front of him. They were unbelievable. There were fresh bread rolls covered with honey, a few slices of potatoes with something sprinkled on them, and a piece of sausage! "I must be in heaven," Toby said with wide eyes. He looked at Gina's face and knew he had said the right thing.

She bent to him and kissed his temple. Ella came in the door just then and smiled. "Good morning, Tob'! I hope you're feeling better. Gina told me about the tobacco. I guess that's one way of discovering it!" Gina giggled and watched Toby eat furiously. He swallowed several mouthfuls and finally spoke to Ella.

"It's all so good! I can't believe it! Maybe you *can* make a cook out of Gina!" It was her turn to take a swipe at his head. He didn't even try to duck. But she missed completely.

"Did you husband come in last night?" Toby asked, looking around for signs that he had been there.

"Oh yes—he's been here and gone! He only stays about four hours and then he's back to the boat. He can sleep on the way down the river to the Landing, so he doesn't stay here too long at night." Toby thought of how lonely it must be for Ella, but she seemed to be so happy.

"Eeeeeyut!" Ella said. "He comes and goes, short and sweet!" Ella smiled and winked at Gina, then went outside. Gina grinned at the comment and went to the counter. She poured two cups of hot water and added a spoonful of the ground tea leaves and some honey to each. She placed the cups on the table and sat in a chair. She just smiled at Toby and watched him finish the food. He used pieces of bread to mop the plate clean.

"Uh, Toby?" Gina said. He looked up at her with a mouthful of food. "Do you think we could stay here a couple of days?" she asked. "It's so nice here. And Ella's real nice. It's almost like being part of a family again...." Her voice trailed off as she saw the look on his face.

"We have to get that still delivered," he said. He saw the disappointment in her eyes as they started to well up with tears, but she quickly blinked them away. "I have to go on with..." Toby wasn't sure what to offer at that point. He stopped and changed his words: "*We* have to go on—and get the still there." He searched her eyes again to see if the second answer better suited her.

She smiled, but lowered her eyes. After a moment she spoke haltingly: "It's just that—this is the first time in six years that I've felt like I count for something.... I like Ella so much and I can learn..." She trailed off again.

He nodded and reached for her hand, curling his fingers over hers. He chose his words carefully: "I've seen that you're happy, and it makes me happy, but we *have* to go on! It's what I was trusted to do...."

"No, that's what *Lew* was trusted to do!" she quickly reminded him.

But Toby shook his head. "It's up to me now. I have to be counted on! An' I *will*! It's mor'n I can explain to ya…." He gave her a pointed look and nodded at her, hoping she'd understand.

She looked down at her cup of tea with tears still in her eyes and nodded. In a quiet whisper she said, "I know, Toby. I knew this was the way you'd be—and I agree that it's the right thing to do. We can go when you say." She looked up at him and blinked away the tears.

He felt he should do something more than just squeeze her hand—something a grownup would do to show his appreciation. "We'll stay till tomorrow if Ella says it's alright. And—if her man will allow...us. Will he be back today?'"

"Yes! And if he's as nice as she is then he'll allow us—I know it!" Gina said and began clearing off the table. She started washing the dishes in a pan of water on the counter. Toby realized that she was wearing the dress she wore when they first met at Lucca's farm. He looked at her, the outgrown dress—and her slender legs that he was learning to like a lot! He thought that she looked a lot nicer in the dress than the worn-out pants and shirt she'd been wearing for the last several days. He wondered how long it had been; he'd lost count of the days.

That afternoon they helped Ella turn over some ground for a garden. They were taking a break, sitting on a big rock in the yard when they heard a shrill whistle. They hadn't seen the large flat boat arrive on the other side of the rock. Toby turned quickly to see two men using long poles to manage the craft towards shore. Ella waved and walked to the riverbank

Gina and Toby followed at a distance. The barge bounced against the shore and a man jumped to the ground, carrying a rope. He tied it to a driven steel ring in the ground. Toby noticed how much the river had receded just over night. He and Gina waited to be introduced.

As the other man jumped to the ground, Gina gasped loudly and covered her mouth with her hands. He was younger than the first man and looked just like *Lucca*!

He stared back at Gina with a stunned look on his face. Toby didn't know what to think. This couldn't be Lucca—he was too young. But he was the spitting image of him! Toby felt tense and noticed that this guy was a few years older than him and had a few more muscles. Toby thought of the whip and remembered that it was back on the seat of the cart.

Ella was the first of the others to realize that something was wrong. The Lucca look-alike stared at Gina a moment longer and then shifted his eyes to Toby. He looked Toby over quickly and then acted as if nothing was wrong. Ella knew differently! But since nothing seemed to be happening, she proceeded to introduce everyone.

"Toby, this is the man in *my* life: Ernie Mack." Toby removed his hat and shook Ernie's hand. It was strong and callused, and so large that it covered Toby's hand completely.

"Howdy, Toby!" Ernie's voice was deep and friendly. "Ella tells me you two have been on quite a journey." He turned to Gina and offered her his large hand as he removed his hat and smiled.

"And that is Gina I tol' you about," Ella said. Gina smiled back at Ernie and nodded.

"She's *prettier* than you tol' me!" Ernie said and laughed again with his infectious laugh. Gina blushed.

"And this is our Firs' Man on the boat, Luke!" Ella said proudly and pointed to the boy from the boat, keeping an eye on the three youngsters.

Luke stepped forward and gave Toby's hand a one-pump shake. He looked at Gina, took off his cap, and nodded curtly. Toby studied Gina's face as Luke moved away. She seemed frozen, with a lost, abandoned look on her face.

Noticing the lack of warmth, Ella decided to steer the group towards the porch. As they walked Ernie put his arm around Ella's waist and kissed her cheek. She laughed and chidingly tried to push him away.

Luke strayed off to pet a goat but turned his head and looked straight at Gina. Toby saw Luke staring at her and looked at Gina, too. He saw her look quickly from Luke to the ground.

They reached the porch and Ella brought out two chairs. She and Ernie sat down in them and Toby and Gina settled on the steps. Everyone turned towards Ernie.

"I didn't expect you till later, near dark," Ella said to him.

Ernie leaned forward and put his elbows on his knees. "They've got the Landin' closed. Can't move anything in or out. They sez they're looking for a man or two. The magistrate sent men from Butler to look for them, so we can't haul anybody out of the Landin' till they get here." He shrugged.

Toby looked at Gina; she was looking at her hands in her lap. Toby looked to Ernie and asked, "Does that include everybody?" Ernie nodded to him and then shifted his eyes to Luke, who was still petting the goat.

He looked at Ella and frowned. She'd been watching Luke, as well. She glanced back to Toby and then to Gina before patting her knees and saying, "Gina, I 'spect these men are starvin'. Let's put some magic in that kitchen!" She tilted her head sideways towards the house. Gina stood up quickly and followed her inside.

"Toby, why don't you get Luke and go fetch those two planks out of the boat? We'll make up a place to eat," Ernie said before he stood and went inside.

As Toby crossed the yard, he tried to think of something to say to Luke. But it seemed like there were more things he probably *shouldn't* say to him.

◊ ◊ ◊

# 22

## ~walkin' the plank~

It wasn't long before Toby and Luke were struggling up the riverbank carrying the long, heavy planks on their shoulders. Toby was in the lead with Luke behind, the planks stretched out between them. Luke moved with a deliberate bounce that caused the planks to bow up and down as they walked. It made it hard for Toby, as their paces weren't matched. The weight of the planks came down on his shoulder as his foot was in the air. Several times he nearly lost his balance and slipped in the grass (or on goat droppings). They were nearly to the porch when Toby realized that it was a mean trick Luke was doing on purpose.

Toby pushed the planks from his shoulder and they hit the ground. They jammed into the soft dirt and he heard Luke curse him. "You carry them!" Toby said without another word. He was just a few steps from the cart. When he heard Luke's end of the planks hit the ground, Toby quickly took two steps and had the whip in his hand. He lifted it slowly, showing it to Luke. Luke's eyes widened and he paused. Neither said a word.

Ernie had placed two barrels on the porch and hadn't noticed the scene in the yard. "Well, bring them on!" He patted a barrel top and then turned and went back into the house. Toby put the coiled whip into his waistband and walked to the plank. This time he took the plank and faced Luke. Walking backward, he kept his eyes glued to Luke's—which were glued to Toby's! Together they got the planks into place and still, neither of the boys spoke. Luke sat down at the bottom of the steps and Toby sat four steps up.

Ella served dinner and she and Ernie were the only ones who spoke. Gina and the boys ate in silence. Ella gave Ernie a questioning look about the silence, but he just shrugged. After dinner, the men sat on the porch and Ernie told Toby stories about river work. Luke sat quietly, looking towards the river.

The women were in the kitchen and Toby noticed that Luke stole a glance inside each time he heard them speak, especially Gina. Luke seemed disturbed. He finally stood and stretched, and clearly faked a yawn. "I reckon I'll bed down in the boat," he said. Without another word he stepped from the porch and left.

"Guess I put him to sleep with my yarns!" Ernie said, smiling at Toby. Ernie filled a pipe and offered it to Toby. Toby shook his head quickly. He'd had enough tobacco for one day!

"So tell me," Ernie said with a purposeful pause to draw on the pipe," about your trip." He puffed the pipe several times and smiled at Toby. Toby told him about the trip, about seeing Butler and the Stone House Tavern. Toby noticed that Ernie gave him a strange look when he mentioned Butler, but Toby shrugged it off and kept going. He told Ernie about the roads, the rain, and Bea, all the way up to arriving at the farm in Boyers and meeting Gina.

At that point in the story Gina appeared on the porch with Ella. Ella whispered something to Ernie. He looked towards the boat that sat in the dark and then turned to Gina and said, "Toby here's just been tellin' me 'bout his trip so far to Boyers. I understand that's where he met up with you. How 'bout you take over the storytelling from there? How'd you end up on that farm, anyway?"

Gina hesitated a little. But then she told Ernie and Ella everything about her time at the farm and how she ended up there. She even included details that she hadn't told Toby. He sat motionless, listening to everything Gina said, and began to understand even more clearly why she hated Lew and Lucca so passionately.

The hardest shock to handle was when she told them, quite openly, about how both men had touched her and abused her. Toby already knew a little about this, but, only then began to understand how awful it had been for Gina. He saw the disgust in her eyes as she stared into the lantern light.

Toby noticed that Ernie had given Ella a pointed look when Gina mentioned the brothers. Toby watched to see what else aroused their interest, but the rest of the story passed—even the meanest parts—without interruption.

Toby thought he heard a stick break in the yard, but it was too dark to see what had made the noise. Gina was just finishing the story of their trip down the gigantic hill that brought them here. Ernie leaned forward and spoke very softly: "You're headin' to Sligo, right?" Toby nodded. "And you think both of the men are after you?" Toby and Gina both nodded. "Then you'll go through Foxburg, head up to Alum Rock, an' head to Callensburg from there. Then you'll be back on the same road to Sligo! It'll take a day longer, but the road's much the same. We'll load up the cart and the mule and have you across the river into Foxburg before sunup! They won't know you went that way, and you'll be pretty close to where you're goin'."

Ella curled her arm through Ernie's and looked pleased at his devious plan. Toby asked him how they would handle Bea if she didn't want to ride in the boat. "We ferry horses, mules, and other cattle all the time! It can be done."

With that Ernie rocked forward into a standing position. He straightened up and said, "Time for sleep. I'll wake you both when it's time to leave. Pack your things and be ready to go."

Toby headed off to the outhouse and then went to bed. Gina spoke with Ella for a short time and then went to the outhouse, as well. Toby woke when Gina crawled into the bed. He wasn't sure how long he'd been asleep, but it seemed like a long time. *What had taken Gina so long in the outhouse?*, he wondered. Gina was still dressed, and she shivered when she lie down beside him. He thought something seemed wrong, but he drifted off to sleep again. He slept in short naps and kept waking, each time thinking someone was calling his name. He rolled over and bumped into Gina. She jolted and pulled away from him.

◊ ◊ ◊

# 23

## ~two jerks on a pole~

When it was time to leave, Gina and Ella hugged goodbye, and Gina stepped onto the bow of the boat. It had taken an hour to load the cart and blindfold Bea and get her into the boat. Luke used the long pole to push off from the river's bank, and Ernie used his to direct the other end of the barge to face downriver. The darkness surrounded them as the lantern Ella held faded away. They decided to travel without lights. Ernie described how he and Luke could hold their poles in the water and tell if they were in the faster flow of the river.

Gina sat near Toby, but said nothing. She stared straight ahead and wouldn't look at either Toby or Luke. Toby didn't know what had gotten into her. They traveled slowly, using the drift of the river and the poles to cross. It should be a short trip to Foxburg. You could see the town from here during the day and Toby reckoned it couldn't be more than a mile away. Toby could see several lights in the distance. He leaned towards Gina and was about to whisper to her, but she quickly pulled away. Toby stood, and the barge tilted slightly.

"Easy!" Ernie's voice cut through the darkness. Toby wobbled; he was near the edge of the barge and could sense the water. Just then one of the poles touched Toby's arm. Then with a sudden forceful push, it knocked Toby off balance and into the water! His head went under and he kicked to the surface. "Here!" he gasped. The pole came down on his shoulder and pushed him under again! This time Toby grabbed the pole and jerked it as hard as he could. He felt the splash beside him and thought he heard Gina scream. With quick movements, Toby swam two strokes and grabbed the edge of the barge. He dug his fingers into the boards and held on.

The pole slammed down again very near his fingers. Toby grabbed the pole and held it under his arm. He could feel Luke at the other end of it! Now Ernie was at the side of the boat. With one hand he pulled Toby onto the deck of the barge. Ernie instinctively knew where the pole was and used it to haul in Luke.

Toby sat on one of the crates and coughed up water. Luke sat nearby, catching his breath. Toby felt Gina's hand on his wet shoulder, rubbing back and forth. He jerked away from her touch.

"He shoved me!" Toby said with a snarl after he could breathe normally again.

"I tried to keep you from falling overboard!" Luke spat back.

"You liar!" Toby hissed. He went to make a move but Ernie's hand stopped him cold.

"Enough! Both of ya! The nex' one of ya that yaps…I'll throw over!"Ernie's voice sounded menacing and it scared Toby. There was silence on the barge.

"Luke! Man that pole and guide us in!" Ernie commanded. It was the last of any conversation until the barge was unloaded and Bea stood waiting to pull the cart away.

Ernie gave Gina a hug and turned to Toby. Luke was busy putting the planks back into the boat. "Toby, I'm not sure what happened back there, but I'm suspicious of things. I hope you two have safe travel. You remember the directions?" Toby nodded. His teeth chattered, but he couldn't tell if it was from cold or anger. Ernie looked at Gina and then back to Toby. "Come back this way. I know Ella would like that, an' I think I would, too. Now get! Both of ya!"

Gina drove the cart with Toby sitting beside her, wrapped in the blanket. In the breaking light, they both looked at Luke. He was watching them. He didn't seem bothered by his wet clothes or the cold air. He just stood rigidly and watched them go.

◊ ◊ ◊

# 24

## ~it's hard to fly with muddy legs~

Bea stumbled and jerked the cart, jolting Toby from his sullen thoughts. He grabbed the reins from Gina, who didn't try to stop him. Neither of them had spoken so far. He still had the blanket wrapped around himself even though he was now dry and warm. Actually, he was overheated, but didn't bother to unwrap himself. Gina just stared ahead and didn't say a word.

Toby realized that he was hungry and that Bea must be, too. He wasn't sure he cared about Gina at the moment. He watched the roadway, and when he found a suitable spot to stop, he guided Bea into the trees. Toby unhitched her and led her away from the wagon to a spot where she could get to some sparse grass. She seemed grateful and sniffed at the ground. He returned to the cart and tried to lift the seat, but Gina was still sitting on it. Toby still didn't say a word. He waited quietly until Gina finally moved from the cart and walked into the woods.

Toby put the last of the grain into the bucket and gave it to Bea. He found a suitable spot under a big tree and decided to nap. He chewed at the green stem that he'd cut from a larger branch and used it to scrub his teeth. He worked at it for awhile and his mouth soon felt cleaner.

He unlaced his boots and pulled them off. His socks were still damp so he pulled them off too and hung them on his boots. He leaned back against the tree, trying to enjoy the warmth of the spring day.

His mind was fully awake now and he started to think about all that had happened last night and this morning. Toby decided that Luke *had* to be Lucca's son; there was no other way to explain how much they looked alike! And it was obvious that Gina and Luke knew each other. Toby saw her recognize him as soon as he stepped off of the boat yesterday. But why had she seemed so upset? Was it just because Luke was Lucca's son? Toby wondered what their relationship had been. A dozen questions swam in his mind: *Had Luke been close to her? Why had Gina kept so quiet about Luke? Did he really try to kill Toby when he pushed him off the boat? Or was he trying to save him? Was it a mean joke or was it a real murder attempt?* But, most of all, Toby wondered where Gina had been for so long after he'd fallen asleep last night. There seemed to be only one answer: She'd gone to see Luke! *Why?*, Toby wondered. *What had they discussed? Did she plan to help Luke kill him?* Toby's brain felt like it was exploding! At the moment, he thought he most hated Gina for going to Luke in the darkness of night!

Toby drifted off to sleep, but woke a short while later, thinking that he was swallowing river water again. He sat up quickly and drew several deep breaths. He looked up at the sky and tried to figure out the time of day. He decided that it was early afternoon, which meant he'd slept for a couple of hours.

The deerflies were starting to appear. Bea slept standing up, swaying a little from moment to moment, yet her tail swished at the flies that came near her. The deerflies were starting to appear bury their blood sucking bites into her! A couple tried landing on Toby, but he brushed them away. He pulled on his now dry socks and then picked up his boots. He checked inside and felt the money he kept wrapped in cloth and tucked into the toes of the boots. It was safe. With his boots laced, he rose and led Bea back to the cart.

The nap had only softened his new feelings for Gina. She lay on the blanket beside the cart. He hitched up Bea without trying to be quiet and was almost ready to leave. He went into the woods and relieved himself. When he returned, she still hadn't moved. He noticed a new bundle of clothing on the ground beside her. He figured Ella must have given it to her.

Toby thought about leaving her there. He was so angry that he felt he could— maybe even *should*—just leave her and go on his way. After all, it wasn't *her* job to deliver the still…. And it wasn't her that needed to endure the hardships of this trip.

Still, she'd saved him from Lew and Lucca's plan to steal the still and leave him to walk back to Pittsburgh or kill him! And she'd helped get him this far. Plus, she wasn't bad company.

Could he just leave her here? Toby thought about it some more and his anger rose again. It wasn't that far back to Ella and Ernie's shack, he reasoned. They could put her up! It wasn't his worry! He paced around thinking about it and couldn't decide what to do.

He just couldn't ride away and leave her helpless and stranded—*that* was the only thing he could decide. He walked over to her and in a flat voice said, "It's time to go." Gina immediately rose without saying a word, put the bundle back onto the cart's deck, and crawled up beside it. Toby thought maybe she didn't think she should sit on the seat with him—and that suited him fine! He climbed onto the bench-seat and pulled the reins straight back. Bea obliged by backing the cart out until he turned her back onto the path.

A few hours down the road they started to see areas where the trees had been cut down. Toby could make out small campsites in the distance and figured they belonged to loggers. A little further down the road Toby saw something he'd never imagined: trees so large that six men could join hands and still not reach around them!

Trees grew all around the road, blocking out the sky. The spring leaves were tiny, but the forest canopy seemed to swallow the blue sky. Small roadways led off of the main road in many different directions. Toby assumed they were paths cut from hauling the large logs out of the forest. There were so many of these other paths that it was getting harder to determine which one was the original roadway.

Spring flowers grew in patches of sunlight where a tree had died or been cut down. There were also mushrooms growing here. Toby decided it would be good to gather some to eat along the way. He took his hat and walked to a stand of mushrooms and began picking them. With the hat nearly filled, Gina walked up to him and said, "Not those! They'll kill ya!" She took his hat and pawed through the mushrooms, tossing some back onto the ground. She finished filling the hat and handed it back to him.

Toby looked in the hat and then looked at her, waiting for her to say something else. He felt like she still owed him an explanation about Luke. But she remained silent. Toby took this as her refusal to offer any excuse for what had happened. He spun on his heel and returned to the seat of the cart. Then, without a word, he got Bea moving. He didn't turn, but felt the weight of Gina's body as she jumped onto the cart.

He ate a couple of the mushrooms as they continued towards Alum Rock. He thought that they should be coming close to it by now. It seemed like they'd traveled far enough to be there. He looked at Bea. As always, she was content to just pull the cart. Toby decided he could be content to simply ride. He looked around at the huge trees, still in awe of their size. He softly said, "Whoa" at a particularly big one. As he opened his mouth in awe, a deerfly hit the back of his throat and Toby hacked to cough it up.

The air temperature in the shade of the forest was just right and the flies began to attack in large numbers. Toby couldn't even count how many were on Bea! They seemed to cover the poor mule from her head to her tail, which she swished furiously. She trotted a little, thinking she could get away from them, but it was useless. Toby swatted and cursed at the flies and scratched at the bites on his body. They were everywhere now. He didn't know what to do. It was maddening! He looked back at Gina and saw that she had covered herself with the blanket.

Toby had an idea and stopped the cart. Bea danced among the swarming flies. Toby grabbed the oilcloth and—still swatting at the air—covered Bea with it. The deerflies continued to attack her exposed legs. Nearby, a rut from the dragging of logs was filled with water. Toby scooped up a two handfuls of the muck and returned to Bea. He covered her legs with the mud and it seemed to help.

He covered each of her legs and her face with mud and decided to cover his own exposed skin, as well. The flies still attempted to bite , but it was harder for them. The mud also seemed to provide a cooling effect to the bites he already had. Bea seemed calm enough to travel now. He looked back at Gina, but she hadn't moved from beneath the blanket. That was fine with him!

◊ ◊ ◊

# 25

## ~too many trails and another man's face~

Toby didn't know if they could get away from the deerflies or if they'd get thicker, but he knew they had to move on. As they went, it did seem that the flies thinned—or maybe they were giving up. Toby hopped off the cart and walked Bea up the next hill. They were nearly to the top of the hill when Toby looked back and saw Gina leaning on the rear of the cart, helping to push. His mind was still full of questions that he wanted to scream at her, but he felt kinder towards her at the moment. They were now walking due east and the sun was low in the sky behind them. The late day warmth felt good, and Toby wondered how cold it might get in among these huge trees at night. Even though the trees were now spaced further apart, Toby saw only a sparse sign of tracks here and there. He realized that there was no longer a trail! He swept his eyes along the ground, searching for a trail to follow.

Toby knew there wasn't much daylight left and realized that it was up to him to decide whether to try going further or to camp here. He continued to lead Bea since the ground was uneven and she would have a harder pull carrying him. He looked back and Gina still had her hands on the back of the cart and continued to push.

Toby began to realize that they may be quite a distance from the path and could be going in the wrong direction! He either had to admit it to himself now, or stop for the night and decide what to do in the morning. There was no sense in continuing in the wrong direction. Toby pulled Bea to a stop in a clearing. Some nearby fallen trees would be good for firewood. He wished they had found water, but the last valley they crossed had a dry streambed. There weren't even any ruts filled with water here. Things looked worse when he realized that he had no feed for Bea. *What else could go wrong?*, he wondered, shaking his head in dismay.

Toby unhitched Bea and started dragging firewood to the camp. He got a fire burning and had several piles of wood ready to keep the fire going for the night. He hadn't paid any attention to Gina until she appeared from the back of the cart carrying the small cooking pot. She set it into some of the hot coals, wiped a stick clean on her pant leg, and then stirred the pot several times. She kept her back to Toby and got up without talking to him. She rose and went over to Bea. She stayed there and petted the mule. Toby thought he saw Gina hand something to Bea to eat. He was sure of it! What had she found to feed to the mule? Out of the corner of his eye he watched Bea chewing on whatever Gina was giving her.

Gina returned without saying a word and without looking at Toby. She stooped to the fire and stirred the pot again. This time she licked the stick and tasted what looked like a thick sauce on it. Toby had yet to smell anything and wondered what was cooking. Gina had a small pan and two spoons that they had used before. She dipped the small pan into the cooking pot, filling it with soup. She put a spoon in it and walked to Toby. Without a word, she placed the soup on the ground beside him. Finally, he smelled it: It was the mushrooms they'd picked earlier, and they were in a fine stew! He tasted it and realized that Gina must have added something that Ella had given her. It was delicious. He chewed at the hot mushrooms and drank the broth.

When he was done eating he realized that Gina hadn't eaten anything. He took the pan to the fire and set it beside the pot, then returned to where he'd been sitting. Gina filled the pan again and set the pot away from the fire. She carried her soup to the rear of the wagon and sat down in the near darkness.

After making a trip to relieve himself in the woods, Toby came back to the fire and put more wood on it. He saw that the blanket was sitting where he'd sat before, but he didn't see Gina. He figured that she had crawled inside the still. He knew that she had clothing and the oilcloth to keep warm, so he curled up with the blanket and fell asleep watching the flames of the fire.

Toby woke once during the night and put more wood on the fire. As he warmed up, many things kept working on his mind. He thought about his mother and sisters again and hoped they were alright. He also wondered if Lew and Lucca had given up searching for him and Gina and were headed back to their farm. What if they weren't? What if they were coming after them? And worse yet, what if they *kept* following them? Toby thought of Gina's story about Lew viciously slaying the Indians and taking their scalps! He shivered. He thought about that for awhile and then thought of Gina. He wasn't sure if they would ever talk again. He finally fell back asleep looking at the stars that shone through the trees.

He woke in daylight when he felt someone kicking the bottom of his boot. He quickly threw the blanket from his head and looked straight into a man's face staring down at him!

◊ ◊ ◊

# 26

## ~a face full of dirt and a chesty wabbit~

The man squinted down at Toby. He was grizzly and dressed in filthy clothes. Toby could smell him without moving. The man's stench wafted down to Toby and seemed to envelope him.

Toby pushed himself up on his elbows and looked up at the man's wrinkled face. His legs were still flat on the ground and he was in no position to move. The man hunkered down to close the gap (of fresh air!) between them. Toby drew shallow breaths. The man smiled and showed a few remaining teeth that looked like brown and yellow Indian corn. "Wish way ya headin', son?" the man asked. Some of the missing "corn" caused him speech problems.

It wasn't only the man's body that smelled bad! His breath reeked. Toby looked at the man's beard, which was a motley shade of grey, reddish brown, and something that definitely looked like charcoal and a day old meal!

Toby cleared his throat and wished he could clear the air as well. In a raspy voice he answered: "Uh, south, I guess. Uh….—Or east maybe!" Toby needed to get away from the man's smell and didn't think he was a threat, so he rolled away and stood up. He blinked at the surroundings; things always looked different in the morning. "Where exactly is this place?" Toby asked as he looked at the large trees surrounding them.

"Boy, you be in the Firs' Woods. Kinda near the so-west o' it!" the old man said and looked around like he'd never seen it before either.

"The what? We—uh—I was heading to Alum Rock! It's supposed to be near here."

"Nope! It ain't here. More o'er tha' way. Looky." The man turned Toby around by the shoulder and pointed across an opening in the trees. "See them big-uns o'er there? Way yonder?" His grubby hand held Toby's jaw and turned his head slightly.

Toby nodded at the bigger hill-line that was a misty-blue in the distance. "Yes, sir."

"Left o' that un, an' 'bout six miles, but, you ain't gonna make it with *tha'* cart!"

Toby looked at the cart like it had fallen apart. "Why not? I've made it from Pittsburgh to here in it!"

"No doubt, you come a long way. Jus' saying you ain't gonna head *tha'* direction in *tha'* cart. Too man-nee gullies and washez, bo-ey!" The man sprayed Toby with spit with each "*tha'*." Toby stepped around him and made like he was busy with the fire. He pushed some hot embers into a small pile and added some branches.

The fire began to burn brighter and Toby rubbed his hands together.

The man stepped to the other side of the fire and squatted, too. "You got any cof-fee, son?" he asked. Toby didn't look up and just shook his head while he stared into the fire. His stomach grumbled. Last night's mushroom soup was good, but it just didn't last.

"You et lately?" the man asked, and then snorted and rubbed his sleeve across his nose.

Toby just shook his head again.

"I'm clearin' my traps and takin' fur," the man announced. Toby glanced over where the man had indicated and saw some rolled pelts.

"I see. You got some food?" Toby asked him.

The man eyed him suspiciously, "No. I kept da one rabbit whole though!"

Toby didn't understand the man at first, but then he eyed the dead rabbit like a hungry wolf.

"Trouble is, I can't find my flint so I couldn't cook her up!" The man laughed and shrugged his shoulders. "Guess'n I'd get los' myself if'n I wasn't crazy!" He laughed again and looked across the fire at Toby. Each time the man spoke Toby heard his spit sizzle as it hit the fire. (He was thankful for the barrier between them.)

Toby laughed. "We'll I'd be willin' to share my fire *if'n* you'd share some rabbit," he said, mimicking the old man's dialect.

"DONE! And done—Boy, you drive a hard bargain. We'll cook up that fat ol' girl right now!" The man pulled out a wicked looking bowie knife that was razor sharp. He deftly parted the rabbit and the fur in under a minute. He proceeded to cut the raw meat into small chunks Toby studied his moves and made a note to remember them in case he ever needed to cook a rabbit.

It suddenly dawned on him that Gina was still in the pot. Toby wasn't sure what to tell the man about her. He still had no notion that the man was dangerous, but he had to watch.

The man stripped the bark from a small tree branch and threaded the bits of rabbit meat on it. When he finished placing the skewers around the fire, he spoke again. "What I was tryin' ta tell ya earlier is that the direct path to Alum Rock is too rough for a cart. Yeah there's paths, an' open areas, but you ain't gonna make it. It's best to go back and catch the road!"

Toby looked back the way they came and asked how much time it would take.

"No mor'n a day, mebe two."

"And there's no other way?" Toby asked, his eyes imploring the man's wrinkled face of dirt.

The man looked at the cart again and then studied Toby's build. "Boy, I jus' don't think you can get across them gullies an' washez. An' it got some steep hillsides! That cart an' its load would lay ov'r." He turned the rabbit skewers again to cook evenly.

The man sat quietly, chewing on his lip like he was thinking of something. He turned the rabbit again and said: "There iz a easier path, but the bog....It'd be too wet this early in the year. Your mule just couldn't pull that cart!"

"But it's not that heavy of a load. And if I could save some time, that would be useful," Toby said.

"Son, forget I tol' ya that. I don't want to see ya in trouble. I ain't goin' that far or I'd help some way."

They sat in silence, watching the rabbit cook, swallowing frequently as their mouths watered at the sight and smell of the cooking meat. Toby spent the time thinking of a way to get Gina out of the still and fed without having to talk to her. Finally he went to the cart and climbed up. He looked inside the still and saw that Gina had put her hair up under the hat and was wearing the men's clothes she'd worn before. Toby nodded to her and said, "Brother, wake up! There's a rabbit here to feed ya!"

He returned to the fire and saw that the rabbit looked nearly cooked. He offered a couple of branches to the man. "Here you go…. You know, I didn't catch your name."        The man looked up at him, seemingly confused about why Toby would care to know. "Oh yeah," he finally said. "I'm forgettin' my manners. Sorry. I'm Wilbur." Toby shook his hand (and then wished he had some water to wash his hand in). Just then, Gina stepped out of the still and jumped from the cart. She walked into the woods and returned about five minutes later.

Gina returned to the fireside and said good morning, but Toby was playing with the fire. "I'm Gene, his older brother," Gina announced, pointing at Toby. She took Wilbur's hand and shook it like any man would do. (Toby noticed her wiping it on her pant leg several times as she squatted down near the fire.)

Wilbur looked at "Gene" and studied "him" for several moments before he returned his gaze to the fire. He spoke some of the First Woods and said he'd been here about twelve years. "The trappin's real good here," Wilbur said. "I take all my pelts to a man in Foxburg. Good man, he is. Does lots o' bidness on the river, he does. Goes by the name o' Ern-ee." Toby realized that Wilbur was talking about Ella's husband Ernie. "Good man! Good man!" Wilbur kept repeating.

They ate until the bones were clean and then talked for another hour. By then Toby began to get antsy. He wanted to make up the time they'd spent getting lost. He still hadn't said anything to Gina/Gene and let Wilbur do most of the talking.

Soon it was obvious that Toby wanted to get on the road. Wilbur tapered off his stories and helped with putting out the fire. Toby asked him if he needed a piece of flint, but he declined: "I can be back to my camp by morning, and I won't eat till then anyway!"

Gina was carrying some of the tack in her arms and it became obvious that her chest wasn't that of a man's. Toby looked at Wilbur and saw that he noticed. When Wilbur's eyes met Toby's, he simply nodded in understanding at him. Then Wilbur gave him a stern look and repeated his earlier warning "Listen to me, *go back* the way you came. You can't make it through there!" He pointed his greasy hand south and looked again at Gina struggling with Bea and the tack.

Toby nodded his thanks and smiled. Wilbur was on his feet and shouldering the furs. "The longer way around is the shorter!" he said, loud enough for Gina to hear. He turned to leave, waved goodbye, and wandered off.

Toby looked wistfully in the direction they had been traveling and then turned Bea around. With the silent help of Gina they turned the cart around. They backtracked through the First Woods and were now in a large meadow that was clear of trees but filled with winter-dried, waist-high goldenrod. It was beautiful and easy travel for them, but the cart caused dust from the flowers to float in the air.

They soon arrived at what looked like a main path. They spent the rest of the day in complete silence. Toby rode in the driver's seat and Gina rode on a crate in the back. The only sound was the two of them coughing and sneezing from the goldenrod dust. Their eyes itched and watered from all the pollen.

Finally, they arrived at a place where three paths connected, but there was no sign! Toby felt sure that this must be Alum Rock, but except for a flat layered shelf of whitish rock, there was nothing else here. He walked to the start of each road and studied them for a moment. He finally kicked at the dirt and pulled Bea to the road on the right.

Gina jumped off the cart and leaned into the back rail, pushing. The way ahead looked to be full of long, rolling hills and open areas that would make easy traveling. Toby looked at the panoramic view and wondered which of the hill-lines ahead held their destination. How many would they have to cross before they reached Sligo?

But first they had to reach Callensburg.

◊ ◊ ◊

# 27

## ~Bea's dance and a throaty growl~

The day went as usual, with Toby and Gina helping to push or pull the cart through areas that were too hard for Bea to do it by herself. The long rolling hills weren't too bad, as they ran mostly in the same direction that the trio was going. Toby saw smoke rising on the horizon and figured that it had to be coming from Callensburg. He estimated that it couldn't be more than two, maybe three, miles away. He felt better to be this close to the town and hoped they would have easier travel from there on—on a road instead of a path, for a change!

But Toby worried about being back on the main road to Sligo. If Lew or Luca were still looking for them that might be where they'd find him and Gina. He kept an eye out in every direction, even glancing backward every so often.

Despite the possible danger, Toby really enjoyed the clear skies and fresh air. He'd miss these when he got back to the city of Pittsburgh. He saw two eagles soaring high above them, flying about a mile apart from each other. Toby wondered if they could communicate with each other at that distance, and if so, how?

Of course, he and Gina hadn't spoken now for two days. Toby still wasn't able to sort out the mess. He just couldn't understand her, and right now he didn't care to! He glanced at the back of the cart and saw Gina lying down, curled up and holding her stomach. He wondered if she was hungry or if she might be sick. He didn't say anything but thought about his own hunger. But they were out of food and he hadn't seen anything edible along the trail; it was still too early in the season for berries or wild vegetables.

Toby looked at the sun's position and figured it was now midday. They had been following a border of crabapple trees for several hundred yards and he hoped that they didn't form a barrier ahead for them to have to cut their way through. He knew their thorns! He'd had enough worry about things he couldn't control, so he followed Bea's example again, and just dealt with what was.

As they topped a small knoll, Toby saw the wash ahead. It started as a small spring on the hillside above them and ran across the path ahead. It didn't seem too bad, and Toby was glad to find fresh water. But as they drew nearer, he was disappointed to see that the banks on each side were about two feet high. Bea drew up to the edge and stopped.

Toby studied the area around them. He could see quite a way up the hillside to his left, and he noticed that the crabapple trees ahead all had bare limbs near the ground. Every limb was stripped to the exact same spot just above Toby's head. He remembered how the goats had eaten everything at Ernie and Elle's place along the river. Maybe there were wild goats nearby! Toby pursed his lips and remembered the older, aggressive goats and wondered if wild ones would be harder to deal with.

Keeping an eye out for wild goats, he unhitched Bea and scouted the area for mushrooms or some small critter that might make them a meal. He looked again at Gina and saw that she hadn't moved. Bea was now in the spring water run and drinking merrily. After each long drink of water, she looked skyward. Toby imagined that she was letting the cool water slide down her throat. He took the canvas bucket to the stream to get a drink for himself, and then decided that he might like to bathe, too. His shirt was smelly and he could use clean socks. He left the bucket on the bank, along with his boots, and lowered himself into the water. It was cold, but the air was warm and getting warmer in the noonday sun. Toby peeled off his shirt and socks to let them soak in the stream. He figured he might as well have a wash himself, and he rubbed the cold water over his body. He knelt down, put his head into the water, and rubbed it briskly. Coming up for air, he shook his head and squeezed the water out of his hair.

He thought he'd get a look at the source of the water and stepped gingerly along the rocks in the water. A rock rolled over as he stepped on it and he saw something underneath it. He'd seen them in the river in Pittsburgh: a crawfish!

He grabbed it and held it so the pinchers couldn't reach his fingers. "FOOD!" Toby shouted joyfully to no one in particular. He went back for the bucket and put the lobster-like critter inside. He diligently turned over rocks, searching for more. In less than a half hour he had twenty-two crawfish in the bucket. His mouth watered as he returned to the cart. He sat the bucket on the ground and the canvas side started to collapse under the weight of the crawfish. Toby scooped up the bucket and hung it from the front of the cart's drawbars instead. Next he gathered up some dried grass, twigs, and heavier sticks for a fire.

He used the flint and steel to get a fire going and sat the cooking pan across two rocks by the fire. He wasn't sure how to cook these creatures, but he was going to try! They were small, only as long as his hand, so he figured they'd cook quickly. Toby carefully tipped out some of the extra water from the bucket and then poured the rest—water and crawfish—into the cooking pot. The water heated up and started to steam.

He heard a noise behind him and turned around to see Gina pawing through the seat-box. He ignored her and turned back to the fire. He remembered his shirt and socks in the stream and went to fish them out. He hung them on some sticks to dry. Suddenly a loud boom erupted behind him. He turned in time to see Bea jump and trot several rods away.

It took Toby a minute to realize what had happened: The cold rocks had heated up and exploded! His meal was strewn around the grass and in the fire. He ran back to the fire and began searching the area for escaped crawfish. He picked the hot critters out of the grass, juggling them in his hands as he carefully returned them to the bucket. He made a trip to the stream and put cold water into the bucket. He even managed to fish a few of them from the fire. After a thorough search and recovery effort, he had eighteen crawfish remaining. Not bad, even though some were a little fragmented.

Gina was sitting in the grass a little distance from the cart, with her arm still wrapped around her lower stomach. "There's a little food here," Toby said without looking in her direction.

"No, thank you," Gina replied in a quiet voice. She got up and walked along the bank of the stream, away from the fire. Toby shrugged and pulled the first of the meal from the bucket. It only took him three crawfish to figure out the best way to pull the meat from the hard shell with his pocketknife. He was happy not to have to share the food, as it was just enough to take away his hunger. Each crawfish yielded the same amount of meat that was in his little finger.

After he finished eating, Toby went back to the cart and sat on the ground, leaning against the wheel. He loved the sky out here in the country. He thought he could see rain clouds far off in the south. His mind drifted to Gina and he wondered what was wrong with her. She'd looked so pale and weak. He rose and walked in the direction she'd gone. A short way down the stream he saw her sitting in the cold water; she had removed her dress and her bare back faced him. She moved her arm in the water, letting her hand slowly drag back and forth. Then she rubbed her lower back with both hands.

Toby decided to give her time to clean up while his shirt and socks dried. He returned to the cart and sat against the wheel again. He closed his eyes and fell asleep. About an hour later he woke and stood up. He looked downstream and then to the back of the cart and saw Gina again asleep where she'd started the morning. He went back and looked at her. She seemed ok, but he noticed a smear of blood on her ankle. He looked closer but saw no wounds. She was breathing normally, so he thought no more of it.

Toby hooked Bea back up to the cart and led her to a place that he thought would be an easy crossing. The cart rocked hard as they crossed the stream, and Toby glanced at Gina. She had grabbed one of the tie-down ropes holding the crate. On the other side of the wash, they encountered a thicket of the crabapple trees, just as Toby had feared. But it wasn't as bad as he thought it might be. There was only one spot that was a tight fit for the cart to pass through. Toby noticed a lot of animal droppings in the thicket and again thought of the goats.

After about half an hour of winding their way through the trees, they came to an open area where the larger trees had been cleared. The remaining stumps were about two feet tall and four feet across. Some of the treetops were lying around, and they were also picked clean. The grass was too short for Bea to chew on and she pawed at the ground. Toby wasn't concerned about her as she'd eaten a lot of grass earlier.

Here the trees began to switch from crabapple to hemlock. The ground sloped downward, and Toby realized that another stream was ahead. He judged the distance and guessed that traveling to it would burn up the rest of the remaining daylight. He was disappointed. Another day was gone and they were still on the road. He tried to remember how many days he and Bea had been traveling, but he'd lost count. Through the hemlocks he could see the reflection of sunlight on the water. The stream looked to be of considerable size! Toby worried that they might have trouble crossing it.

He pulled Bea up to a stop, surveyed the area, and decided to make a camp. Bea nosed around looking for food as Toby foraged for firewood. He took the whip along, as it seemed that there were snakes where there were the hemlocks and rocks. "Hemlocks and rocks and snakes!" he said to himself as he wandered around. Then he thought of Ella's story that goats eat snakes and felt a little safer.

When he returned to the cart, Gina had started a small fire already. Neither spoke as Toby approached and dropped the wood by the fire. He turned and reentered the woods. He searched for a path to take them to the larger stream and for a way to cross, but found nothing. He returned disgusted, trying to imagine how far they might have to move to find a suitable spot to cross. He sat down sullenly.

Suddenly Bea began braying. Toby and Gina and exchanged quick, startled glances and stood up to look around. Bea was getting more agitated and started stepping in circles. Toby decided it best to remove the remaining harness and went to her. She wouldn't stand still. She snorted and brayed loudly as he tried to comfort her. He pulled her by the harness closer to the fire, all the while scanning the woods around them.

He saw nothing, but continued staring into the ever darkening forest. Gina stoked the fire and it shone brightly. She stood with her back to the flames looking in one direction while Toby, holding Bea's head, did the same on the opposite side. A low throaty growl came from the woods, but neither Gina nor Toby could determine what direction it came from!

Toby tugged Bea to the front of the wagon and tied her there. She danced around, plainly terrified. Her eyes were wide with fear! Toby picked up a burning limb from the fire and held it above his head. His other hand gripped the whip tightly. Gina glanced around wildly and picked up a torch from the fire, as well.

In a barely audible whisper, Gina very slowly said Toby's name: "Toobeee!"

He turned his head and saw what she saw. It stepped from the wood line, each foot moving ahead ever so slowly, tenderly stepping onto the soft pine needle floor of the woods. The fire's light made its fur shimmer, revealing its massive muscles. Toby had never seen anything so strong looking. There wasn't one area of softness on its entire form. The low growl came again. Toby could see Gina shaking. He spoke very quietly to her: "Don't move or talk."

Toby had never been so scared in his life. He looked into the eyes that reflected the firelight and shuddered. He doubted that there was anything he could do to save them now. Bea fussed furiously and danced in a semicircle, frantically pulling at the halter rope. The growl came again like a low, throaty snarl.

◊ ◊ ◊

# 28

## ~a chief chef~

The large cat's dark fur reflected the firelight, making its shape stand out as a separate darkness from the background. Toby could hardly breathe; he knew that nothing could stop so much strength. The mountain lion moved forward one last time. Then in short steps with its back feet, it shuffled into a stance preparing to leap! Each of its paws tested the ground for traction again and yet again. Seconds dragged as the great cat prepared to spring!

Toby motioned for Gina to move behind him, but she was frozen. Just then they heard a whizzing noise. Then a thud! The large cat screamed in pain, curled into a ball, and began flipping in leaps. Another thud and it made another horrifying scream and fell into a twitching mass. Toby's legs were about to collapse beneath him when he heard another arrow strike the large cat. A moment later everything around him fell into deafening silence.

Gina grabbed at Toby, collapsed onto her knees, and sobbed. Toby looked around for the archer. He saw a movement. An Indian and a white man slipped from the forest. The Indian approached the large, lifeless figure. He had an arrow notched in his bowstring, ready to release another shot if necessary. Toby's hand was on Gina's head and he used it to steady himself.

The white man entered the fire lit area. Bea was dancing a bit slower now, but still highly agitated. "A bit too close, for my blood!" the man said, his eyes on the big cat. "I'm sorry, but if we'd made a sound, she'd spooked and pounced—or ran off. Then we'd a' had to track her again." He pushed back his hat and looked at Toby and Gina. "You two alright, then?"

Toby nodded quickly and looked at the top of Gina's head; he felt her nod against his leg. He nearly lost his balance from her trembling and the grip she had on his leg. "Guess so," he finally replied, drawing a deep breath. He watched the Indian—who had said nothing so far—pat the head of the large cat. There was a sad respect in the Indian's eyes as he stroked the cat's jaw line.

"We've been trackin' this big girl for three days. She's been hangin' round the sheep farm on the next hill," the white man said. He jerked his head to the hillside on their left. "There's another one with her, a larger male. He probably caught our scent and is holdin' himself off somewhere." They all glanced back into the woods. Gina slowly stood and Toby let her hang onto his arm.

"You think he'll come in to follow her?" Toby asked.

"Not likely. We heard your mule and rode as fast as we could in the trees and the dark. We're gonna skin her and drag her carcass off into another direction. By the time he figures out what happened he'll move on. Pity though. They mate for life. But we'll have him too—soon enuf."

Toby began to understand why the Indian looked sad. He heard Gina sniffle. The Indian took out a knife and skillfully began to skin off the cat's fur coat. It was quite a process and they all watched the beast's naked form appear.

"We can't offer you anything to eat or drink," Toby said apologetically. "But you're welcome to share the fire," he added. He hoped the men would stay, thinking they'd be safer with them around.

"We'll take you up on that one, son, soon as we get a scent-trail dropped and bring in our horses." With that he strolled off into the woods.

The Indian finished stripping off the cat's hide and tied a strap of leather around its waist. He made an incision in the cat's belly and reached inside. He felt around for a moment and then passed the knife to the hand inside the cat. In a decisive move he pulled out something that looked like a red bag. Another plunge inside and he retrieve something else. He handed both to Toby and motioned that he could eat them. Toby nodded and passed the warm meat into Gina's trembling hand. She hesitantly took the meat and put it into the pot.

The other man returned riding a chestnut colored horse and leading a smaller horse without a saddle. Both horses balked a step or two at the sight of the cat until the rider commanded them forward. He tossed one end of a piece of rope to the Indian, who tied it to the belt on the panther. "I'll be back shortly," the man said. "The chief here will show you how to cook up them parts!" The man turned the wide-eyed horse and headed into the woods.

Toby watched as the Indian prepared the meat. He cut several slices into the parts and sprinkled them with some leaves from a pouch he wore. Gina offered the pot to the Indian, but he frowned and tossed the meat directly into the fire. Gina and Toby exchanged glances and then looked back to the Indian, who seemed to be chanting something softly into the fire.

◊ ◊ ◊

# 29

## ~mind that missy and the knife~

The white man surprised Toby and Gina when he returned silently in the dark, but the Indian didn't seem surprised. The meat was cooked and the Indian had carved several small tree limbs into fork-like utensils to hold it. Gina ate one piece of meat and the men ate the rest. She disappeared for a short while and then returned wearing her dress and a pair of pants.

Toby thought this was strange, but didn't say anything to her. He continued his conversation with the men, with the white man acting as an interpreter between Toby and the Indian. Toby asked enough questions to know almost exactly where they had yet to travel. Gina sat demurely and said nothing. After awhile she looked at Toby and guided his glance to the still. She went to the cart and climbed inside.

Toby liked talking with these men. He felt that they respected him for holding his ground in the face of the big cat. They seemed to share a special "kinship of the kill." After another hour of translations, the white man's concentration began to falter. He begged off translating anymore and mentioned sleep. Then hHe spoke something to the Indian and they both nodded.

Then the man went to rest; he placed his head on his saddle and started to snore softly. The Indian stood and slipped into the woods. Toby placed several pieces of wood onto the fire and crawled onto the back of the cart. He looked down into the darkness of the still. He couldn't see anything and decided that Gina was asleep. Toby lay down on the deck of the cart and covered himself with the oilskin cloth.

He was asleep within seconds but didn't sleep well. He tossed and turned and once woke himself as his fist hammered against the deck of the cart. He sat up and looked towards the fire. The man had disappeared, but the Indian sat by the fire with his head tipped slightly forward. He looked peaceful, but Toby would bet his life that the Indian wasn't asleep. He laid his head back onto the cart and looked up at the sky. The stars were dimming and Toby knew that dawn was near.

Toby woke in morning to the sound of the Indian's horse whinnying. He slid off the cart and went to the activity at the fire's side. The white man's horse was already saddled and the Indian was checking the horses' legs. The men were nearly ready to mount when Toby approached.

The two men smiled and nodded to Toby. Toby rubbed his head and yawned. He guessed the men had been waiting for him to rise before riding off. Toby couldn't think of anything to say except to thank them profusely. He shook their hands and they climbed on their horses. The white man looked at Toby for a long moment and said, "Mind that missy. She'll do you right, ya hear?" Toby looked to the still and nodded, but he wasn't sure that he wanted much to do with her. He watched the riders as they wove their way into the hemlocks and then disappeared.

When he turned he saw the dark fur from the cat hanging on the wheel of the cart. They'd forgotten it! He wondered if he could whistle and catch them before they were out of hearing range. He ran into the woods, but there was no sign of them. Since this was the direction he was headed next he studied the path for a bit, seeing if Bea could travel through. He'd been gone about half an hour when he made it back to the camp.

Gina was standing at the cart's wheel and looked scared. Her eyes were wide and she looked at him, but she said nothing. Toby started to ask her what was wrong when he saw a movement. Someone stepped around the cart.

It was Lew!

Toby immediately pulled the whip from his belt and unfurled it. He moved to put the fire between him and Lew. Lew just grinned and stepped forward.

"Toby! Just run!" Gina shouted. Lew backhanded her across the face. Her head dropped to her shoulder and blood trickled from the corner of her mouth onto her dress. She moaned and spit the blood at Lew. Toby realized that her one hand was tied to the cart.

Lew ignored her and kept his eyes glued on Toby. He pulled the now rolled-up cat's hide from behind his back and held it towards Toby. "So, the

Baby Grape is a killer!" Lew spat the words at Toby.

Toby's first instinct was to be honest and explain the hide, but he caught himself and decided to use Lew's assumption to his advantage. "That's right!" Toby said. "And I'm about to kill a snake!"

Lew sneered at him and tossed the pelt onto the cart's seat. Toby glanced behind Lew and saw his horse. It was lathered and soaked in sweat. Toby imagined that Lew had punished it severely trying to catch them. It angered him further. "Toby, please. Just go! Get away!" Gina said as blood continued to run down her chin.

Toby was distracted by Gina's pleading and realized almost too late that Lew had stepped closer to him. But Toby quickly stepped to his left and kept the fire between them. He figured Lew wouldn't jump across it to get to him, but maybe Toby could just reach him with the whip.

"Baby Grape! You want this little pig-dropping?" Lew's head tilted towards Gina. "You didn't know her plans, eh?" Another step along the fire. Toby matched it, staying directly across from Lew. "She has plans—you didn't know? She was to ride with you until you delivered the load and got the money, and then she was going to lead you back to the Landing and join up with Luke!"

Toby's mouth dropped open and he looked at Gina who shook her head violently. "It's a LIE!" she blurted out. "Toby, it's a LIE!" Toby was stunned. He looked at her and then at Lew; he wasn't sure what to believe.

Lew stepped back to Gina and grabbed a handful of her hair. He twisted her head to look at Toby. "Look closely, Baby Grape! She's the one that lies. We had a long talk. Luke told me and Lucca how he and Gina planned it. And that Ella, what a woman!" Lew kissed his fingers and pushed them into the air. "It took some persuasion—from each of us—to get her to talk!" Lew looked at Toby and realized he didn't quite understand his full meaning. But Gina did. With her free hand she reached out and scratched his face. He flinched and stepped out of her reach. "You'll pay for that!" he snarled at Gina as he stepped to her and backhanded her again. She dropped to her knees.

At that moment Toby stepped to the edge of the fire and cracked the whip at Lew's hand. The knife he was holding dropped to the edge of the fire and Lew grabbed his hand in pain. He looked at the knife, and Toby could see he was trying to decide if he could get to it before Toby could reach him again with the whip. Lew ducked for the knife but Gina grabbed his foot and tripped him. His outstretched hand was the first to fall into the hot coals of the fire.

It was enough of an advantage for Toby. He struck one blow with the whip and then another! Lew tried to roll away from the fire but Toby kept up a continuous rain of whip blows. Each strike cut terrible holes into Lew's shirt and the skin beneath. Six, seven blows landed. Lew had no way to escape! He'd roll out of the fire only to receive a lash, and then roll back into the fire to avoid the whip. Toby's arm worked the whip mechanically. He sidestepped and lashed again without thinking. It was nearly a dance now, the rhythm following each move. Lew quivered. He was curled into a ball and his shoulder was burning on the hot coals. He screamed curses at Toby and Gina.

Meanwhile, Gina had untied her hand and now grabbed Lew's knife. In one quick move she was on Lew with vengeance that exceeded Toby's. He stared openmouthed as Gina slashed and stabbed Lew with the knife. Her face contorted in hatred and blind rage. Lew looked like a bloody piece of meat. The blood from Gina's split lip dripped down and mingled with the bloody mess beneath her.

Bea stirred as badly as she had the night before from the terror of the huge cat. Toby was frozen in place, panting, and shocked at the sight. Gina finally slowed her attack as she grew tired. She started to regain a sense of the present, and then she withdrew slowly and knelt beside Lew's bloody body. She spat blood at him and said, "Filthy pig! Filthy pig!" She repeated it over and over again until it turned into a whisper, and then into silent mouthing of the words. Finally she looked at Toby and her face turned into shame. "He lied," she said and dropped the knife. "He lied." Her voice pleaded with Toby to believe her and her eyes filled with tears.

Toby felt helpless. He wasn't sure he believed her. He looked at Lew's mangled body. Part of it burned in the fire and the smoke smelled terrible. Toby went around the fire and dragged Lew away from it. As the body passed Gina a wild look came over her face and Toby thought she was going to jump on Lew again

A few moments passed and the crazed look in Gina's eyes faded. She looked around confused, like she wasn't sure where she was. Finally she came back to her senses and motioned Toby away from the scene. She walked towards the water at the bottom of the hill. Toby followed her at a short distance, looking back several times to make sure Lew was really dead.

For a long time they both just squatted in the cold water and let it cool them off. Gina slowly regained herself completely and finally turned to Toby. He'd stayed several feet away, but kept a watch on her. "Toby, I *was* planning to see Luke when we got back to the Landing. I wanted to know why he hadn't come back to the farm to get me! It was two years ago when he left and *promised* to come back for me. Then he found work and a place to live." She shook her head, disbelieving her own words. "And then he told me he had a wife!" She sobbed at that last word. "He just never came back! He left me with Lucca! And that PIG used me, too!" She searched Toby's face to see if he completely understood.

Toby understood. He lowered his eyes and couldn't think of a reply…

◊ ◊ ◊

# 30

~asses to ashes to Anna ~

They wrung the water and blood out of their clothes and put them back on—still wet. Toby found Lew's horse and brought it to the campsite. Since they were going to be there awhile, he unsaddled the horse and hobbled it with a short rope at the front knees. Bea and the horse sniffed at each other and then went about foraging for food in the underbrush.

Gina leaned against a tree, far away from Lew's body. Toby noticed her staring at the corpse and said, "We should bury it—him. It would be better if he isn't found."

"It's too good for that pig!" she said without looking at Toby. "Let the crows find him, and eat those horrible eyes."

"Well, that might be true. But I would feel better if *nobody* found him, and we git as far away as we can." Toby studied Lew's lifeless form. "Maybe we should bury him and cover the spot with ashes from the fire. That would hide where we dug."

Gina was silent for a moment and then said, "Strip him first!"

"Why?" Toby asked. He looked at the body and then realized that it made a lot of sense. "Yeah, you're right! We could use some of what he's got." Toby stepped over to Lew and gazed at him. They could take his boots, his belt, and maybe his pants. Toby squatted down and hesitated for a few seconds before pulling on Lew's arm. As the body rolled over it made a rude sound. Toby looked at Gina. She was chewing her fingernail and looking at the grizzly sight. Toby gingerly felt in Lew's pockets. He found several coins, which he put in his own pocket. Next he pulled off Lew's belt and boots. In the right boot was a small knife inside a sheath.

Toby tossed the boot to Gina. She took out the knife and untied the sheath from the inside of the boot. She studied them and looked for a way to fasten the sheathed knife to her waist. Finally she just laid it on the cart.

Lew's shirt was covered in too much blood and was stabbed through with too many holes to be of much use, so Toby tossed it into the fire. "Get those two bars from under the seat. We'll use 'em to dig with," Toby said. He kicked some of the ashes back into the center of the dying fire, then took one of the bars and began digging.

Within an hour they had a hole large enough for the body. They unceremoniously rolled Lew into it and pushed the dirt back into the hole. After covering the body with earth, Toby used his bar to drag ashes over the grave. When he was satisfied with their work, he sat down on the back of the cart.

Toby sat silently, rubbing the dirt off his hands and looking into the distant hills. Gina joined him and sat quietly with him on the cart. They sat like this for a long time. Finally Toby broke the silence and said, "Is there anything else that you need to tell me? 'Cause I don't ever want to talk about this again—ever!" He looked at her for a long moment and then she slowly shook her head.

"Toby, a real ugly part of my life just got buried there. I'm leavin' behind things that I'll never tell anybody about. If you *want* to know anything else, ask it now. 'Cause I won't remember it from this day—or this spot—EVER!"

Toby watched her speaking. When she finished and looked at him, he shook his head and looked down at his feet. For a long time he studied the mud on his father's scuffed boots. Gina leaned over and kissed his cheek.

They took several minutes to wash off the dirt and ash, and then Toby saddled the horse and hitched up Bea. "With any luck, we could be in Callensburg in a couple of hours," Toby said.

"I feel lucky, Toby," Gina said brightly as she climbed onto the cart's seat and took the reins.

*I wish I did*, Toby thought as he mounted Lew's horse. He looked at her, then into the distance, and shrugged as he led the way. After crossing a wide but shallow stream, they found the road—finally! Looking in the opposite direction, they saw another cart going away from them. Toby thought of how it might have helped to talk to the driver and get some knowledge of what was ahead.

Traveling on the roadway was ridiculously easy compared to the last several days. Toby shook his head at himself, at getting lost the way he had and the stupidity of it. Then he realized that things might have turned out differently with Lew if they hadn't gotten lost. Just maybe they *had* been lucky! He took a deep breath and looked at the beautiful sky.

Gina handled the cart as if she'd been born on that seat. She looked over at Toby and smiled. Lew's horse was a "stepper," full of energy and more inclined to run than match Bea's slow plodding. Toby let the horse trot a little further ahead, but held him in check. He turned to look back at Gina and saw that she had stopped the cart. She was standing and folding something to sit on. *Women*, he muttered to himself.

They climbed a small hill and were relieved at what they saw when they reached the top. There were several homes ahead. They were of rudimentary construction: log homes chinked with mud and with wooden plank roofs. They passed several small plots of land, each surrounded by tree-limb-fencing, and then came to the intersection of two roads. A sign, properly painted, hung from a post. The sign indicated that Parker's Landing was to their right. Another arrow pointed left and read Sligo. Neither gave a distance, but it didn't matter. Toby and Gina were relieved to see the name of their final destination.

Across the street was a building with a sign above the door: *Post and Supplies, J. A. Callen/proprietor.* They pulled up alongside the building where there was space to park the cart and tie up the horse. They walked to the front of the building and Toby showed Gina the money. "This is all we have," he said. "Get what you can for supplies. We'll get some more money when we deliver the still and can make do with it later. I need some paper and postage to send two letters, so take out for that." Gina nodded and followed him into the shop.

A very tiny woman came to greet them and eyed them up closely before speaking: "Hello. You look a little road weary—come in, come in." She turned before Toby could ask for mailing paper and walked to the counter where she poured two cups of water. Toby and Gina gratefully accepted them and drank slowly. "You two sure got yourselves some sun! Been riding far?" Gina nodded, but said nothing else. The woman was obviously hungry for a story, but they weren't about to give her one.

Before the silence could be considered impolite Toby asked her if she had two sheets of postal writing paper. "Sure do, son," the small woman replied, looking up at Toby's face. "You had a black eye lately?" she added. As she turned to get the paper, Gina gave Toby a sudden sharp look.

"Uh, no." Toby rubbed at his eye and offered an excuse: "Probably just dirt."

The woman looked at his eye again and slowly handed him the paper. "You're right, probably just the shadows in here," she said. She didn't sound any more convincing than Toby had. The tiny lady looked at Gina's swollen lip.

"And you, miss?" she asked.

Toby interrupted before Gina could speak. "I guess I'll need some ink an' a quill, too." He saw some on the desk, but the woman didn't offer to let Toby use them. She looked to a shelf and pointed at the pens and ink she had for sale. Toby gave her a disappointed look and looked at Gina, who held the money in her open hand and chewed at the inside of her cheek.

After an awkward moment, the woman spoke again, "Well I *guess* I could loan these to ya." She pursed her lips as she handed the ink and quill to Toby and swiveled her eyes again to the money Gina held. Toby thanked her and went outside. He sat on the ground and used the wooden deck of the porch as a writing surface. He could hear Gina inside haggling and ordering supplies. Toby finished a short letter to Mr. Rodgers and explained that he was near the destination. He said nothing about Lew or the trip. Next he wrote a longer letter to his mother, leaving out the same details. He told her how much he had seen, that he was fine, and about the clear skies. He was out of things to say, but still had half a sheet to go. He wrote a little larger and told her of the towns they passed through and about crossing the river—without the incident between him and Luke. When he was finished, he folded them and addressed each. He corked the ink bottle and took everything inside.

The two women had finished doing business and were now making small talk. Toby couldn't understand how women could always find something to talk about. He placed the letters on the counter. The woman started to take them when he asked her for sealing wax. She half-hid a disgusted look on her face and quickly added: "O'course! Woulda done it in a minute."

*Yeah, after you'd read them!*, Toby thought to himself. He just smiled and watched as she melted the wax and sealed the letters. She placed the letters in a large leather pouch hanging on the wall. It had the word *Post* across it. Toby sighed with relief.

Gina smiled at him and winked. "I was just telling Anna, here, that we're on our way to see your family—and to tell them about our upcoming wedding!"

"Oh, yes dear, congratulations!" Anna sparkled and trilled the words. "A fine looking girl you're getting! Better treat her well, ya know!"

When Toby recovered from the initial shock, he smiled and nodded.

"An' just which family is yourn?" Anna asked. "I know just about everybody in these parts."

"Well, we're just headin' a bit further east to deliver a load to the Hattenfelt place. Then we'll be headin' to my folks," Toby lied.

Gina coughed to cover a snicker.

◊ ◊ ◊

# 31

## ~purple arms and a toll~

They rode out of town and into a long valley rimmed with low hills. They were heading down a slight slope when Toby rode up beside the cart and said to Gina, "Funny how she looked at me when I tol' her who we were deliverin' this still to!"

Gina nodded without looking at him and said slowly, "I was thinkin' the same thing...."

By now the day was mostly spent, and the sun was low at their backs. The road was clearly well traveled and was marked with ruts from wagons and carts, but they hadn't passed anybody since they'd left Callensburg. About three miles down the bumpy road, the cart took a big dip, bouncing Gina hard in her seat. She re-made her folded blanket-cushion several times, but still squirmed uncomfortably in her seat.

Just about the time they hit the big rut in the road, they saw two small children carrying sticks and herding sheep in a nearby field. Toby waved and the kids waved back. Toby noticed something strange about them: Their arms were blue!

All four of their arms, from the elbows down, were just as bright blue as the sky could ever be! Toby looked at Gina with a puzzled face; she returned the puzzled look and smiled as the kids kept waving.

It looked like they were all going to converge in the same spot on the road ahead. Toby didn't want to have to follow them, so he sped up the horse and Gina matched his speed. But the cart and load bounced too much, so she slowed back down. When Toby turned around to check on her, he was about twenty yards ahead. His shoulders drooped when he realized they were going to finish the day's trip at a snail's—or rather, a sheep's—pace.

Another child arrived from the opposite side of the road and ushered across a single sheep that had been separated from the flock. When it saw the other sheep, it darted ahead and blended into the herd. All the sheep were freshly shorn and looked funny. Instead of being the round, fluffy balls of wool that you think of when you picture sheep, they looked more like off–colored and naked dirty goats!

The single herder was just at the side of the road when Gina stopped the cart for her. The child climbed aboard and smiled proudly next to Gina. The girl had the same blue arms as the children in the field. Each time Toby looked back, she and Gina were gabbing away. Once more, Toby thought: *Girls!*

The other two children walked with the sheep in front of Toby's horse. They moved slowly, and Toby was forced to ride slowly, too. The slow pace, the baying of the sheep, and the clopping of his horse's feet were too much for him. He grew sleepier and sleepier until he nodded off.

A sharp whistle woke him from his half-sleep. He turned in the saddle and saw that the herd and the cart had turned down a lane. Toby turned his horse and rode back to them. "We've been invited to stay at this farm tonight!" Gina said in a happy voice.

Toby looked past her at the buildings coming into view, raised an eyebrow, and shrugged.

They wound their way along a stone wall, past a stone well, and between stone-bottomed buildings containing wagons. Several large buildings dotted the farm. Inside, bleating sheep looked out through nicely built fences. *There must be hundreds of them!*, Toby thought as he glanced around. From a pipe in its base, a wooden windmill poured water into a large series of waist-high wooden vats. A little further along Toby saw stacks of sawn wooden boards. That explained the nice buildings, and the even nicer house just beyond.

Two of the children ushered the sheep into pens inside the buildings and then ran ahead to the house. The small blue-armed girl on the cart stayed seated beside Gina.

As they pulled up at the house, a woman came to the door and looked at them. She smiled and waved. Toby nodded and Gina waved back.

Toby asked where the outhouse was and excused himself quickly. What a relief after days in the woods! Besides, he was happier to let the chatting to Gina. After a rather extended visit, he left the privy. As he approached the house, a man appeared and greeted him.

"These are the O'Malley's: Samuel and Grace," Gina said, gesturing to the man and woman. Toby stepped forward and shook Samuel's hand. His arms were purplish-blue, as well! He nodded his respect to Grace. He noticed an interesting smell and realized that everything around him—including the man—smelled like sheep! He had the oily-lanolin smell of the natural wool.

Their hosts ushered Toby and Gina inside the house. As usual, the men went one direction and the women another. Samuel, with Toby in tow, wandered through the house and out the back door. He gave Toby a grand tour of the farm and told him how they raised the sheep, cut their wool, dyed it (*That explains the blue arms!*, Toby thought), and shipped it to Pittsburgh on the boats at Parker's Landing. When Toby mentioned knowing Ernie, Samuel stopped in mid-stride.

"Funny you'd know him," Samuel said. "I send all my wool through him. He's a good man—never cheats me, always pays on time. He takes all I'll sell him." Samuel trailed off and furrowed his brow before adding: "Was just there yesterday, but Ernie wasn't! Just that kid helper of his."

"Luke?" Toby quizzed.

"Yeah, that's his name.... I don't like him much, and I don't trust him. Still, it was funny Ernie wasn't there. First time in years...." Samuel was lost in thought as he stared out across the fields.

Toby did the same as he thought about the missing Ernie.

Samuel broke the silence. "Well, there's work to be done before supper. Let's say you and your girl help us out a bit. Grace'll be cookin' up a fine meal that you don't wanna miss." Toby followed Samuel back to the house where he gave orders to his children. "They'll show you what to do," he said to Gina and Toby.

After an hour of helping around the farm, they sat down to a large meal with the O'Malley clan. The seven blue-armed children were very polite and curious about the guests, but ate like a pack of wolves. Gina seemed to be happy to be back in the midst of a family and Toby couldn't help but smile at their antics.

Samuel invited Toby and Gina to sleep inside, but they declined the invitation, not wanting to intrude in an already crowded house. Grace showed them to a large hay mow in the barn. After checking on the horse and Bea, they bedded down for the night, finally feeling well-fed and safe after so many days of hunger and fear on the road. The night grew cold and they snuggled down into the hay. Toby woke when Gina rolled over and curled up against him. He slept almost as comfortably as if he was in his own bed that night.

They woke before dawn. The small girl (was it Beth or Abby?) that had ridden with Gina on the cart came to the barn and invited them to breakfast. Toby waited as Gina made a trip to the outhouse and then walked beside her to the house. Unlike dinner the night before, breakfast was a hurried ordeal. Toby thought it would have been nice to sleep in and eat later, but he was thankful for the coffee. The strong brew hadn't crossed his lips for so long!

Toby had forgotten to tell Gina that Samuel knew Ernie and said so at the table.

Grace quickly added that she had spent time with Ella, as well. "Both are welcome in this home anytime!" Grace said. She added a few other comments about Ernie and Ella as she passed around the food and watched her family and guests eating with a hawk's eye. Toby mentioned to Gina about Luke being the only one at Ernie's boat a day before, and she looked at him with shrewd consideration. Samuel told her much the same as he'd told Toby last night.

As they finished eating, Gina said, "Samuel? Could we leave the horse with you for the day and pick it up tomorrow?" She gave Toby another one of her *tell-ya-later* looks.

The O'Malley's exchanged a funny look when Toby mentioned the name of the person they were delivering the still to, but both of them bit their tongues. Toby didn't think they'd say something bad about anybody, so he didn't pursue it.

Samuel said they were welcome to leave the horse at the farm overnight and pick it up the next day. He helped Toby and Gina get Bea hooked up to the cart and back onto the road. They were just a few paces away from the farm and headed towards Sligo when Toby finally asked Gina why they left the horse.

"The shopkeeper in Callensburg told me of a toll bridge we'd have to cross this side of Sligo," she answered. "So I figured there was no reason to pay extra for both the cart *and* the horse." Toby nodded in appreciation and they rode on. Reliable as ever, Bea plodded steadily ahead into another fine morning.

Or it was, until they reached the toll bridge.

◊ ◊ ◊

# 32

## ~who's countin' hussy?~

At the edge of the town they could see a wooden bridge. It was made of stout timbers and large cut-stone and spanned a stream no wider than a couple they'd already crossed. But the banks of this stream dropped steeply, ten feet to the water below. Toby looked as far upstream as he could see, but saw nowhere else to cross. It looked like they would be stuck paying the toll.

When Toby saw several heavy coal wagons crossing the bridge, he understood why it was built so sturdily. At the moment, he and Gina were the only ones going east this morning. The coal wagons were headed west to Parker's Landing.

Toby asked Gina how much money they had on hand while he read the price schedule posted nearby. He didn't know how much they'd have to pay, because none of the descriptions were anything close to what their load would be considered.

"I—uh, we have three half-penny pieces," Gina answered, also looking at the sign. But it didn't seem to matter. It was then that Toby realized that Gina couldn't read *or* count money!

"Great! We have one and a half pennies! The lowest price on the sign is two cents for a single rider!" Toby said forcefully. "You mean to tell me we're less than two miles from getting this load delivered and we *can't cross*!?!" Bea's ears swiveled as Toby's voice rose in anger.

At the far corner of the bridge was a small shanty built above the top of the bridge's railing. It overlooked the bridge and the approach on either side. A man sat inside the small box and watched them through the window. He was no more than fifty feet away and seemed to be looking at Gina closely.

"You'll need to pay, a'fore ya cross!" he hollered to them.

"Now what?" Toby asked from the side of his mouth.

"I'll take care of this one," Gina answered. "When you see that window's shutter close, you and Bea go quiet as you can. Just get across, and keep going. I'll catch ya."

"That ain't gonna work! What are you going…?" Toby turned to Gina as she lifted her dress up her leg and stepped onto the foot rail of the cart. "Just do it!" she whispered harshly.

Toby watched as she climbed the steps to the watch house. She looked back once at Toby. Gina said something that Toby couldn't hear, and after several more minutes of discussion, the man smiled. In a minute, the shutter closed. Toby looked behind him; nobody was in sight.

Toby got Bea moving and she shuffled her feet silently across the bridge. He kept a watch on the shuttered window. They had just reached the other side when Toby looked back and saw Gina running down the steps. The man was bent over and Toby couldn't see what he was doing. Gina hopped onto the cart and said breathlessly, "Move!"

Toby had Bea in a trot and the bridge disappeared behind them. He heard a shout from the man at the bridge and he turned to ask her, "Why did he call you 'Huskey'?"

Gina looked back and her smile faded a little. She kept wiping her hands on her dress, smoothing it down her thighs. When Toby tried to ask her about the incident, she replied, "It was just some harmless flirting." He kept looking at her, but she didn't meet his eyes.

They hurried along the town's main road as quickly as they could without causing any suspicion. In the center of town another bridge crossed a small stream. Beside the road was a place to pull off. They saw that a building was under construction here. Two stone masons pried a stone apart, and it looked like they were opening a large book of white rock.

Toby stepped from the cart and approached the men. They were too occupied with their work to notice him as they wrestled the flat stone up on its edge. Then the largest man walked the stone to a wooden plat on the ground just beside a large sawn stump. He single-handedly hefted the stone onto the stump-turned-worktable. Toby was amazed; that stone had to weigh over three hundred pounds!

Toby walked up behind the other man and said, "Sir? I need some directions." The man never turned around. He continued to look at his coworker. The man with the stone dumped a bucket of water onto it and then picked up a square stone and started rubbing it in long-figure-eight motions over the big stone. Toby watched the process and realized that the man was smoothing the surface of the larger stone. The muscles in the man's huge back rippled with each movement.

Toby spoke to the man beside him again. "Sir?" When he received no reply he touched the man's large arm. The man swung around quickly with a fierce expression on his face. It quickly softened when he saw the boy.

Toby spoke again. "We need your help." The man shook his head and pointed to the other man. Then he pointed to his ear and shook his head again. Toby realized that he couldn't hear.

The other man noticed Toby now and walked over to him. "Mornin'," he said to Toby.

"Mornin', sir. I'm needin' directions. To the Hattenfelt place?"

The man's face broke into a large smile and he let out a huge belly laugh. The deaf man stood by, looking curious. The big mason looked at the deaf man and seemed to talk to him using hand signals. He pointed at Toby and then into the distance. Next he pantomimed grabbing the brim of a hat and wobbling it back and forth. The deaf man grinned and grunted a laugh in a panting cadence. Toby looked at them both and waited; he wasn't sure what else to do. The big man finally stopped laughing and said, "So! Ya goin' to see *Mad Hattie!*?!" Toby paused and then nodded and grinned back at him.

From the cart Gina watched the huge man waving his arms and pointing east with curving gestures, first up and then down, like a three dimensional map.

She sat with her elbow on her knee and her chin in the palm of her hand, amused at the men's exchange. Toby returned to the cart after several more minutes of arm-waving direction-giving, and Gina asked him what on earth had just happened.

Toby looked a bit mischievous as he turned to her, pushed up the front brim of his hat, and said: "We're off to see *Mad Hattie!*" Gina raised her eyebrows and gave a wary smile. Toby started to laugh and Gina joined him. Bea cocked an ear at the laughter behind her as Gina flipped the reins and they moved forward again.

◊ ◊ ◊

# 33

## ~ruts & rudesters~

As Gina drove the cart as Toby clowned with his hat, acting out different impersonations of the so-called Mad Hattie. He tired different accents and postures, all the while making different faces. Gina howled with laughter until tears ran down her face and her ribs ached. They had no idea what the real Mad Hattie would be like, but they were having fun imagining!

They covered two small hills and came to a turnoff. It was another heavily rutted trail! Toby and Gina groaned when they saw it, remembering how much trouble it had been for Bea to pull the cart along the last deeply-rutted road. But this was the way to Mad Hattie, so they had no choice. They set out, bracing themselves for the bumpy ride ahead. At each rut, one cart wheel suddenly dropped into a deep ditch and then rode up out of it, only to drop the other wheel into the ditch on the other side of the cart. The cart rocked and jolted Toby and Gina in the seat. Sometimes the ruts were so deep that they got down and pushed the cart to help Bea.

After a few of the bigger ruts,they just stayed off of the cart and helped Bea along. They could see that past travelers had tried to improve the road by placing rocks in some of the soft spots, but it didn't make much of a difference. As they were pushing the cart, a large coal wagon pulled up beside them. The two men on the wagon were young, no more than eighteen at most. They were dirty and sweating, and both of them seemed to be captivated by Gina. They eyed her up luridly.

"Howdy, missy!" the driver said, touching the brim of his hat. He glanced between Toby and Gina, apparently trying to figure out if Toby would be a problem.

Gina nodded slightly at the man, her face set in a stern expression.

"And howdy to you, lad!" the driver added. The other man on the wagon snickered stupidly at the insult to Toby. Toby kept his eyes glued to the driver.

"A fine morning," Toby replied without warmth. While he looked at the man, he also surveyed the road and the clearance of the cart's path. He felt very calculating and briefly wondered if he'd picked this up from his time with Lew. He wondered how quickly Bea could cross the ruts if they had to get past these two bucolic buffoons. Toby removed his hat, taking the opportunity to hide his eyes just long enough to quickly survey the area.

Something in these two just bothered him. They were clearly hardened men. Toby imagined them shoveling coal into the wagon and then shoveling it out again when they delivered it, thus the muscles under their dirty shirts.

"Yeah. 'Spect it is a fine mornin'—'specially when I git to see a pretty girl," the driver said, his eyes still on Gina. Again, the passenger snorted. Toby wiped the sweat from his forehead with the back of his forearm and replaced his hat. He decided to let the rude comment pass. "Can either of you tell us how to get to the Hattenfelt farm?" he asked.

That stopped both of the young men. Their eyes widened and they straightened up in their seats. "You headin' to see Mad Hattie?"

"That's right!" Gina interrupted and shot Toby a glance. "She's family and we're heading there, if you could be *kind* enough to tell us how to get there."

The driver's voice changed and he became respectful. He glanced between Toby and Gina and offered directions most politely. "An' when ya get there, ya tell Missus Hattie that we helped ya. We gotta go now!" He cracked his reins on the back of the two large horses and the wagon pulled away. "Tell her John and Michael helped ya!" he said loudly over his shoulder.

"I can't wait to meet this Hattie, whoever she is!" Gina said.

"Me, too," Toby replied.

The directions the stone cutter had given them were perfect. They looked for a road to the left and quickly found it. Half a dozen very small shacks bordered the road. All of the houses looked very much alike and were equally spaced. Their weathered, wood siding had turned a dark blackish-brown. Ropes hung between the houses to hold laundry, and some clothing and bedding—all the same dirty-grey hue—hung on the lines.

There were dogs everywhere! A group of mangy mutts glanced at Bea and the cart, but they were accustomed to travelers on the road and went about sniffing and marking anything that was taller than six inches above ground level. Among the shacks were another three dozen "three-legged" dogs, doing a marking dance and giving a random yip at Toby's crew. Gina pointed at another pack of puppies that were looking around to see what the excitement was all about. She turned to Toby with a gleeful look.

"I think we're in for a special treat to meet these Hattenfelts!" she said.

"I think you're right there, Gina. Those two idiots sure acted different when you told 'em you were family to Mad Hattie!" Toby said with an occasional glance at her.

Gina was quiet for a minute and then said, "Toby?"

"Yeah—?"

"I'm just curious, but did anybody ever tell you how much you're to receive for the still and the delivery?" she asked tentatively.

Toby thought for a moment, frowned, and then thought again. "No, I uh... never heard a price." He looked at her and pushed up the brim of his hat. "I never thought I would have to be the one to ask for the money."

"That's what worries me. Suppose we don't get the proper money? I mean, what if they just make up a number? We wouldn't know, and it would all be for less than what's right."

Toby hated to admit it, but she was dead right. He had absolutely no idea what amount was to be charged. He remembered the paperwork in the seat-box, but was sure there was no invoice with it. He pulled Bea up to a stop.

"I don't know," he said, the realization of the dilemma washing over him. "How do we do this?" he said to no one in particular.

They sat for awhile and thought in silence. Another coal wagon was approaching, and Toby guided Bea off the cartway to the side of the road. These drivers were huffing and puffing—trying to catch their breaths. Their clothing was drenched in sweat. *They must have to hurry with the loading, and then rest when they ride*, Toby thought before his mind drifted back to his own predicament.

Another half hour passed while they sat without thinking of a solution. Bea was starting to get antsy, so Toby started her moving again before speaking. "I doubt the amount is anywhere but in Lew's head. And he's not tellin'."

Gina looked at him and said, "Lew who?"

Toby gave her a one-dip nod of the head and held the reins steady.

They followed the road as it wound through the trees and came to a bridge crossing a small stream. This bridge was built of stone and spanned the water with an arch. Small flowers grew along the abutments, looking out of place with the surrounding muddy roadway. Before long they reached a fork in the road where they turned left and began to climb a winding grade. This roadway was clean and obviously wasn't used by the coal wagons, but it was part of the directions the stone cutter had given them.

Toby and Gina knew that whatever was ahead, it was going to be significant. And they weren't disappointed when they turned the last curve into the front yard of the Hattenfelt farm. A large brick home stood to their left and a barn to the right. Situated between the two were a wagon shed, a chicken coop, and two other small buildings. They were all lined up neatly and in excellent repair. An old dog walked towards them, wagging its tail, and seemed comfortable with strangers' visits. Even Bea dipped her head to sniff at the old hound.

A man stood near the chicken coop and held a bucket that he'd been using to toss grain onto the ground—one handful at a time. Toby and Gina rode directly to him and Toby prepared a formal introduction in his mind.

"Morning, sir," Toby said in a voice that betrayed his nervousness.

"An' mornin' to you—both," the man replied.

"We're here to see Missus Hattenfelt…." Toby said.

"Well, welcome! And to you, miss!" The man removed his hat and nodded to Gina. "We been 'spectin' ya for 'bout a week now!" He replaced his hat and reached to shake Toby's hand. "We—Miss Hattie, that is—tol' me to keep a watch out fer ya…. But you both look weary. Miss, why don't you go to the house and introduce yourself while me and your…mister unhook the cart?" Gina nodded and took his offered hand to climb down from the cart's seat. She smoothed her dress and fluffed her hair as she gave Toby a reassuring nod.

"My name's Jericho, miss, but you can call me Jerry," the man said as he released her hand.

"Hello, Jerry, it's my pleasure to meet you." With that, Gina turned and walked towards the house.

Jerry motioned Toby and Bea ahead as he sat down the bucket and led them to the wagon shed.

◊ ◊ ◊

# 34

## ~clean, fed, and in love~

"Have a seat there, Toby." Mad Hattie pointed to the rocking chair she'd been in when they arrived. Gina was already on the porch and smiled at Toby, but didn't give him any indication of what had gone on during his time at the wagon shed with Jerry.

"Gina is gonna clean herself up, and I'm gonna get some cooking done. But if you'd be kind enuf to keep an eye on them fellers down there and count the loads, I'd be right happy. I like to know what my employees are up to in my own coal mine!" With that Gina and Hattie left the porch and went inside.

Toby didn't mind at all. He was glad for the rest and welcomed the treat of not worrying and wondering what was next. He watched the men working for awhile and then picked up a spyglass from the nearby table. When he swept the telescope from one end of the valley to the other, he could see other small houses dotting the far hillside. He also saw the mine entrance, where the dirty tailings spilled out in piles across the flats.

The men invented ways to entertain themselves amidst the menial labor. They hurled rocks at the helpers and insults at each other, all the while working hard in the sun. Toby counted two wagons that were nearly loaded and two just coming in by the road he and Gina had arrived on.

By Toby's estimate, it took half an hour to hand-shovel the coal onto the large wagons. Several men brought pushcarts of coal out from the mine. Toby wondered why they didn't build a ramp and drop the coal into the wagons instead of having to shovel it in. He thought to mention it to Hattie.

The fourth wagon was just pulling out. Toby drew another line in the dust on the tabletop to mark the fourth wagon's departure. That made two hours that Gina had been gone! *What was she doing?*, he wondered.

The sun was topping the crest of the western rim of the valley when Toby realized that the men were slowing up. Some of the miners came out of the mine, pulled on jackets and hats, and climbed aboard the last wagon. The rest of the men finished shoveling in the last of the coal and climbed up, as well. Both of the loaded wagons left and nothing else moved in the valley.

Hattie appeared at the doorway. She had cleaned up and looked to be wearing a basket on her head! Toby looked again and realized that the basket was actually her hair, black with grey streaks, braided, and wrapped tightly around her head.

"You hungry there, Toby?" Hattie asked as she sat down a glass of water for him.

"Yes, ma'am. I worked up a big appetite countin' to four!" He sat up and grinned at her.

"Well from the tales that Gina told me o' your trip, I can't imagine some rest would hurt much. An' we got plenty of food out, so you can put some fat on them scrawny bones o' yo'r!" Hattie erupted with a hearty laugh.

"It wasn't so bad—the trip I mean. We had a couple of close scrapes, but it was ok," Toby said.

Gina walked out on the porch and stood beside Hattie. Toby couldn't believe his eyes. She was cleaner than he'd ever seen her! And her hair had been trimmed and hung softly around her shoulders. She even had a bow in it and was wearing a dress Toby hadn't seen before. She looked like a completely different girl than the one Toby had been traveling with. Gina carried herself differently. She seemed unsure of how Toby would react to her new look. She stared into the distance, but stole glances back at him, seeking his approval.

Hattie smiled and seemed to read his thoughts. "Got her shined up and she's a looker, eh, Toby?" she said, giving Toby a wink.

Toby regained his sense and nodded at Hattie, but kept his eyes glued to Gina. He noticed the shape of her body underneath her dress. He'd seen her naked, but this was more interesting somehow.

"Well Toby, bring that FOOD appetite of yours inside and we'll eat," Hattie said. She turned her back to Toby and gave Gina a wink.

They sat in a room dedicated to just eating, which was unheard of in most houses along the frontier area. (But Hattie had her ways.) A girl, about twenty-five years old and missing at least two teeth, served them. Hattie had called the meal "the usual," but it wasn't usual to Toby or Gina. They had roast chickens, a clear soup, potatoes, and several types of bread, all made with different grains. There was even fresh coffee and a pitcher of wine. Toby devoured two plates of everything and couldn't keep his eyes off of Gina during the meal. She was lovely to look at, even as she gnawed at chicken bones and licked her fingers!

During the long meal, Hattie talked of how she and her husband had first settled in the valley, clearing the land and building first a small shack to live in. She told Toby and Gina how the cattle had died from the harsh winters and then how they'd discovered the coal seams. Gina asked Hattie of her husband's whereabouts. Hattie held up her wineglass, toasted him, and said, "He just plain worked hisself out, bless 'im. But, he was smart enough—and loved me enough—to set me up so's I'd be comfortable." She smiled as she spoke, but there was sadness in her eyes.

"There was the first timber, and the game—Lord we had game! Then we planted corn, and wheat, some oats. It was all for him to make the 'shine, o' course. He loved makin' whiskey! Those were good days, they was! Had our health, both of us strong and grateful for the next day o' work. We couldn't have children—not that we didn' try!" Hattie barked out another laugh. "So, we helped out some of the families that had too many! Brought them here and put them to work on the farm. Got one—Jamie—up near Clarion; he's a stone cutter. Another girl married and lives over the next hill; her husband runs the mine you were watchin' today, Toby."

Toby blinked at his name and sat up straighter in his chair. That second glass of wine had made him a little too mellow.

"Oh, I've been an ol' blabberin' woman!" Hattie said. "I plum forgot how tired you two must be. It's off to bed with you both! I can blabber more in the mornin'. I hope you don't mind, but I only got one spare room I can put you both up in, but the bed's soft and warm." Hattie didn't wait for a reply; she stood and turned to the kitchen doorway. "Up those steps and first room on your right," she said.

After several weeks of living on the ground, Toby and Gina were both excited about sleeping in a real bed again. Toby followed Gina upstairs and into the bedroom. She set the oil lamp on a table and handed him a long nightshirt that Hattie had given her. "I'll be right back. You can put that on."

Toby used the washstand and cleaned himself up before putting on the long shirt. He got into bed and was hoping that it'd warm up quickly under the covers when Gina returned. She, too, wore only a nightshirt and the ribbon in her hair. Toby watched silently as she untied the string of the shirt, shrugged it off her shoulders, and let it fall to the floor. It was the loveliest he'd ever seen her look! As Toby tried to catch his breath, she blew out the lamp and crawled into bed.

The two nightshirts lay together in a heap on the floor while their former wearers lay in a heap on the bed. Every time Toby tried to move he was trapped under a leg or arm that Gina had draped over him. He tried to think of a better way to go to sleep, but couldn't imagine one.

◊ ◊ ◊

# 35

## ~one "nightstand" and two prices~

The next morning, Toby found himself alone in bed. He looked at the floor and saw only one nightshirt—his own. The bright sunshine coming through the window told him that sunrise had come and gone. He used the bedpan to relieve himself and got dressed in his traveling clothes. Every muscle in his body was more relaxed than he'd ever known, and he felt refreshed in both mind and body. But, as was always the case, his empty stomach grumbled. Even after last night's meal he felt he could eat twice that much.

He walked down the staircase and outside and saw Hattie and Gina walking back from the wagon shed. Hattie continued her random watch of the valley's workers as she nodded at what Gina was saying.

Toby suddenly remembered the bill-of-lading he'd found the day before when he and Jerry had unpacked the crates. It contained figures regarding the cost of the still and the delivery price. Toby realized that he'd forgotten to tell Gina about it in the midst of everything else that had happened last night.

He thought about Hattie's generosity, the wonderful food, and the warm bed. She'd given them so much already. Then he thought of how it was his job to deliver the still and that he had to return with the money. He knew he had to make certain that the money was enough to cover their expenses. After all, they still had to make the hundred-mile trip back to Pittsburgh.

As the women approached the house, they both smiled at Toby. Gina looked a little sheepish, which was something Toby had never seen before. Hattie said, "Gina's been giving me help lookin' over that fine copper still ya brought; my husband would have felt like cryin'. It's well done—you tell your boss that! I'll send him a letter and let him know what a good job you two did deliverin' it, too."

Now Toby felt a little shy and embarrassed. He smiled at the compliment and nodded. "I guess we need to get the papers signed and get the payment," he said.

Gina perked up at that and said, "Toby, I discussed a price with Miss Hattie, and included the deliv—"

Toby interrupted her: "I think *THAT'S* for Miss Hattie and me to discuss, since I represent the company!" He was furious about Gina's presumption, and at the moment he didn't care about her feelings or what had happened last night. *It wasn't right for her to say anything!*, he thought. He gave Gina a sharp look and turned to Hattie. "I would like to discuss this with you—*alone*, Miss Hattie."

Hattie looked at Gina and patted her arm. "Honey, why don't you get Toby a cup of hot coffee from the kitchen and bring it to the porch?" Hattie nodded encouragingly at Gina with a faint smile on her lips. Gina turned and walked away without looking at Toby.

Back on the porch, Toby gave Hattie the seat facing the valley. He cleared his throat and spoke: "I, uh, wanted to thank you for the dinner and the nice bed. It was, um, nice…very generous of you. But I have to collect what's rightfully due for my boss. He did a lot for my family, 'specially since my father passed."

Hattie was nodding and glancing at the workers in the valley. "Toby, I have me a copy of the letter your boss sent with a price on the still. But he could only estimate a price for the delivery and asked me to be 'fair with the driver,' which in this case is you *and* Gina." Hattie smiled at him and nodded her head encouragingly again.

Toby pulled out the packet, opened it, and handed the papers to her. "This is what I have," he said.

Hattie looked it over and nodded again. "Yup, that's the same amount as I saw: a hundred forty for the still. That leaves the delivery charge. Your boss included an estimate figure, but it's up to you to decide on the exact right price."

Toby thought about it for several moments, remembering what Lew and he had spent, how much feed Bea had eaten, and then what he and Gina had used up. Toby did the math in his head and decided to double the amount to account for the trip home. "I guess that would make it around twenty two...." he stammered, still doing the math as he spoke. "Maybe twenty five—figuring food for the mule."

"Done, and I'll throw in a sack of feed!" Hattie said quickly, slapping her knee. She pulled a pouch from her apron. Toby had never seen so many gold coins in one place before! "First is the hundred-forty for the still," she said as she counted out seven twenty-dollar gold pieces. "Then FIVE, five-dollar gold pieces, for your work in deliverin' it."

Toby's hand sank under the weight of the coins. He'd never held a gold coin before and was amazed at how heavy they were. He wasn't sure where to put them; he only had the one pocket that he used to carry his father's pocketknife. Hattie noticed the dilemma and said, "I think you ought to hide some on the cart. I can get Jerry to help you cut a slot beside the seat, ok?" Toby nodded, still holding the coins. "And maybe Gina could sew a couple into your britches?"

Again Toby nodded. That all made good sense. He put the money back into the pouch with the papers for the time being. Gina came out carrying the coffee and placed it on the small table. Without saying a word, she turned and went back inside.

Hattie was looking through the spyglass and watching the workers load the coal onto wagons. "Toby," she said softly. "Gina asked for thirty dollars for the delivery, and I think you should give her the other five. Sound fair to you?" She slid another five-dollar coin across the table to him.

Toby had been bested again! At first he was angry, but then he realized that Gina had made a better deal with Hattie and *she* was still happy. He had to admire the women; they had done a fair deal, and everybody was satisfied. He nodded his acceptance and picked up the coin.

"And Toby?"

"Yes, ma'am?"

"You got a good woman there; you need to treat her right." Hattie was still spying on the valley, but Toby felt like she was studying *him* through the spyglass.

"Yes, ma'am, I intend to do just that."

◊ ◊ ◊

# 36

~hoops and a Hattenfelt story~

Toby spent the rest of the morning in the shop building with Jerry. They decided to hide the coins in a wooden board along the front floorboard under the driver's feet.

Jerry started the work, showing Toby how to use the wood chisel to make the cuts. Next they made a false cover to hide the pocket made for the coins. It fit nicely and was invisible to someone who didn't know it was there. When the coins were couched in the carved pocket in the wood, Jerry dripped candle wax onto them to lock them in place and prevent them from rattling.

Jerry also showed Toby how to remove the wheels from the cart with the wrench that was in the seat-box. They pulled off each wheel and used the can of bear-grease that Lew had put in the box before they left Pittsburgh. Jerry showed Toby how to properly lubricate the axles so the wheels turned freely— and without making any noise!

They also mixed up a solution of varnish and soot from the stove and made a black paint to match the color of the cart's paint. They used this to touch up any faded or nicked spots, and more importantly to hide the coins for the trip.

They decided to treat the panther's skin, and Jerry showed Toby how to scrape the hide and put salt on it to keep it from rotting. He rolled it up and tied it with some leather. "Leave it for about a week that way. I'll give you some paste to put on it. Leave that on another week," Jerry said. "That's a fine treasure, that pelt! Strange them fellows left it." Jerry showed him the paste and explained how it was made from the acid of tree bark and leaves. "When you get back to the city, it'll be soft and make you a fine carpet. *And* you'll have a fine story to tell everybody about it!"

Someone called Jerry's name and he went to the house, leaving Toby behind in the shop. Toby found some leather soap and used it with some soot to blacken his boots. The leather on the boots was almost brittle from the salt of his sweat and from being wet and dry so many times. The saddle soap helped to soften the leather and the boots looked nearly new.

The back of the cart looked so empty now without the still on it. The oilcloth and the blanket that Gina had brought with her were folded neatly on the bed of the cart. Toby wondered what they would use for shelter during the nights and during the next rain. He thought about some way to build a cover for the cart, something to keep them warm and dry. He glanced around the shop and saw some large, bent wooden hoops behind several barrels. They were covered with white-grain dust, chicken droppings, and cobwebs. He pulled a rope along them to gauge their width. They matched the width of the cart perfectly!

Toby couldn't wait to ask Jerry if they could buy the hoops from him and fit them to the cart. In addition to giving them shelter from the night and rain, they would also provide shade from the hot summer sun that would follow them back to the city. Toby thought that Gina would be pleased. He paced around the shop considering the work to be done.

He stopped pacing abruptly with the sudden realization that Gina may not want to go back with him! They really hadn't discussed what was to happen next. All along they'd been focused on the goal of delivering the still.

Toby also hadn't thought through the fact that Gina was more of an orphan than he was. At least he had his mother and sisters to return home to. Gina had nobody! She'd told him this—ages ago, but he didn't think to ask her to come back to Pittsburgh until just now.

What if she didn't want to leave the countryside? These couple of weeks in the frontier had changed his outlook on living in the city: The clean air, the endless hillsides, the people—all had changed him, one at a time. Maybe Gina wouldn't want to leave all of that for a city she'd never seen.

Toby wondered *why* he was thinking of Gina as being with him at all; he had no right to assume that she would come back with him. But he also realized that he didn't like to think that she might go and leave him to travel the long road home alone. That idea depressed him.

He snapped back to the decision at hand. Regardless of Gina's decision, the cart would be better for the trip if it was covered, with or without her. *But it might help her to decide!*, Toby thought. He glumly paced the shop again. *Life without Gina?* It didn't seem to be possible to travel without her.

Jerry returned with several items from the house to be repaired. He showed Toby how to use strips of leather to clamp a chair that he glued with hide glue. Toby sniffed at the glue and Jerry told him that it was made from the gelatin in the hooves of animals. "You can use in cooking as well,but if you keep cooking out the water, the glue gets stronger," Jerry said.

As they worked away the morning hours, Toby again thought of the hoops and asked Jerry about them. Jerry stopped and looked at them. "Toby, I'd near forgot 'bout them; they been there since Mr. Hattenfelt left."

"Left? I thought he died, or was kilt. Miss Hattie never said he left."

"Oh, he was," Jerry replied. Toby looked at him with a puzzled expression. "Toby, I been here for fourteen years now, and worked with Mr. Hattenfelt when we cleared the grounds. Even went to join up an' fight Indians with him, but they had that battle solved. So we came back and we planted corn, tobacco, and o' course the food garden. Well one winter we had a great excess of corn and decided to make some whiskey with it. An' for two years, we made some really fine whiskey. But that was when the Tax Revenuers came round. Next thing they told us we had to pay them a tax! BEFORE we sold it!" Jerry shook his head and spit on the floor. "Well that kinda stuck in the Mister's craw. One thing led to another and there was plenty of people all over the frontier fightin' them tax people. A lot of people died—on both sides!"

Jerry carved on a chair leg, blew off the shavings, and continued his story. "You see, the government didn't do much for us folks out here. We fought the Indians ourselves, built our own roads, kept the law—best we could! And all they wanted to do was tax our land and whiskey and give nothin' back. People's folks fought for this country's independence from the Brits. And now their own government was taxin' them, jus' like the Brits was!"

Toby listened closely and nodded. He watched Jerry work as he talked and helped when he could. Jerry continued: "Jus' wasn't right! Not right at all! Then one day a sheriff and two others came and arrested Mr. Hattenfelt. I 'member Miss Hattie cryin' her eyes out."

Toby tried to imagine Mad Hattie crying.

"Back then there weren't any courts here in the wilderness. So they took him cross the state, keer back to Philadelphia to stand 'fore a judge. Course they found him guilty and cut off'n his right ear." Jerry used a stick smeared with glue to make the motion of sawing off his ear. "They did that to everybody back then, just to show all the others that they was a thief. Well, after they kept him two months in jail, they let him go. He was three hundred miles from home and without money. So this is where the story gets dark, and nobody but Mr. Hattenfelt can tell it." He paused to clear his throat and spit on the floor again.

"Story goes that he tried to work his way back here, but most folk, out east, wouldn't hire a man without his ear. Figured that he was a thief, and stole from them by not paying his taxes. Word is that along the way he got himself jumped and kilt. It wasn't right, a man like him who cleared and built all you're seein'." Jerry waved the stick in a broad sweeping motion and shook his head in disgust. "Them damn folk back east charged us folks out here TWICE the tax that they paid themselves! Yeah, they live their soft lives while folks out here die workin' for THEM!" Jerry tossed the stick onto the workbench and pulled out a cigar from under his hat. He lit it from the fire pit and remained silent for awhile.

Before Jerry could compose himself, they were called in for the midday meal. It seemed that Gina had been busy in the house, as well. She'd spent the day sewing and hiked up her dress to show Toby the leather knife holder she made to strap Lew's knife to her thigh.

Toby always needed to gulp a breath when he saw the white skin of her legs. Gina hadn't seen Jerry behind Toby and quickly dropped her dress when she saw both men gaping at her. She showed Toby the coat he'd worn on the trip and how she'd sewn a few coins to the inside of its collar. Last, but not least, she lifted a belt that Hattie had given her and showed him the pocket she'd slit into it for additional coins. Toby was pleased at her cunning. But he still didn't know if she was planning to travel back with him, so he said, "You should have to carry some, too—'case we get separated." Gina gave him a startled look.

Hattie interrupted, saying, "That ain't gonna happen, you two are gonna have a good, safe trip. Let's eat!"

Toby hoped this meant that Gina was going to go with him. He mentioned the wooden hoops for the back of the cart and noticed Hattie and Gina exchange another one of their meaningful glances. He was really beginning to hate the way women seemed to communicate without saying anything!

◊ ◊ ◊

# 37

## ~Longy's revenge?~

A middle-aged woman, probably around 30 years old, named Longy served them their meal in silence. Hattie, Gina, and Jerry talked about what they had accomplished that day, but Toby kept quiet and watched Longy; he noticed that she never spoke. When Hattie saw him watching her, she told the story of how Longy arrived at Hattie's house one day, wearing a scarf around her mouth and ears. Toby glanced at Longy, watching for her reaction, but she gave none.

"Both her eardrums had broke and they were caked with dried blood. Her husband had cut her tongue up real bad, trying to cut it out," Hattie said. Gina shivered at the story.

"Well my husband was so outraged he went to the man's house and beat him near to death. He worked in the mine and did the best work a man could do, but he was crazy-mean to her. She showed us scars from other beatings, poor darling. We nursed her back to health. She's can't talk or hear, but she's been here ever since." Hattie smiled at Longy, who smiled back, completely unaware of the storythat had just been told of her condition.

Toby realized that Gina was gripping his hand. He saw fear in her eyes and realized that she sympathized with Longy's ordeal. He knew she was thinking that she may have ended up like Longy if she'd stayed at the farm with Lew and Lucca. Hattie saw Gina's condition and quickly offered her some more tea. A tear slid down Gina's cheek as she smiled at Hattie's offer.

After a few sips of tea in silence, Gina smiled at Toby, and then at Hattie and Jerry. She finally spoke to them all: "It's been so nice here. You helped us, even though you didn't have to! When Toby and I leave, I'll miss you both. But

I know Toby wants to get back to Pittsburgh to see his family. And tomorrow, we should probably leave, right Toby?" She turned to see his response.

Toby sat down the pewter cup he was drinking from and nodded slowly. "Gina's right. You've been so nice to us. And given us so much great food! I won't have to eat till we reach Pittsburgh!" he joked and they all laughed.

"Oh, you'll be hungry before we get to Sligo!" Gina said and they laughed again. Toby felt his face blush.

Hattie smiled, burped, and said, "Oh dear, 'scuse me!" She burped again.

Jerry burped louder, and they all laughed louder.

That's when they heard a shout and the sound of horse's hooves coming towards the house.

"Miss Hattie! MISS HATTIE!" a boy's voice called out.

They were instantly on their feet and out the door. The boy on the horse rode into the yard and jumped down. He was out of breath, as was the horse. "In the mine! The MINE! The roof let go!" He gasped for breath. "They hit a dome pot and it fell. Dropped on Mr. Holtz, it did! Crushed both his legs! They are diggin' him out now. He's hurt BAD!" The boy bent forward and put his hands on his knees, still gasping for breath.

"Jerry, get the wagon ready. Toby you help him. Gina, you can help Longy—she'll show you what to do." Hattie barked orders as she grabbed Longy's arm and made gestures towards the table and the kitchen. Longy's eyes widened as she glanced at the others and nodded. She clenched her jaw and set her face, and seemed to understand everything that was happening.

Toby ran after Jerry and shouted that he could have Bea hooked to the cart quicker than hitching up the wagon. Jerry stopped in his tracks and nodded in agreement. They quickly turned the cart around and got Bea into a harness. The mule seemed to realize that she had a job to do and perked up.

Hattie mounted the horse and the boy climbed up behind her. They dashed across the lower field towards the mine. Jerry threw some empty feed sacks on the cart and ran to the barn. Over his shoulder he shouted to Toby, "Bring the cart over here!" Jerry came out of the barn with a pitchfork speared into a huge bundle of straw. As Toby pulled the cart up in front of him, Jerry tossed the straw onto the cart bed and jumped on as Toby got Bea into a trot and then into a run down the lane. They made the round-about trip on the wagon road and arrived at the mine five minutes after Hattie and the boy.

Two men sat on a spoil pile, catching their breath. They were black with coal dust from head to toe except for their eyes and teeth. They wiped sweat from their foreheads, making streaks across their faces. Hattie disappeared inside the mine, accompanied by two other men.

Toby listened as the men gasped out a story to Jerry. They were played out and simply couldn't move. They'd been removing the stone from the man's legs and it was now up to the others to get him out of the mine.

Toby turned and saw Hattie holding the man's head as the other two carried him towards the cart, which was as close as it could be to the mine's opening. He watched as Jerry scattered the straw on the back of the cart. The man's legs hung like limp, bloody laundry. They were bent high above the knees and his feet pointed in unnatural directions. *It wasn't right!*, Toby thought. That was the only way he could describe the scene: *It wasn't right!*

Hattie was clearly in charge. No one gave a second thought to anything as they followed her orders. "Head back to the house, Toby!" She and Jerry were on the back of the cart, cutting off the man's pant legs and using strips of cloth to make tourniquets.

Toby had Bea at a good trot and they reached the house in short measure. He swung the cart as close to the front porch as possible, and before he could hop down to help, Jerry and Hattie were lifting the man off of the cart. Toby ran to their side and helped carry the man onto the porch.

It was getting dark now, and Toby saw Gina inside holding a lantern. He noticed lights in the dining room, as well. Toby drove Bea and the cart back to the shed and quickly unhooked her. He looked at the mess on the cart and paused a brief moment—trying to decide if he should rinse off the blood now or if he was needed at the house. He looked over at the house; all seemed quiet, even though he knew there must be a lot going on inside.

He decided to tend to the cart. He raked off the straw and saw the bed beneath covered with a sticky coating of blood. It seemed to be everywhere! Toby used a bucket of water to rinse off most of it. He used a clean handful of straw to scrub at the rest of the blood before rinsing the bed again with a second bucketful of water.

He started for the house but glanced at Bea. She had performed what was required nicely, and was now as unconcerned as ever, eating some grass she'd missed earlier that day. Toby shook his head and quickly trotted to the house.

He walked inside and saw everyone circled around the dining room table where they'd just eaten. The man from the mine was stretched out on top of it. Longy was working over him in silence, and Hattie seemed to be reading her mind as she assisted her. Jerry held the man's chest in case he woke up, but he was out cold from shock. Gina held a small mirror to the man's lips and watched his breath condense on the glass.

Both legs were crushed so badly that hardly any bone was left. Gina glanced nervously at the work Longy was doing. Longy slid her hands along the crushed meat of the man's leg, probing until she found a solid end to the bone. She stopped at mid-thigh and marked the leg with her bloody finger, giving a pointed look to Hattie. Hattie gave a small nod in agreement.

Longy did the same on the other leg. When she reached about the same spot as on the first leg, she marked it in the same way. She checked the tourniquets, took a long look at the man, and then nodded to Jerry and Hattie.

Toby watched the slow process of the amputations in horror. Both of the bones were sheared so cleanly that Longy didn't have to saw through them at all. She cut through the flesh of the man's legs with a large knife and then staunched the bleeding with the hot irons that Hattie fetched from the kitchen. Longy then pulled patches of meat and skin over the stumps and sewed them together.

Nearly four hours passed until the operation was finished. One at a time, the others each backed into a chair and sat down, slumping in exhaustion, watching as Longy finish wrapping the man's stumps. They took turns watching the man's breathing with the mirror and cleaning up the area.

Finally, they went out onto the porch. The fresh air helped to revive them a bit, but they remained quiet. Hattie made more hot tea and handed a cup to Longy. She took it with a tired, trembling hand. She sipped at the tea and stared vacantly at the floor. Every so often she glanced up at the light coming from the dining room window and tried to get up. But Hattie's hand on her shoulder kept her seated.

Only once did she look directly at Toby, just long enough to nod an appreciation. Then she gave a long approving look at Gina, before she smiled another very tired smile.

The long night passed wordlessly, even when they went inside again and sat looking at the man. Toby drifted off, but awoke when he heard a quiet sob.

Longy was holding the man's hand and crying. Toby realized that the man had died and that all their work to save him had been futile.

Toby and Gina quietly left the room and sat on the porch in the cold morning air, watching the sunrise in silence. A long while later Hattie came out onto the porch. She leaned her hip against the porch railing and gave a long, tired sigh. "Longy is a better woman than I ever knew," she said. "You couldn't know this, but that man she worked so hard to save? That was the same cruel man who made her deaf and cut her tongue. I reckon she still loved him—a heap!"

Toby glanced at Gina and Hattie and saw tears sliding down their cheeks! *How could they have feelings for such a man?*, he wondered.

◊ ◊ ◊

# 38

## ~the framework in a round world~

Toby offered to help with digging the grave and burying Longy's husband, but Hattie just wanted him to help by carrying the body in the cart. Jerry built a coffin during the night and dug the grave in the morning. Gina helped Hattie and Longy sew the burial shroud.

Toby and Gina spent the next day with Jerry in the machine shed. He showed them how to use the fire pit and anvil to forge brackets to mount on the cart's edge and hold the hoops. Once they seemed to have the hang of things, Jerry left them alone to make more brackets.

Toby cut, heated, and forged the strap iron pieces into brackets and then tempered them in water. Gina kept the bellows pumping and watched him forge. She used some cloth sacks to handle the tongs and carry the hot brackets to the water barrel. When Toby had eight of them made, he used a measuring stick to mark the places on the sides of the cart. Then he hammered in square, handmade nails to hold them in place.

A couple of the brackets were too small, so they shaved the wooden hoops to fit. By midday, all four hoops were on the cart. Toby and Gina stood back admiring it. Gina hooked her arm through Toby's and leaned her head against him.

They took a break and sat in the shade along the shop's wall. Toby leaned back against the building and stared into the sky.

"What are you thinking about?" Gina sat cross-legged nearby.

He looked to the house and shook his head. "I guess I was thinking of something my father once told me." He pulled at a grass stem and then looked at her. "He said once that 'the world is round and everything comes back to you.' I was just wondering if that's what Longy was facing." He shrugged at the thought and pulled at another long stem of grass.

Gina was cleaning the dirt from under her fingernails. She paused and glanced at Toby. "You think it goes that way?"

He shrugged again and added, "I think it *must*. My father believed it. Yes... I think it must—somehow."

Gina watched him a moment, considering it some more. "Then why do you worry about it?"

"I was just thinking about Lew. If that's the case, then we have something coming our way."

Gina rolled to her knees and quickly took his hands before speaking. "Toby, you don't know what he did to me; what came *around* was what *he* deserved, *not* something that is going to come back on us! Don't you see?"

Slowly, a glimmer of understanding crossed Toby's face as he looked into Gina's convincing eyes.

"I guess I do. I was just worried that we'd have to face something terrible. I can't remember what my mother called it. It's in the Bible.... Ret-tri-bu-tion. Retribution, that's it!"

"I don't know about that, but I do know it's what he deserved!" Gina rolled back into a seated position on the grass and looked towards the mine. No one was there today, and Toby wondered if the people would come to a wake, or some kind of prayer service.

Gina changed the subject. "Hey! Let's put the oilskin over the framework and see how it fits," she said. They worked the rest of the day. They made leather tie-downs for the cart cover and fashioned hinges of leather for one of the crates to make a carrying case. It would be a good place to stow their personal items. Toby took a brace-and-bit and drilled four matching holes in the crate bottom and in the deck of the cart, and then secured it with large cotter keys that he'd made from hard pieces of wire he found in a box.

"It would be nice to have a lock on it," Gina mused, admiring the work.

"They'd just cut the leather hinges!" Toby said as he pushed her gently and swatted playfully at her arm—missing on purpose.

"Oh. Yeah." Gina laughed at her foolish statement.

Toby put away the tools they'd used and wiped off the deck of the cart. There was still blood in the crevices of the wood grain, and flies gathered along those spots. He frowned and wondered what he would tell them back at Howard & Rodgers Company. The condition of the cart was definitely *not* the same as when he'd left Pittsburgh.

There was another thought troubling Toby. "Gina?" he said. "I've been thinking about the horse. If we go back to get it at the sheep farm and then go on to Parker's Landing,don't you think that Luke might see us? And if he does, he could call us horse thieves! We could go to jail. Get our ears cut off!" Gina almost laughed at Toby's dramatic delivery, but realized on second thought that it *could* happen! They didn't have rights to the horse. If they were caught, they could even hang!

"I was thinking that we should go back to Foxburg and see Ella. I didn't like the way Lew talked about her," Gina said. "I think he lied, but I'm afraid of what he might have done if Ernie wasn't there. I know you're really trying to get back home, but we kinda owe it to Ella and Ernie."

"I guess you're right, and we could leave the horse with her." Toby considered the proposal and then said, "Gina! We have to get back ACROSS the river!"

"I've been thinking about that," Gina said. Toby rolled his eyes and she punched his arm. "*I have been*! It'd be safer to go back the way we came. I think there's less chance that anybody who knew Luke, or heard about us, would see us."

Toby nodded and agreed with her. "But we *still* have to get across the river!"

"I have a plan for that, too," Gina whispered with a smile and leaned in like she was going to kiss him.

"Go ahead," Toby whispered back, his eyes half–shut.

"I don't remember if I told you, but Ella and Ernie had this message system. When she needed him to come across the river, she'd hang out a white flag—basically any strip of white cloth. He could see it with a spyglass from his boat. So I figured that if we could stop at the top of the hill across the river from the shack, and hung up a white flag, she'd see it and come across to get us." She looked hopefully at Toby for an answer.

"It might work. But what's to make her look up to the top of the hill?"

"We can start a smoky fire. People *always* see smoke!" She nodded to validate the point.

Toby looked at her from the corner of his eye and shrugged. "I guess. Or we can come up with another plan along the way." He thought of the spring leaves coming out that might possibly hide the smoke, but he didn't mention it to Gina.

Toby placed some of the items from the cart deck into the new carrier crate. He came upon Lew's boots and held them towards Gina. She sneered at them and said, "Give them to Jerry!" Toby tossed them onto a nearby workbench.

Hattie whistled from the porch to let them know that supper was almost ready. Toby and Gina washed up and then joined Hattie, Jerry, and Longy at the table. Although she wore a black work dress, Longy held her head up and smiled at them as they sat down. She was a completely different woman from the one they'd first met.

Gina held Toby's hand under the table as Hattie said a blessing.

As they passed around the food, Gina spoke quietly to Hattie and told her what they planned to do on the return trip. Hattie seemed pleased and impressed. "You two are gonna do jus' fine, jus' fine. But Gina, you watch that Bridge Master. He's a wily one. You just pay him like I tol' ya, and tell him I said hello! That will keep him friendly!" Hattie winked at Gina and passed her a slice of bread.

◊ ◊ ◊

# 39

## ~a burial, a promise, and something nice~

They buried Longy's husband on a hill above the house just before dusk. None of the other workers showed up, so it was just the five of them. They spent the evening lounging on the porch, quietly swapping stories. Gina was completely absorbed in Hattie's stories of the early pioneering days here. Hattie talked about the dangerous wildlife, illnesses that people got, and how many new people had moved in to the area. Some of Hattie's "closest" neighbors were miles away! But the way Hattie told it, it sounded like they were crowding *her* wilderness.

Longy hummed to herself and smiled whenever someone looked at her. She reminded Toby of Bea: living quietly within herself and seeming to be content with whatever the present situation brought her. He wondered if surviving such horrible abuse had made her that way or if she simply had a steely resolve within her.

When the time to retire came, they all parted and went their respective ways. Toby followed Gina up the stairs to the second floor and playfully tugged at the hemline of her dress. "I hope you're always there, Toby," Gina said softly.

"I hope so, too." He followed her into the bedroom and gently turned her around to face him. She pulled back to set the lamp on the table. She walked back to him and replaced his arms around her waist. "Let's enjoy the last night we'll have in a bed—for awhile!" he said. Toby didn't bother putting on his nightshirt. He looked at Gina over the top of the lamp and softly blew out the flame as he winked at her.

Later on Gina whispered something to an exhausted Toby, but then realized that he was sound asleep. She smiled and nestled into his chest. They slept like dogs after a hunt.

They woke the next morning at dawn to the smell of hot pan bread and fried slices of hog belly. When they got down to breakfast they also found ground corn mush, basted eggs, fresh milk, and brewed tea.

Toby wolfed down his first plate and tucked into the second helping that Longy served him. He joked to Hattie that Bea might not be able to pull him and Gina in the cart, as full as they would be this morning. Everyone tried to be lighthearted, but they were sad that Toby and Gina were leaving.

After loading up the cart, Toby and Gina made Jerry put on Lew's boots and promise to take Hattie dancing in them. Then with hugs, handshakes, and much waving goodbye, Toby and Gina started their long trip back to Pittsburgh.

Toby was charged in a way that Gina had never seen before. He chatted in a steady stream, telling her of Pittsburgh and all there was to see. He put aside her fears of not knowing what she would do in the city. He told her about the jobs and that there were so many things she was capable of doing. "There's taverns to work in, houses to clean," Toby said. "Or maybe you could do laundress work, or maybe even work in the Howard & Rodgers Company!" Gina doubted that last one, but listened intently, all the while wondering if any of it was true.

Toby described the huge riverboats built in Pittsburgh and explained that they ran on steam. Gina shot him a skeptical look. He talked about the fancy homes of the rich people in the city and the marketplace with stalls of food that went on for a whole block!

He told her that there was always a festival of some sort going on because people from so many countries lived in the city. There were Germans, Italians, the Polish, English, and Irish—and some group was always celebrating something. Toby described wagons full of singing immigrants being pulled into the city by teams of huge oxen. When he described how big the oxen were, she punched his arm and called him a story teller.

As Toby talked, Gina sat quietly. She started to wonder what his mother would think of her, a poor country girl who couldn't even read or write. She knew that her tanned skin marked her as a lowly field worker. She worried people would think she was too rough and ragged for the city. Still, she couldn't help but get caught up in Toby's enthusiasm. She knew that whatever else happened or wherever else she went, it wouldn't be without her Baby Grape!

They soon reached Sligo and crossed the town area. Toby nodded to other drivers and the people they passed on the street. He saw the stone workers that they'd asked for directions and waved at them as they drove past. They were a little nervous when they got to the toll bridge, so Gina hid in the back of the cart, which was now covered. Toby paid the fee to the bridge master, who studied him and the cart for a minute, but didn't seem to recognize him. They made it to the O'Malley's farm just before midday.

Only Grace was there. She said that Samuel had taken a load of the dyed wool to Parker's Landing to be ferried across the river to one of Ernie's warehouses. Grace and the kids were glad to see Toby and Gina. She fed them lunch and they talked about the events of the past several days. When Gina apologized for leaving the horse with them for more than a day as planned, Grace waved her hand in the air and said, "Don't you worry 'bout that. One more animal ain't no trouble on this farm." Neither Toby nor Gina mentioned that they planned to travel back to Foxburg. They had decided to tell no one in advance. The just wanted to get to Ella's before anybody else saw them.

By 2:00 they were on the road again. An hour later they were in Callensburg. The horse didn't seem to mind being tied to the back of the cart and trailing along behind it. They stopped at the store in Callensburg again and bought some additional supplies. Each only wished that Anna, the nosy shopkeeper, wasn't around to see them leave on the road to Foxburg.

They were surprised to be nearly at Alum Rock by nightfall. Toby realized that they had lost three days being lost and traveling the way they had. But he also thought of how they'd "lost" Lew in the process.

They backed the cart to face the fire and made a comfortable bed under the canopy of the cart's cover. Gina made a fine meal as Toby tended to the horse and mule. He tethered them nearby in case of any prowling animals. He now wanted to be beside Gina all day, but thought of how he would have liked to have the horse to ride last week, when they couldn't stand each other. He smiled as he looked at Gina, who was stirring the pot and humming to herself.

Toby looked across the nearly dark hills and thought that they were somewhere near the spot that Wilbur the trapper had met them. He pondered the man's life, alone in the First Woods, living as opportunities arose, wandering among the critters, as he'd called them. Wilbur was at home here, and Toby began to wonder if he and Gina might be, as well. It didn't make sense, yet it seemed like it did.

Toby had talked himself out on the trip and ate in silence, but didn't understand Gina's silence. He asked her about it and she just shrugged. When he pressed her, she began to talk.

"It's just, well, what if I don't like the city?" she said. "All those people.... And I might not fit in. There are so many things that I don't know and maybe can't learn."

"That's wrong, and besides, I can teach you to read and write!" Toby said enthusiastically. "I could also teach you to count and add. There's enough time on the trip, we could get started."

"That's not all, Toby. I might not fit in with other girls, other women. They'll be so proper. And I'll be....Well, I'll just be *me*."

Toby looked up from the fire and smiled. "That's all I want you to be, Gina. You're more than you think!"

She shook her head in doubt.

"You ARE!" Toby said loud enough to startle Bea. He lowered his voice and continued. "Gina, did you think we would get here? I mean, we got the still delivered and got the money. We're safe, and on our way home."

"To *your* home, Toby. *Your* home." Gina picked up a stick and poked at the fire, slowly shaking her head. "Toby, you can do so much better than me. And what if we get to Pittsburgh and you get tired of me? I'd have nowhere to go." She stabbed the fire harder each time.

"Gina, I *promise* you that won't happen. I'll stay with you. And if you don't like it there, we'll go somewhere else—together!"

"Toby, we're *kids*! They aren't gonna let us just *go*!"

"I don't feel much like a kid anymore. And I promise that *we'll go* wherever we choose! And I mean *we*!" She was still looking at him with disbelief, so he added: "Maybe since we got the still delivered I can make other deliveries, and you can go with me! We just have to get Bea, the cart, and the money back to Mr. Rodgers. If we tell him all that we had to do to make this trip, he's sure to keep us working for him."

Gina hugged her knees to her chest and propped her chin on top of them. She stared into the firelight and mulled over what he said. "It would be nice, for awhile. I'd like to travel, and see what there is to see." She rolled her head towards him and looked into his eyes. "Will you make me a promise?" He nodded once and waited. "Tob', will you promise me that you won't just leave me somewhere, without money or a place to stay?"

Toby nodded.

"It's because I don't want to have to…do things, again, to stay alive. I have no family and no money, and I don't have anybody to help me."

"Gina, *I'm* your family. And I *won't* abandon you. We've already saved each other's lives. And hey! I might need you to save me again sometime!" He laughed and put his hand on her shoulder. She pressed her cheek against his hand and smiled back.

She stood and walked into the darkness, returning after a few minutes. "Maybe I could do something nice for you right now," she said, taking his hand and pulling him towards the back of the cart….

◊ ◊ ◊

# 40

## ~a wait by the river~

It was late morning when they reached the hilltop above Foxburg. The leaves on the trees were out, but not fully. It was difficult to see Ernie and Ella's shack from their location, so they moved the cart along the road to look for a better spot to start their signal fire. Toby rode the horse to places where they couldn't take the cart. He circled the area along the ridge, first one way and then the other. Still, he couldn't find a suitable spot. When he returned to the cart, he shook his head in disgust. Gina sat on the cart's seat and looked down at the river below.

In case Luke was in Foxburg and not in Parker, they backed away from the hill's edge and stayed out of sight. It didn't seem to be a good idea to go down the hill, as it was a one-way trip. They would never be able to get Bea and the cart back up if they were chased. They made a small fire and fed both of the animals.

Toby offered to take the horse down the long, steep hill and see if there was any sign of Luke, the barge, or anybody else that could give them away. When they hadn't come up with a better idea after an hour, Toby saddled the horse and left Gina, the cart, and Bea hidden in some low brush. He wasn't too concerned as they hadn't passed another person since Callensburg.

He descended the steep road and entered the cluster of small houses. When he felt that he was too visible, he dismounted and tied the horse to a tree. He covered the last fifty yards on foot to a spot still hidden from the landing where the barges tied up. There were no boats there now. Toby looked downriver in the direction of Parker's Landing. Nothing was in sight, so he ventured out in the open and looked upriver towards Ella's shack. He could just make out one side of the shack and the porch roof. He was amazed at how much green there was. The leaves covered everything and blended into the hemlocks they had traveled through on the other side of the river.

He thought that if he could just ride upstream a bit along this side of the river, he could get a better look at the shack. But the steepness of the riverbank prohibited a horse from traveling along it. Plus, Toby knew that it would just take one snake to spook the horse and throw him off. He gripped his whip tightly and decided to try it on foot. If he could get just a short way up, he could tie the two white flags that Gina had torn from some cloth. He looked downriver again and saw no barges or boats heading in.

Toby made his way among the large rocks and slippery moss. Everything was so damn green! But soon he was in a good spot and looking nearly directly across the river to the shack. There was also a white flag hanging there! Toby selected a spot where his flags couldn't be seen from the Foxburg side and tied them to a tree branch as high up as he could reach.

Toby soon realized a snag in the plan. *If I wait on top of the hill with Gina,* he thought, *how are we going to know when they're down here? Or how will Ella let us know if she's here?* He paced along the ground and tried to think of a way to leave a message or a sign. But no idea came to him, so he returned to the horse and rode back up the hill to the campsite.

He scouted both sides of the hillside road, but couldn't find a spot where they could move closer to the dock area, so he made his way back to Gina. She was waiting anxiously for him. She stopped pacing when she saw him approach. She saw the dismay in his face as he dismounted and explain what had happened.

Gina liked that the flags couldn't be seen on the Foxburg side. She suggested that they build the smoke fire and wait. That didn't sit well with Toby; he wasn't in the mood to wait! Finally, he agreed and went through the woods to cut green, leafy limbs to make smoke. Even with an axe in his hand, he glanced around a lot to watch for snakes.

They started the smoke fire, rested, and waited. Towards the late afternoon they were bored. They could sit here a day or two at this rate! Gina finally broke the silence and asked, "Toby? Was there *any* place down there that we could tie up Bea and the cart and hide them with tree limbs? At least we'd be there when Ernie's barge made it in."

Toby thought about it and slowly shook his head.

"Think! There must be an area where they would store stuff, waiting for a barge?"

Toby again shook his head, pursed his lips, and poked a stick into the fire. "You're right...they *would* want to unload only once. They wouldn't want to move the loads twice." He was thinking out loud now. "Maybe they'd stock lumber and things when the boats weren't in. *But I just didn't see any!*" His head still wagged back and forth. "I could go back and take another look, since it's only half a mile or so." Gina nodded and looked at the sun to calculate the time.

"There's still a couple o' hours till dark," she said. "And with any luck you could see the barges for quite a ways before they might see you. I just don't want Luke to see you if Ernie isn't with him."

Toby nodded as he rose and re-saddled the horse.

"Toby, wait! Let me go this time!" He was just putting his foot into the stirrup, but paused. Gina walked up and took the reins. He hesitated for a moment before handing them over to her.

"Gina, be careful. And if that bastard Luke sees you...." He didn't need to finish the statement. She pressed against him and kissed him on the lips.

Once in the saddle, she turned the horse and looked at him "When I get back we'll play a game." She smiled and winked, then rode away. Toby liked the aspects of that and spent some time considering the possibilities.

Toby spent the next hour walking off his desire for her. Suddenly he heard the horse's hooves pounding the ground as it approached. Gina pulled to a stop and quickly slid from the saddle.

"I think we can do it!" she said. "I found a spot surrounded by trees where we could wait. If we stay here tonight, we might miss the boat when it comes in and leaves early in the morning. But if we were down near the dock already, we'd be able to catch Ernie before he leaves again!"

Toby thought the plan sounded good. "It'll be dark in half an hour, so let's get goin'," he said. It was a safe and quiet trip to the bottom of the hill. The spot that Gina had described was perfect. They cut some hemlock branches and covered the side of the cart. It was enough to break up their outline among the trees. They left Bea and the horse tied to the cart and gave them some feed to keep them occupied.

Gina and Toby walked along the river's edge and kept an eye on the water's horizon for any sign of a barge. Darkness came without any sign of a boat or barge. They sat on a large rock near the river's edge, watching for stars to appear in the sky. The temperature dropped quickly, and they sat close together for warmth—and comfort.

They heard a lot of sounds here by the river that neither of them had ever heard before. Raccoons splashed in the water as their small, human-like hands searched the shallows for freshwater oysters, crawfish, and salamanders. Sounds of small battles for life and death broke the silence of the riverbank when one creature became another's dinner.

It was getting close to midnight and they decided to give up for the night. Gina picked her way along the stony water's edge, holding tightly to Toby's hand. She didn't let him go even when they arrived back at the cart. Bea didn't seem to mind the cart's rocking; it held her attention only long enough for her to sigh and close her eyes again. Even though Toby and Gina were exhausted, they each slept with one ear listening for any activity near the dock. But they didn't hear a sound all night.

◊ ◊ ◊

# 41

## ~flat rocks and fog~

Toby woke to the sound of Bea relieving herself on a flat rock. When he sat up in the cart, he held onto one of the hoops and realized how damp it was. With the oilcloth cover on, only the rear and front of the cart were open. The air moved through it like a tunnel and he felt the dampness in his hair. The blanket was wet on the outside, as were his clothes when he picked them up to get dressed. Gina was still sleeping as he slid to the end of the cart and onto the ground. A thick fog had drifted into the river valley during the night, making it impossible to see more than two or three feet in any direction.

Toby moved silently along the cart and went to where Bea and the horse were tied. They were ok, but their coats were drenched with the fog. Toby had never seen fog so thick, not even along the Pittsburgh valley with the three rivers passing through it.

Toby relieved himself on another flat rock nearby, but despite his best attempt, he couldn't do it quietly. When he finished he listened to the absolute silence around him. Nothing made a sound. He thought he could hear noises from the river, but as he listened more closely he realized that it was his imagination.

He stepped around the cart again and tried to remember exactly which direction the dock area was and how far it was to the river. The grey fog was so dense that he could barely see the ground before his feet. Each step was like a baby's first. He felt his way along slowly and stepped between two rocks that he remembered from last night. He became a little surer of the direction he was going and proceeded to look for the docking area.

There was nothing to see or to touch in the grey expanse—except the ground—and he held his arms out ahead of him. The air's moisture collected in his hair and started to run down his forehead. He moved ahead slowly and tried to estimate the distance he'd covered, but couldn't guess. He knew that if he turned one direction or another from the path he remembered, he probably wouldn't be able to get back to the cart without whistling for Gina to help—and he didn't want to let anybody know they were here. He wanted to be the first to find anybody else, rather than someone—like Luke—waiting for him!

Not five minutes into his search, he began to doubt his choice of direction and realized how confused his senses were in this haze. He could find a place to sit and wait for the sunshine to burn off the fog, but that could take the better part of the morning. Or he could keep moving and attempt to scout the area.

His stomach growled loudly, but he didn't think the noise could penetrate the fog. Still, Toby began to get frightened; he imagined Luke standing close by with a heavy club ready to hit him! Or worse yet, a knife to stab him!

Could they have come upstream last night and landed without Toby or Gina hearing them? Wouldn't they have made a loud noise hitting the dock in the foggy darkness? Or had they made it in before the fog set in? Did they sleep on the barge, or did they come ashore? The questions swam in Toby's head and the answers weren't much clearer than the air around him. He had broken out in a cold sweat from the fear and the fog. His clothes were soaked and he was getting cold. His nose started to run and he sniffed as quietly as he could and then ran his nose across his sleeve. But that was just wet on wet!

Now he wished he hadn't left the cart and Gina's warm embrace. *No!*, Toby thought. He couldn't allow his attention to wander from the task at hand; he had to know if others were around.

Then he heard something! It was a kind of thud; the sound of wood against the dock. Toby's stomach flipped in fear and he wondered why he hadn't brought the whip with him. He felt completely helpless. If he didn't find the barge there, fine! If he did, that might be good, too! He thought of finding a stone and tossing it out ahead; it *should* hit the river. What would a splash tell anybody else? It could be a large fish jumping, or a turtle! He squatted down and felt around for a rock when a knee hit him full in the face!

◊ ◊ ◊

"Ow!" Toby inadvertently grunted out loud. He grabbed his cheek and rolled away. The other person was just to his left. He heard a movement and jumped back just in time. Something had just swung past his head! Now what? He stepped back again into the fog. He was breathing hard and knew the other person could hear him. But he could hear them breathing, as well. Toby guessed the other person was about five feet away. If he could only quiet his breathing, he might be able to get the upper hand.

He was preparing to jump to the side and shout, when he heard the voice whisper menacingly, "I'll kill you...."

Toby stopped. He knew that voice. "Ella?" he whispered. "It's Toby."

"Oh my God! Toby!" she whispered back.

He saw two hands reaching through the fog and then saw Ella's face closing in. They hugged each other.

"I thought you were Luke," Ella said in Toby's ear.

"Yeah, me, too!" Toby said softly. Ella still had him in a bear hug and he was embarrassed to be so close to her. It was too good! She was so warm and soft. He tried to step back a little, but she held him tightly.

"Listen to me," Ella whispered into Toby's ear, sending a ticklish shiver down his back. "Luke's here. I heard them come in last night. I saw your flags in the tree yesterday. I waited until dark and came across, but I got here about the same time they did. I couldn't think of a way to warn you, so I waited in the boat, and then the fog set in. I have been creeping around in this damn fog for an hour, trying to imagine where you two might be. Is Gina alright?"

"Yes, she's in the cart asleep." Toby whispered back into her wet hair. (*God, this is nerve-wracking!*, he thought.)

"We have to get to Gina and warn her."

"She won't sound out," Toby offered.

"Probably not, but we can't afford a mistake. Oh Toby, there's *a lot* to tell you!"

"Where's Ernie?"

"I don't know. *That's* the problem. I haven't seen him for four days!"

There was a soft noise somewhere near them. Ella put her hand over Toby's mouth. They stood in their tight embrace as they strained to listen. With each slow breath, her chest rubbed against his, and he was having trouble slowing his breathing all over again!

They heard the sound again. Almost inaudibly she whispered to Toby, "Which way to the cart?"

"I...I don't know!" he breathed backed, realizing that he'd lost his sense of direction when he took her knee to the face and spun away. "I don't know!" There was a tinge of fear in his voice.

"We'll find her. Don't let go of my hand! I think I'm still going the direction I was when I heard you pizzle."

Toby flushed at her mention of it, but she tugged him into the fog. They stepped forward quietly. Once he accidentally stepped on the back of her foot, causing her to stumble. He caught her from falling and she regained her footing. They proceeded again, slowly and quietly. There didn't seem to be any change in the fog. It was still dimly-lit and the sun felt imaginary. Toby shivered again.

"Here!" he whispered, his voice was barely audible. He tugged on Ella's hand and she stopped. "These two rocks. They were near the cart." She squeezed his hand as an acknowledgement.

He stooped and felt the two rocks, trying to remember how they felt when he crossed them earlier. There was a sound ahead. Toby and Ella stayed still. It didn't sound like an animal or like Gina moving around! They waited.

"Mmmnnffffff!" There was a commotion ahead. Then came another grunt and a scream that sounded like Gina!

Ella's hand crushed Toby's in the ensuing silence. She wanted him to stay quiet and not move. They were frozen in mid-step.

◊ ◊ ◊

# 42

## ~Bea makes an enemy~

Toby was sure they weren't more than ten feet from the cart, but they had no idea what to do. They heard another muffled cry! Toby thought he could just see the edge of the cart's covering against the thick, white fog. He pictured how the cart sat and where the whip was. Getting to that whip was his only fighting chance!

He slowly pulled Ella to him until her wet hair was against his face and then whispered, "I'm going to the front of the cart to get my whip. When I have it, I'll start talking to whoever is there. Stay back so you stay clear of my whip." He felt her nod against his cheek. She slowly opened her hand and let him slip away.

It took only a minute for Toby to creep to the front of the cart. As he felt along the seat for the whip he drew a deep breath and prepared himself. He found the wet handle of the whip and closed his fingers around it. He pulled it towards him, but the loose coil of the whip fell to the floor of the cart and made a wet thump.

He felt a hand fly past his face and land behind his ear in a glancing blow. He instantly pulled back and missed what he imagined was a second attempt. Toby pictured the area that they had pulled into last night, roughly sketching the tree spacing behind him. He stepped back to what he thought was the right distance and cracked the whip!

"The little snake bites, eh? How about I cut your lil' hussy's throat?" Luke's voice snarled into the fog.

Toby misunderstood Luke. *Huskey?*, he thought and cracked the whip again just to the left of his last shot.

"Maybe I just choke her quietly, and then I come after you," Luke hissed.

Toby knew his advantage at that moment: "Keep quiet and strike from a different direction." Again he cracked the whip to another imaginary spot near the source of the voice.

"I'm putting her in front of me," Luke said. "Maybe you'll tear her eye out!" No sooner had Luke said those words than Toby heard a loud crack and a curse. Luke had been hit and fell to the ground. Toby didn't lose a second; he cracked the whip into the air in the direction of Luke's groan.

Toby heard something behind him. "Ella?!" Toby said sternly, drawing back the whip again, poised to strike. He thought he heard Luke trying to get to his feet.

"I'm fine Toby!" Ella said from behind him. "He's between us! Keep him there!"

CRACK! The whip hit something, and Luke shouted curses, but his voice seemed to be moving away from Toby. The next thing he heard was Bea braying and a thud, followed by the sound of something falling to the ground! Toby realized that Bea must have kicked out when Luke stumbled into the mule's business-end. Toby listened intently, but all he heard was the sound of Ella climbing into the back of the cart and helping Gina. Toby wasn't going to move until he knew that Luke was not getting up!

"Toby!" It was Gina's voice and she was ok. He knew it without her saying so.

Toby closed in on the spot where Luke had fallen and slowly reached into the grey expanse of the fog.

He could just make out Luke's shoulder and watched for any movement. But Luke was completely still. Toby got Luke's hands behind him and used the whip to tie them together. Then Toby tied him to the cart's axle. He felt his way to the back of the cart. As he rounded the corner of it, Gina threw her armsaround his neck. For a split second Toby thought it was another attack and attempted to protect himself. When he realized it was Gina he dropped his arms and pulled her towards him. She was out of the cart, standing on his foot, and kissing him madly!

Toby, Gina, and Ella sat on the back of the cart, listening for any movements along the river. The fog began to clear, moving away in a soft breeze. It looked like smoke drifting around the edge of the cart's cover. First the tops of the hills appeared; then bright sunlight glistened off of the wet tree leaves. As the fog lifted, the valley radiated in wet, green beauty. They watched the fog clear the valley until they could see the river. The fog seemed to drift along with the river, thickly clinging to the water's surface.

It had been a long morning, and Toby was hungry. Ella poked her elbow into Toby's side and nodded towards the barge. Luke's dumber-than-an-oar helper was just waking up. He sat on the floor of the barge under a coat, blinking at the sunlight.

"I think I'm about to get some answers—the easy way," Ella said. "Keep an eye on Luke!" With that she hopped onto the ground and strode to the barge.

"It looks like the captain is about to take her ship back!" Toby said and smiled at Gina. She had just pulled away from him and was tying the knife to her leg.

"I'm *never* sleeping without this on—*ever*!" she grumbled.

"Never?" Toby asked with a teasing grin.

"Well, we'll discuss it," she said with a grin. "I think it's my turn to watch Luke," she added. She walked around the corner of the cart and kicked him in the leg. Luke barely stirred. (Well, it was her turn to watch him!)

Toby couldn't have been prouder of himself or either of the women. His belly groaned again, and he thought of how nice it would be if one of them could cook breakfast right now!

◊ ◊ ◊

# 43

## ~Stefan's story~

Toby and Gina waited for awhile before going to the barge. They checked on Luke, but he was still in a fog of his own. They walked towards the river until they were within earshot of the conversation. They heard Ella being diplomatic with Luke's young helper, Stefan.

"…an' that's the last time you saw Ernie?" she asked.

"Yes, ma'am." The boy nodded, repeating, "Yes, ma'am."

"He and Luke were the only people on the barge?"

"Yep. Like I said, they tol' me to stay in the warehouse and restack the grain bags, which I did!"

"Stefan, what exactly did Luke say when he came back alone?"

Stefan looked at her for a long moment before replying. "I think he said that Ernie was going to stay the day—with you! I didn't think 'bout it much. He's done that before."

Ella nodded, her eyes glued to his. "Stefan, Ernie never came to the shack. He wasn't here either. Think! When they left, did Ernie say anything other than for you to restack the grain bags?"

Stefan smiled as a light went on in his head. "He tol' me they'd be back by dark!"

"Ok, Stefan, was there anything on the barge when they went upstream? In this direction?"

Stefan frowned and thought hard before shaking his head.

"Did you see them leave in the barge?"

Stefan nodded again. "Yes…."

"Did anybody else? Was there anybody else around? Maybe others working nearby?" Ella was nearly out of patience by now and blew air out of her puffed up cheeks. Stefan shook his head.

Gina stepped up to Stefan, smiled, and asked, "How long did you watch them pole upstream?"

Stefan shook his head and said, "Not too long. I was supposta stack the grain bags."

"I know, I know," Ella said. "But did you stay and watch—just for awhile?"

"For awhile…." he agreed and lowered his head.

"That's ok, Stefan. Can you remember how far upriver they were when you went inside?" Ella asked sweetly.

Another moment passed. "I reckon, 'bout a mile. They was past the flat island, then I couldn't see them no more." Stefan looked back and forth between the women and shot a glance at Toby.

Ella asked, "Did either Ernie or Luke say why they weren't bringing you along?"

"They said they was goin' to pick you up and would be back by late afternoon, or dark, that's all. But Mr. Ernie tol' me to pack my clothes 'cause we was takin' you downriver!" Stefan smiled as he remembered another detail.

Ella looked at Gina and Toby and then back to the boy. "Did he say why? Why we were going downriver?"

Stefan had that blank look again. He shrugged his shoulders.

"Stefan, was Luke there when he told you this?" Ella bent to Stefan's height and looked him directly in the face.

"He was at the other end of the barge."

"Could he have heard you or Ernie at that point?" Ella's head pivoted towards the cart. Toby could see that her blood was starting to boil. She seemed to be piecing everything together.

Stefan shrugged again, but offered no answer.

Ella paced back and forth; Toby could see her eyes darting from one object to another. He knew her brain was racing, as she eliminated possibilities and organized others. She did this for several minutes before she returned to face her new crew of three. "Here's what were gonna do. Stefan, you're gonna row me to the shack; there's some things I need to get. When we get back—in maybe an hour—Toby, I want your cart here on the barge. We'll bring on the horse and mule when we're ready to leave. Then see if you and Gina can get that piece of goat manure you got tied up down here and tied to the barge." She motioned Stefan to the rowboat. "And use a rope to tie him, cause I'm gonna need that whip of yours when I get back," she added. With that she stepped into the boat and Stefan pulled at the oars.

Gina turned to Toby and said, "Let's get started."

"Let's EAT!" he said and playfully swatted the air near her arm.

"We'll do that, too. I just think that Ella's plan is going to be fast and we'd better be ready!" Gina swatted back at Toby's arm. She missed, too.

Toby pouted on the way back to the cart. He really wanted some breakfast after the crazy morning he'd had! But he watched the sway of Gina's dress as she walked in front of him, and that cheered him up a little.

His good mood evaporated like the fog when they reached the cart and discovered that Luke was gone—and so was the horse!

◊ ◊ ◊

# 44

~the river race~

The pace of the plan quickened when Ella and Stefan returned and found out about Luke's escape. Ella threw down the sack she carried and ran to the spot where the cart had been. She kicked at a rock and turned back to the others. "There's a path along the top of the hill that he could use to get to the Landin'. He could get there ahead of us, and I *don't* want that to happen. He'll have to make the horse swim to get cross the Clarion inlet, and then get to the Landin' and cross with another one of the ferry boats. We have to get there first. *We have to!* Stefan, get the boat and tie it to the back of the barge. Toby, blind that mule and bring her onto the barge!"

Everybody moved quickly except Bea. She didn't like the large cloth sack being put over her head or being led onto something that moved. Toby gently led her on and short-tied her in the center of the barge. The cart came next, and they were ready.

When Stefan and Ella used the long poles to back the barge into the river, Toby watched everything closely. He didn't like the idea of things being in someone else's hands—especially Stefan's! He was younger than Toby, and that didn't sit well with him.

"Toby and Gina, I want you two watching the top of the ridge, looking for Luke!" Ella shouted as she used the front rudder to guide them into the faster current of the river.

Stefan and Ella steered front and back, both expertly managing the cumbersome craft. Once it reached the current in the river channel it had a life of its own. It turned and floated quickly southward towards the Landing.

There was nothing for Toby and Gina to do but watch the top of the hills and keep Bea comfortable. The sun's rays were hot, and Toby could feel his skin burning. Gina had tied her hair up, and Toby looked at the stray hairs on her neck; he could see a tan line. He thought of how much she'd changed since they first met. She was a quiet and timid girl before. In two short weeks, she had grown into a keen-minded and bold woman. Her strength seemed boundless, and she fixed her determination on her goal. And at the moment, she seemed intent that she'd be the one to spot Luke and the horse.

Toby was glad Luke hadn't taken the whip, and he couldn't figure out *how* he'd gotten loose. Toby had tied him tightly; plus, the wet leather should have shrunk as it dried. Toby needed to figure it out so the next time he tied someone up they wouldn't get loose!

The next hour passed without incident, and Ella watched the shoreline carefully. It dawned on Toby that she was looking for Ernie—in whatever condition she may find him. Toby watched the hilltop as he was supposed to, but knew that Gina wouldn't miss a movement up on the crest of the mountain. Both women were watching intently for a man: one with love in her heart, the other with loathing. As Toby thought about this, he looked downstream and saw what must be the island that Ella had mentioned earlier.

It occurred to him that Luke might have tried to do to Ernie what he'd done to Toby. He remembered the near drowning, being pushed under the water with Luke's pole. How easy it would be to drown someone if you were lucky enough to catch them just right and force them under the water....

"There!" Gina shouted. "That's him!" They all looked to the skyline and saw the rider heading south. Ella watched only long enough to calculate his progress before returning her gaze to the far edge of the riverbank. "Stefan, I'm going as close to the far bank as we can, you guide her steady...."

"Yes, Mis' Ella." Stefan swept the rear oar and expertly moved the heavy barge slightly towards the river's western bank.

"Toby, when we start past the sandbank in the river, we're going through the chute, where the water moves a little faster than in the main part of the river. So..." She gave a hard push on the front rudder and then continued. "...you glue your eyes to the shoreline on the sandbank.... Don't miss a thing! Ernie could be...lying...anywhere! He might be unconscious...JUST KEEP A WATCH!"

Toby's eyes followed the line of water and scanned about thirty feet up on the sandbank. Suddenly he saw something. "There!" He pointed to a spot along the bank that seemed to be gouged, as if somebody had crawled up onto the drier ground. Ella spotted it instantly and jammed her long rudder into a hard turn. The barge reacted instantly in the quick current, and with Stefan's guidance, it banked not five feet from the mark Toby had seen.

Ella made the bank in one leap and ran into the waist high grass, sidestepping drifted tree limbs that scattered the beach. She hadn't gone twenty feet when the others heard her scream.

◊ ◊ ◊

# 45

## ~a landin' at the landing~

"No! Ernie! ERNIE!"

Toby jumped from the barge and instantly sunk into several inches of silt muck. He slipped his way along the bank and made it to Ella. He felt like screaming, too. Ella was kneeling beside Ernie and gently lifted his head, which was covered with dried blood. He was still soaking wet. "He's alive. Toby, help me get him to the barge."

They tugged and pulled Ernie to the shoreline. By then, Stefan and Gina had laid a pair of planks across and helped get Ernie onboard. Ella covered him quickly with a blanket from the bag she'd brought with her.

Gina lost sight of Luke while she was sidetracked with helping with Ernie. It made no difference, as they could no longer see the top of the far side of the riverbank where Luke had been riding.

"Stefan, get the barge into the flo' again and get us to the Landin'. Hurry!" Ella said. Stefan looked furtively between Ernie and the front of the barge. They were now less than two miles from the Landing and he didn't need to do much with the front rudder except hold it straight ahead. Stefan leaned into the back rudder and guided them out through the chute and back into the main flow of the river.

After they passed the inlet of the Clarion river, Gina was back to watching the far side of the river, but there was no sign of Luke. She remained stationary, holding Bea's halter and petting the mule. But her eyes never left the mountain ridge.

Toby noticed the shacks lining the Parker side of the river first. They were practically nailed together and went on for as far as he could see. A lot of people moved around on the shore and some waved to the barge. Toby waved back, his eyes darting to everything that moved. He saw adults and children carrying every type of goods you could imagine. Dogs chased after the kids and barked at everything.

Toby saw stacks of lumber, some of which acted as housing shelters. Smoke rose from cooking fires and steam from cooking pots. Tattered, grey clothes hung drying in the sun and near the fires. Stacks of purple dyed wool lay in the sun, as well. Some women held babies and talked while men worked at various tasks. Older men worked at lighter tasks and shot longing looks of envy at the younger men who reminded them of what they had  once done— and been—long ago.

At the slow pace of the barge, Toby reckoned that they'd passed nearly half a mile of this sight when he felt the barge start to curve its path to the shoreline. "Gina, mind Ernie till I get the barge in," Ella said as she got to her feet and took the front rudder. "He's bad, but he's gonna be fine," she said to Toby as she took the oar. Fifteen minutes later, they were tied up to the dock that was marked for the "Channel Cat," and Stefan hustled from task to task.

Carefully, they carried Ernie up a set of wooden steps to the main landing level. Several others joined them and started asking rapid-fire questions. Ella, still acting as the captain of the barge, shouted instructions to people. They hurried off in different directions, looking back at the barge as they left. Ernie was loaded onto a cart—much like the one Toby had—and it disappeared. Toby and Gina went back to the barge and watched the far shore. Stefan went through the motions of coiling up ropes and laying out the ramp planks again.

A long ramp, like a roadway, ran parallel to the river and climbed to the main street area. Just above them was a large building with the words, *Channel Cat Trading Co.* printed on a sign above the door. It was a well-built and clean looking building, painted red with blue trim, and was taller than all but one other building. The taller building had two docks beside it and a sign that read: *The Parker Trading, Milling, and Lumber Co.* But it didn't look as nice as the Channel Cat building.

"Toby, come here!" Gina's voice interrupted his observations. He stepped to her side as she gazed across the river. She looked at Stefan first and then whispered, "If Ella gets a sheriff and he starts askin' questions, what are we gonna say? We need a *lot* of answers! We don't have—"

Toby cut her off. "I think you're right, but Ella wouldn't put us in trouble. She just wouldn't."

"But, we were there! And we'd have to tell what we saw and what Stefan said. An' then what about Lew?"

"Shhh! We don't ever say a word about the 'fire pit!' We got separated—plain and simple! You came along with us to deliver the still, an' we got lost from Lew! We spent two days looking for him. *Remember that!*"

"But if Lucca was here, he'd say that we run off. And stole stuff from him. And that he and Lew chased us!"

"Well, *then* we tell them how they planned to steal the cart, the load, and keep the money! It's our word against them. Besides, I trust Ella to cover it. She'll know what to do." He hugged her and quickly kissed her hair for reassurance.

"Toby, there's a barge comin' across," Gina said.

Ella's head appeared above the dock and she whistled. Once she had their attention, she motioned them up. When they reached the top of the steps, she pulled them to the front of the warehouse. "Find me three men who will load the barge for us. I'll pay them a dollar to work tomorrow! Make sure they're here by dawn! And then you two stay outta sight. It's going to be hard in this small town, but the less you're around the fewer questions they can ask you. Got it?" Toby and Gina nodded.

Before they could do anything, Ella grabbed Gina's arm. "Wait. Maybe it's better if Toby gets the workers—on his own. Gina, you wait in the warehouse and stay outta sight! Go inside to the back—there's a door there. After dark, go to the rowboat, and wait for Toby. When he gets there, go downriver about a mile and wait till I get there—tomorrow, or the day after at the latest! Got it?" They both nodded. Toby turned to Gina, kissed her, and went off into the crowd to find men for the barge.

"Get!" She pushed Gina gently towards the door of the warehouse and returned to the barge.

"Stefan, take the mule to Mr. Locke's stable and get her fed. Tell him I'll send for the mule when I need her!

Stefan nodded obediently, coaxed Bea across the planks, and left with the mule.

By now the other ferry barge was in mid-river and Ella picked up the spyglass. She could see Luke standing near the horse at the front of the barge. He looked worried. She doubted he could see her, but she knew he could see that her barge had beaten him.

"You just stay right there in the front of the barge, you little bastard! We'll see how brave you are with the sheriff—and without your papa!" Ella was talking under her breath when she heard a voice behind her.

"What the hell you doin' Miss Ella?" She turned to see Archibald the sheriff standing on the dock and wondering who she was talking to.

"Arch! It's good to see you. I need your services!"

"And why would that be?" he asked as he stepped onto the barge.

"You're gonna have to arrest Luke when he gets off that barge." She jerked her head towards the incoming barge.

"Luke! Your Luke?"

Ella nodded her head and looked through the spyglass again. "Yeah, *my* Luke. The little bastard came upriver with his father, Lucca."

"Lucca! I've got an arrest order on him. He was bringing in grappa to the Landin' and didn't pay the taxes! I normally don't do much except fine them, but he's been in and out several times."

"Well it's *a lot* more than that! This time you can add attempted rape—AND attempted murder! He and his son came to the shack several nights ago and got a little out of hand!"

Arch looked shocked. "That I *won't* overlook. I'll wring his neck myself. Where's Lucca now…?"

"Probably in some wormhole! I think he's probably left town…. You heard about Ernie?"

"Yeah, what happened? Heard he fell into the river."

"Yeah, *after* getting hit by Luke—*or Lucca*! And I'm not sure that Stefan isn't involved. I asked him, and he said he hadn't traveled with the others, but Ernie told me different. I guess you'll have to question him. I'm so mad I could kill him myself!" Ella stared at the incoming barge. By now it was clear that Luke had seen her and the sheriff talking. He stared back at them, holding the reins of the horse.

"Arch, if you take him in on attempted murder for hitting Ernie, he'll deny it. But I'll come in and swear in the additional charges. Will that work?"

"There's a lot to work out, but he's not going anywhere in the meantime."

By now the barge was in direct docking-steerage. Luke stared warily at Ella and the sheriff, who held his wide-eyed gaze and stared him down. Arch said to Ella, "I feel sorry for his wife."

Without dropping her stare at Luke, Ella said, "I'll send her some money, to keep her for awhile. But I'm takin' Ernie to Pittsburgh to see a doctor. We'll be back in a month. Keep an eye on the warehouse, will ya?"

"Done!" Arch stepped to the barge as it touched the dock. Ella watched as Luke, caught in the sheriff's strong grip, was led up the wooden stairs. She couldn't hear his protests—and didn't want to.

◊ ◊ ◊

# 46

## ~a new chest, uh-huh, uh-huh~

"Gina?" Ella said in a loud voice as she walked in the warehouse. "Gina!" She waited and listened for a response.

"Here, Ella."

Ella went to her and described what had happened outside. "I'm going to Ernie right now. The doc said he could be up tomorrow, but I hope he rests. Here's what I'm planning to do."

Gina walked beside Ella and listened to her plan. She offered some ideas of her own, and Ella agreed. Gina seemed happy with the solution that Ella had concocted. They walked around the warehouse while Ella made a mental inventory of things to be loaded onto the barge.

Gina told Ella that she couldn't believe how much stuff was in the warehouse. Ella laughed and said, "Dear girl, this isn't all! We keep another place downriver. In case of fire—'cause there've been two! The first one nearly took out the whole town. It started among the shacks and moved in both directions—wiped out all everybody had. We donated all the lumber we had to get things started again, but the fools just keep re-building one building against another. So when a fire starts it *all* goes up! But now Mr. Parker is demanding that they put separation streets in between every fifth building. The last fire took out his store *and* his home!" She was quiet for a moment and added softly, "Killed his son, wife, and two daughters, it did."

They walked up and down several more aisles and Ella seemed to be satisfied with her count of things. "I'm going to need your help. An' as of now, you and Toby are on my payroll."

Gina's eyes grew large and filled with tears; she'd never been paid in her life! It was a new concept for her to grasp. She looked bewildered and blinked away her tears. "Do you think I could buy a dress for myself?" Gina asked sheepishly. "This one's getting' a little small, and I think it's starting to git a bit gamey."

"Better than that—I have some dresses you can *have*. You can save your money for other things!" Ella put her hand on Gina's shoulder and guided her to an office area. "I keep some clothes here, just in case. We are gonna get you *all* gussied up, gal!"

Gina hugged Ella after deciding which dress to take. She tried it on, and it fit better than anything she'd ever worn. The bodice pulled up tightly and enhanced her figure quite nicely. It wasn't a very fancy dress, but as far as Gina was concerned, it was fit for a ball. She looked at the boots on her feet; she'd been wearing them for months and they looked out of place with the new dress. Ella shrugged and said, "Sorry. Can't help you there, at least not yet. Anyway, I think it'll take Toby some time just to get used to the dress!" They laughed. Gina wiped away another happy tear and then wiped her nose on the sleeve of the dress. Ella frowned a little at Gina's lack of manners, but didn't say anything; she made a mental note to give Gina some guidance in the manner's department—real soon!

Toby entered the warehouse and walked into the scene of Gina and Ella chatting about dresses. When he saw Gina, he was stupefied! He stood with his mouth hanging open, staring at her uplifted cleavage. He swallowed hard and couldn't say anything. Ella broke the spell and asked, "Do we have men coming in the morning? Toby?"

"Uh-huh," Toby responded, but his eyes hadn't left Gina's "new" chest—er, dress!

Ella smiled at the dumbstruck boy and took a step backwards. "Then I'll see you both in the morning. Don't set out tonight like I said before. You wait'll I come by early tomorrow. And stay outta sight!" Ella stepped back again, but didn't turn until she winked at Gina. Gina acknowledged it with a smile.

"I think we can do that, right Toby?" Gina said in a sweet voice.

"Uh-huh. Uh-huh…."

◊ ◊ ◊

# 47

## ~hot river water stew~

The next morning, Gina and Toby woke instantly when the door of the warehouse banged opened and Ella entered. They saw that it was still dark outside.

"Hey you two! Wake up!" she called out. She lit a lamp, and then a second and a third and the warehouse began to brighten. "Toby, you said you found a couple of men to load us up, right?"

Toby cleared his hoarse throat and answered, "Yeah, they said they'd be here before dawn. And they said they knew you." Toby wondered how long it would be till dawn. His eyes were burning and he hadn't slept enough. Gina was up and moving around. She had packed their meager belongings the night before and had them sitting by the door. All she had to gather now was the blanket they'd used last night.

Toby sat on the feed sacks that had been their bed and dangled his feet over the side. He slipped to the floor and tried to put on his boots, but they seemed to be small. He adjusted the laces, but they still felt tight. He took them off and pulled out the wadded cloth that his mother had put in to help them fit. His feet must have grown and he didn't need the extra cushion any more.

He walked over to the women and caught Gina asking Ella about Ernie's condition.

"Oh, that ol' mule, he's just fine. Said he had a headache and his ribs are still sore, but he's coming in later this morning. Anyway, I want you two in that rowboat and down the river *before* sunrise. And it's probably better if you're gone before the others get here." Ella squatted to the floor and brushed aside some straw. With her finger, she drew a curved line in the dust to represent the river. She marked an X at the Landing and made some dots to represent a pair of small rocks past the bend in the river. "You can see them easy," she said. "Behind them is a sandy beach area. It's where you'll wait for us. We'll load today, and should be there by noon tomorrow. Whatever you do, wait there! We'll be along. Now off with ya both!"

In the dark, Gina carried two bundles and Toby carried one and the lantern. They climbed down the steps and into the rowboat. As they pushed off, Toby dipped an oar into the water and let the boat drift quietly around to point downstream.

He pulled the oars silently. At about mid-river, he felt the current pulling them. It was now a matter of just waiting! Toby hated waiting, but he was getting used to it on this trip. They drifted for a couple of hours before the dawn's light showed them the banks of the river.

Gina sat with a blanket over her shoulders, and Toby wore the old coat he'd had since the start of the trip. He felt the collar to make sure that the gold coins Gina had sewed into it were still there. As they drifted along, two eagles circled above them in the sky. The birds were huge and made Toby feel small and lost. He's heard stories of eagles carrying off babies and was glad he wasn't small enough to be plucked up into the sky.

They laid back and watched the birds for awhile. Toby heard some soft splashes in the water and sat up to see what was causing them. Large fish were "boiling" on the river's surface. They swam to the top and then rolled over just as they broke the surface. Toby and Gina watched the water and saw many of these boils along the river. Suddenly one of the eagles struck the surface at a boil and snatched away a very large bass. Gina squealed with delight and the sudden scare. The fish was as large as Toby's arm, and thicker. The eagle never lost momentum as he lifted the fish and flew skyward. Its mate dove down and repeated the process, also leaving the river with a huge breakfast in tow. Toby and Gina laughed and cheered the eagles.

"I wish we had a line and pole," Gina said.

He nodded, and his stomach growled. In their hurry to leave, neither of them had grabbed the bags of grain, dried meat, and potatoes. Toby wasn't hungry for fish for breakfast, but he thought of how good one of those bass would be for lunch, slow-cooked and smoked. He thought back to the times his father had brought home smoked fish.

"There, Toby!" Gina pointed to the shore as the two rocks Ella had described appeared. Toby pulled on an oar and let them drift in. The current was non-existent on the downriver side of the rocks, and they sat still in the water.

After they stepped onto shore they pulled up the boat and tied it off. The sandy spot was clean and level, and about the size of two barges. At the far end, small branches of sun-dried, bone-white driftwood were tangled among the rocks where they had washed up in prior floodings. Toby was happy that he wouldn't have to look far for firewood. Maybe he could even fashion a spear and go after a couple of the tasty bass! There was a small indent in the rocks, somewhat hidden from view, that would make a nice fire area. Gina set about carrying some of the bundles from the boat and gathering rocks to circle a fire pit. "Toby, I could camp here for a week!" she said.

Toby gathered an armload of sticks and brought them to her. They each took their knives and scrapped the dry twigs to make some fine "wood-wool" to use as starter material. Toby used his knife and the flint to get a spark and blew on the shavings to get the flame up. Soon they had a nice fire going and realized all that was missing was food. They had the cooking pot, but that was it. "We could make a stew," Gina suggested.

"With what? All we'd get was hot river water!"

"Toby, I make a mean river water stew!" Gina joked and then sighed. "It's ok. We aren't going to starve with all those fish in the river. And we can probably find mushrooms or nuts in the woods. Oh, and there should be the clams—like you tol' me about!" She went to the water's edge and looked in.

A loud crash broke the silence in the woods behind them. It sounded like a tree limb had fallen down through the branches and thudded on the ground. Gina jumped to Toby's side. They glanced around for the source of the noise.

"Do you think it's a bear? Or another big cat!? What could make that big o' sound?" Gina whispered.

They kept their eyes on the woods, searching for any sign of movement. The noise came again! This time, it was further up the riverbank and deeper in the woods. Nothing moved elsewhere, but Toby and Gina stood guard. Fifteen minutes passed and there was another crash! This one was directly uphill from their campsite.

Every so often another crash rang out from a different location. Since the sound didn't seem to be coming closer to them, they relaxed a little. They didn't jump at each new crash, but they weren't comfortable with the situation. They spent a long time watching quietly.

Now it was getting hot! The temperature rose quickly during the last of the morning hours, and soon they were sweating. Their cold sweat of fear from the noises turned into a hot sweat from the sun's rays. There wasn't much air moving today, which made it even more uncomfortable. They took turns going into the river up to their waists and splashing water over themselves.

As the day wore on, Toby tried to catch a fish with a wooden spear, but it wasn't going well. The near hits educated the fish faster than they did Toby, and he kept jabbing the water and missing. Each time, Gina laughed and he tried again. The sound of Gina's laughter echoed in the river valley, making it sounded like a whole group of people laughing at Toby's efforts.

After awhile, Gina wandered along the bank and looked for crawfish, clams, or some dumb fish. She found a lot of empty clam shells, but nothing else. There was another crash in the forest. This time Toby and Gina just looked at each other, shrugged, and continued looking for food. Gina went back to add more wood to the fire and put the iron pot of water on to boil.

Toby gave up first. He'd passed the point of being hungry and decided he was using up too much energy chasing a meal.

"Let me try there, Baby Grape!" Gina took over spearing the river, which amused Toby.

He laughed and poked fun at her as she tried her best to outdo him and catch the first fish. As she stalked another fish she said, "You know…I'm NOT…going…to… share it…when I do….KILL…*this one!*" The spear came up empty. After a dozen more tries, she returned to sit on the log Toby had been using as a grandstand. "We need some shade, but I'm *not* going into those woods," she said. Toby looked over his shoulder and agreed, even though it had been an hour since they heard the last crash.

"We'll use the blanket," Toby said. He went to the boat and retrieved the oars to prop against a rock, and then draped the blanket across them to provide some shade. Acting the part of a gentleman, he held out his hand and offered her a seat in the shade   "Why, thank you!" Gina said with a mock curtsey. She ducked under the blanket and sat down. She wiggling herself a "butt-seat" in the sand and leaned up against the rock, with just her legs still sticking out in the sun. She didn't seem to mind. In fact she pulled up the hem of her dress to mid-thigh. Toby gazed at her legs and realized how muscled they were. He saw the knife sheath strapped to her thigh and asked if he could borrow the knife.

She pulled it from its holder and tossed it to him. Toby stripped off his shirt and dragged a small stump over away from their tent. He threw the knife at the stump, trying to get the tip of the blade to stick in the wood. Several times the knife hit handle first and bounced off. Soon Toby had the blade hitting the wood and finally landed it in the stump. After each throw, he retrieved the knife, turned and paced three steps, then turned again and threw. In about half an hour, he had the knife sticking more times than not.

Gina had closed her eyes and rested for awhile, but got bored asked to try throwing the knife. "I'm not sure," Toby said and threw the knife again, sticking it into the stump. "It's not really the thing for girls." He knew that statement would put her on her feet.

"It's EXACTLY the thing for girls!" Gina announced. With that she retrieved his next "sticker" and assumed the pose she'd seen him make. "Every good woman should know how to protect herself!"

For the first several throws, the handle bounced off of the stump, just like Toby had done. He told her to think of the point and make it do *one* flip in the air to land on the stump. After a number of attempts she still didn't have it. Finally Toby told her to make it flip once and aim at a point just two feet ahead of her in the sand. She threw the knife at the ground and it stuck point first. Next, he told her to increase the distance a little. After a few more tries, she was making two out of four throws stick properly in the sand. Then they stood eight feet apart and tossed it to just ahead of the other's feet. An hour later, they were getting good at this game. Gina could hit the stump and make it stick one out of three times.

While they played, they kept a watch upriver, hoping to see a barge. They wore out the game and decided to take another swim and maybe try fishing again. Toby pulled off his pants while standing near the water and tossed them onto the beach. Gina made him turn around before she dropped her dress and walked into the water.

The river cooled them off quickly. As Toby dived and swum underwater, Gina turned in circles to make sure he didn't sneak up on her. She giggled in hoots that echoed in the river valley.

All at once Toby surfaced like an explosion! He held a large fish above his head. It wiggled and fought to free itself, but Toby had such a strong grip on it that the fish wasn't going to see water ever again!

They were back on shore in a flash. Toby used the knife to prepare the fish. He had it cut up and on sticks near the fire in a matter of minutes. They watched the fish cook and turned it periodically, their mouths watering. Only after the fish was ready and they were blowing on it to cool it down did they realize that they were sitting on the beach naked!

Both Gina's and Toby's eyes were glued to each other's as they chewed on the fish. They ate silently and looked only at each other's face. When they both finished the last of the meal and sucked clean each finger, Toby spoke in a husky voice: "I think I'll, uh, wash off in the river." Since there was little pretense left at that point, he pulled Gina up to stand against him.

Awhile later they were brushing sand off of their bodies, holding hands, and walking to the river's edge. They walked into the river and stood kissing in the waist deep water.

"Toby, you're shoulders are *very* red. You should get in the shade. It's too hot to be out here." He looked at himself and nodded.

"I'll be right along," she said and swam a few laps.

Toby rested under the shade of the blanket. Gina was walking towards the shoreline and wiping the water from her eyes when she looked up and realized that they weren't alone!

◊ ◊ ◊

# 48

## ~trader Toby by a nose~

"Toobeee." Gina's voice kept its normal tone, but carried a warning. Toby opened his eyes and sat forward quickly. He followed Gina's gaze and saw an old Indian man, smiling and nodding. Beside him stood two Indian girls; one was about Toby's age and the other was maybe ten years old. They reminded Toby of his own sisters near that age. The girls were silent. Their dark eyes seemed void of any expression.

Toby grabbed for his pants and pulled them on. "Toby?" Gina pointed to her dress on the ground. He picked it up and backed over to her, keeping his eyes on the Indians. He handed the dress to Gina and she walked behind him as she pulled it on. When he figured she'd had enough time to get dressed, he stepped towards the Indians. They didn't move an inch. The old man continued to smile and held up a hand, as a sign of greeting. Toby's eyes searched the woods behind them. They seemed peaceful enough, but he was suspicious of the trio.

Gina approached them first, leaving Toby to watch the area. She smiled and looked at the girls. The smaller one leaned against her sister in shyness. The older one stood her ground and didn't move.

The old man continued to nod and grin. He showed both of his open hands in a gesture of "open trust." He looked to the fire and the second half of the cooked fish that had been forgotten. Gina understood his hungry look and saw the same famished stare on the girls' faces. She motioned them to approach the fire and help themselves, which they did!

The old man opened a leather pouch and held out a handful of hickory nuts. Gina nodded and took them. She and Toby took turns cracking them open between the knife handle and a rock. They tasted great! Even though they were from last season, they didn't have the moldy taste that nuts got from being on the ground all winter.

Toby suddenly sat up straight when he saw a dog at the edge of their camp. He nudged Gina. It was a mangy looking rag-of-a-dog with more hunger than trouble in its eyes. It crept into the camp and sat to the side of the Indians. When the old man looked at it he curled his lip and shook his head. The older girl gave a piece of her fish to the dog. Then she picked up the remains of the fish and held it up to toss to the dog. All that remained was the tail, the bones, and the head.

She was about to throw it when the old man's hand caught her hand. He gave her a stern look and took the fish carcass from her. He held it out to Gina, offering it to her first! She leaned back and shook her head. Then he offered it to Toby and pointed at the fish's eyes! Toby also declined. The man gave a slight nod and used his thumb to press each eye loose. He bit into them and chewed each one. Then he casually tossed the bones to the dog, which caught the fish remains and went to the shade to eat.

They sat around the fire and used hand signals and drawings to communicate. With a sweep of his hand to level the sand, the old Indian drew stick figures in it. One was a man, and the other—with two cones on its chest—had to be a woman. He pointed to the figure of the man and then poked his thumb into his chest. Gina nodded. Then he drew another pair of figures below the first and a line to connect them. Gina nodded again, understanding that these were his children.

Beneath the last two figures, the Indian drew another pair of smaller figures, each with cones on their chests. He pointed the stick at the girls beside him. "I think he's saying the girls are his granddaughters," Gina said and smiled at the girls. The older one flashed Gina a quick smile.

Gina thumbed her own chest, and said, "Gina. Gee-na." The old man repeated the sound until he had it mostly right. Gina turned to the girls and said it again. They each took a turn and got it close enough. Then Gina pointed at Toby, saying his name and repeating the process.

The man thumbed his chest and said something that sounded like "Yeah-NO! *Oh good!*, Toby thought, *Yeah-no!* The Indian introduced the girls with the same indifference that he'd shown the dog. It took some time to understand, but the older girl's name sounded like Jaynee. The little one tried to communicate her name, but Toby couldn't pronounce it. Finally the girl touched the red on Gina's dress, rubbed her chest, and pointed to the sky while flapping her hands. They realized she was talking about a bird. Gina's best guess at her name was Robin.

"Yeah-no, Jaynee, and Robin!" Gina repeated the names all around and soon they were being used to address each other. Yeah-no showed them sack full of flint pieces. "That must be a tidy sum," Toby said to Gina as he looked through the stones.

Yeah-no suddenly let out a yelp when he saw the mountain cat's skin rolled up on the ground under their blanket tent. Gina and Toby had been using it as a pillow. The Indian crawled on his hands and knees and looked at it closely. He made a motion, asking for permission to touch it. When Toby nodded, he picked it up and pulled at the paws. He mumbled at the claws, fondling each one. The girls made a clicking sound and looked at the claws. "Grandpa" said something that hushed the girls instantly. They reverted back to their blank stares.

Gina looked at Toby and shot a distasteful look at the back of the old man.

When he returned to his seat near the fire he was still holding the pelt. Yeah-no studied the claws, testing each one in his fingers. He looked at Toby and Gina, and then pointed to the pelt. He pointed to Toby, hammered his fist on his own chest and pointed back to Toby.

"What's he saying, Gina?" Toby asked. Yeah-no was clearly excited about the pelt.

"I think he thinks you killed it," Gina said.

"*Oh!* I guess it *does* look like that's what he's saying." Toby looked at Yeah-no and shook his head. The Indian looked surprised and looked at Gina. She quickly shook her head. Toby tried to indicate that another Indian had killed it and given it to them, but Toby tired of trying to tell the story with hand signals.

Yeah-no seemed to understand that the pelt was not a trophy for the killer and began trying to bargain for it. Both Toby and Gina shook their heads adamantly, declining his offer.

Again, Yeah-no pointed at the cat's claws and then at Jaynee and Robin.

Suddenly Gina understood. "Toby! He wants to trade the claws for the girls!" Toby shot her a look that said, "That's crazy!"

Gina spoke up quickly before Toby could say a word. "Look Toby, before you say anything, did you notice the way he treats them? Like dogs! I remember Lew telling a story once about how Indian girls are considered less valuable than dogs." Toby was looking at her skeptically. "Please listen to me!" she said, gripping his arm tightly. "I know what that's like—to be treated that way. Trade him. Please, Toby." she trailed off, but her eyes pleaded with him.

"What are we going to *do* with them?" Toby asked quietly.

"They're *children*, not *dogs*!"Gina said. "We don't *do anything* with them. We'd *take care* of them!"

They argued for awhile longer, but Gina was persistent. In the end, her logic won out. Toby thought of his sisters being in the same situation and that mental image turned the tide. Toby signaled to Yeah-no that they were willing to trade. The whole process took half an hour and was filled with lots of hand signals while Gina interpreted for Toby.

When the trading was nearly over, there was another loud crash in the woods. Jaynee and Robin looked at each other. Yeah-no said something to the girls. They quickly spun around and walked silently into the woods. One of them picked up a stick and the other a rock. The older one clicked her tongue and the dog followed them.

Toby realized that all three of them—the two girls and the dog—were now his responsibility. They had traded a claw for each of them. *Cripe!*, Toby thought, wondering what he'd gotten himself into.

There was a sudden rash of barking and sounds of thumping in the woods.

The old Indian's lips curled. Without turning, he watched Toby's and Gina's expressions as the girls returned from the dark woods into the daylight. The older one carried a five-foot long rattlesnake as big around as her thigh! It was dead. Toby and Gina shuddered as they looked from the snake to each other. The dog sniffed at part of the dangling snake and wagged its tale. It seemed pleased to have helped kill it.

The kill had a cost for the pair now—another claw! Toby grudgingly cut another one from the pelt and handed it over to the old Indian. Yeah-no took it and left without a glance at the children or dog.

"Another pig!" Gina snarled. "He'll probably use the claws to trade for whiskey, the pig!" She turned to the girls and watched them. Without a word, Jaynee and Robin laid the snake out on the log that Toby and Gina had sat on earlier. The little one went down to the river's edge and returned with a shell. She used her teeth to break off a chip of the shell. They were about to use it to skin the snake when Gina tossed the knife in their direction. The point landed in a log not far from the older girl.

"Nice throw!" Toby said. "Pure luck, though!" He smirked at Gina's smugness.

Gina smiled at him and said in a whisper, "Yeah, but they don't need to know that!"

Jaynee looked at Gina with wide eyes of respect. She nodded and pulled the knife from the log. She moved it around in her hands a few times, getting a feel for its weight and heft, and then proceeded to skin the snake.

Toby wondered what he was going to do with this growing band of women—and a dog! He wiped his face in a tired fashion. When the girls began to chatter, he sighed and went to the water's edge. It wasn't long before the dog was sitting beside him, nuzzling his hand with its wet nose. Toby petted the dog and noticed it was a male. *At least* he'll *be on my side!,* Toby thought.

◊ ◊ ◊

# 49

## ~four too many~

Toby watched the girls working away at the snake. They peeled off the skin, carefully cutting the rattles last. The skin was now about eight to ten inches wide at the middle of its length, and nearly as tall as Toby! The girls fed the snake's innards to the dog and then carefully cut the meat into sections about the size of the smallest girl's fist. They skewered them on cooking sticks, as Gina diced several sections and put them in the iron pot to boil.

Robin walked to the edge of the woods and was about to start in when Gina whoa'd her. Robin looked at Gina with those large dark eyes, as if Gina were stupid. Then Robin clucked her tongue at the dog, which rose and followed her, wagging its tail.

Gina looked at Toby as if he was supposed to say something to Robin, but he just looked at Gina and smiled. Jaynee had only given a glance to the event and went back to preparing the snake meat. Ever so slowly, the older girl cooked the meat; it showed no signs of burning and began to turn an even-tanned color.

Robin returned with a large handful of muck and leaves. She went to her sister and showed her the mess. Jaynee nodded her head towards the snake skin. Robin rubbed a thin layer of muck across the entire skin and then placed leaves along the length of the hide. Jaynee joined her and together they tightly rolled up the skin.

The sun had crossed the v-shape of the valley and was now over the western edge of the ridge above them. They would be in the shade for the rest of the day. Toby felt a shiver on his sunburn and put on his shirt. The temperature dropped and the air finally reached a comfortable level. They heard the sound of another snake dropping out of a tree to the ground. Before Gina and Toby could say anything, the girls and the dog dashed silently back into the woods.

There was another round of barking and club pounding. The girls smiled as they emerged. Another rattlesnake: just shorter than the first, but thicker! They had no sooner placed it on the log to start the skinning process when a large limb in the woods creaked and cracked. Without a sound, the girls ran silently into the woods again. They didn't need to tell the dog a thing this time; it was on their heels, tail wagging furiously.

Toby and Gina worked on the fresh snake, imitating what the girls had done with the last one. Two hours later, their collective efforts showed four rolled skins, all treated in the muck and leaves, and sitting neatly on the log. The girls built a different fire with sticks laced together to hold the meat over smoking leaves.

Toby and Gina were the only ones that had spoken during the entire event. They talked to each other and Gina praised the girls each time they returned. She was like a worried mother every time the girls went into the woods. Toby also worried, but he sensed that the girls were too experienced—and fearless— to try to stop.

It seemed that the noises ceased when the temperature dropped a little lower. Toby thought about the girls for awhile. Most kids would have been too tired or bored here in the wilderness, but they seemed to realize that they had to take advantage of opportunities like this afternoon had presented if they wanted to keep a supply of food on hand.

Gina made everybody go to the river and wash thoroughly before they sat in a circle to eat some of the slow-cooked snake meat. Toby had whittled some makeshift forks from the driftwood and they each had one to use—according to Gina's new rules.

Toby smiled as Jaynee served him first and then Gina. The girls sat with downcast eyes, waiting for the older two to finish eating. Gina wouldn't have it! She motioned them to the fireside to join her and Toby. They reluctantly seated themselves. When Gina offered them food, they shook their heads at first. But with more prodding, they were all eating together. Gina's kindness drew the girls out of their shells, and Toby clowned with the meat, wiggling it on the stick to make it seem alive and then biting at it as it slithered past his face. This made the girls shriek with laughter. Robin imitated him until the snake meat dropped into the sand. She quickly snatched it up and looked terrified until they all laughed again. She wiped the sand off the meat and popped it into her mouth.

There was more than enough for them to eat, and the dog seemed full of the four treats he'd been fed. The young girls even leaned back with the "adults" to relax after the meal. Little Robin crossed her legs at the ankles and laced her fingers behind her head to imitate Toby. Gina tried to converse with Jaynee through sign language. Toby shook his head and wondered why women didn't appreciate the silence of the river, a full stomach, and the smell of the woods.

It grew steadily darker. When it was near dusk, the girls pushed sand around in pockets large enough to lie in near the smoking fire. Toby watched the process, seeing how they had been taught to cover the coals of the fire with sand to stay warm. They were truly masters of their surroundings. They needed nothing except what they had at hand. He thought of how Bea was the same. He wondered about the girls' thin deerskin skirts, though. How warm could they be?

But Gina would have no part of this; she wanted everybody in the boat! Everyone except the dog, that is. He could stand guard. Jaynee tried try to convince her that it was better by the fire, but quickly deferred to Gina as her elder. Toby noticed the longing looks that Jaynee gave the warm sand pockets as she lowered her head onto the blankets Gina had put in the boat for them. The little one made a short walk to the edge of the water and squatted. She gave Toby a glance without embarrassment, then rose and went back to her spot in the boat.

Gina and Toby sat looking at the fire and the stars, but also at the wood line. The dog sat nearby and opened one eye whenever there was movement nearby. "Oh, Toby, they are so sweet—and smart! Did you see...." Gina's voice softly mingled with the crackling of the fire and Toby didn't hear a word. He was still sorting out the day on his own and wondering what tomorrow would bring. But every time he'd wondered that before, the next day always brought a surprise.

"...and then did you see when Robin kept shaking the snake's rattle?" Gina's soft drone continued.

Toby just gave a little wag of his head, a shrug, or a nod—whichever seemed appropriate as Gina talked.

◊ ◊ ◊

# 50

~a river cat~

The morning came with a little fog and lots of shivering. Toby was the first to wake and fed more driftwood to the fire. It wasn't long before a nice blaze burned and he was warm. The dog sat beside him and seemed to enjoy the heat, too.

Jaynee woke next. After a quick trip to the river's edge, she came to the fire and rubbed her arms to warm up. As she squatted near the fire, she smiled at Toby and stared into the flames. Every so often she glanced towards the boat and seemed concerned about Robin and Gina.

Toby noticed this and shrugged his shoulders at her. She held her fingers to her mouth, as if telling him to keep quiet. *It's going to be a long day*, Toby thought as he stroked the dog's neck and smiled at Jaynee. Toby patted his own stomach and looked to Jaynee. She nodded and went to the rock where they'd placed the meat the night before. She opened the cloth cover that Gina had used to protect the smoked snake meat and took out a large piece. She returned to Toby and held it out as an offering.

Toby accepted it and then pointed to her. She didn't seem to understand and just gave him one of her large-eye looks. He reached over and lightly poked her in the stomach and pointed to the rock. She looked at the boat and then back to Toby as he motioned for her to get a piece of snake meat for herself.

She tentatively looked at the rock and back. Toby kept nodding to her until she finally went and retrieved a very small piece. When she returned to the fire, Toby reached for her hand and she looked at him, terrified. He smiled and shook his head. He motioned for her to go back and get another one. She looked puzzled. Toby finally went to the rock and got the biggest piece he could find. He came back and offered it to her. Her eyes were wide with surprise as she slowly took it from him. They squatted again and she waited for him to eat. As he chewed he noticed that she still hesitated. Again, he urged her to eat.

When she fully understood what he meant, she was like a child doing something wrong. She hunched over the food and took sizeable bites, all the while glancing at the boat to see if she was getting away without being caught.

They ate silently and grinned at each other. The two conspirators enjoyed the breakfast and their quiet company. A fish jumped out of the water, probably after a flying bug for breakfast, and birds sang in the woods. Jaynee's dark, calculating eyes watched the river for more fish overtop of her snake meat.

When a stirring sound came from the boat, Jaynee popped the last of the meat into her mouth and chewed vigorously. She gave Toby another sheepish smile. Toby winked and watched as Robin was the next to join the "meat thieves." Toby greeted her with a nod and a smile. Robin, too shy to respond, stood behind her sister. Jaynee reached behind her and pulled Robin around so she could warm herself by the fire. Toby gave Jaynee an upwards nod towards the meat. She rose and returned with a piece of meat for Robin. The little one looked at Toby before she accepted it, but did so quickly when Toby patted his stomach and pointed to hers.

Both of them were licking their fingers clean when Toby stood and raided the sack again. He returned with three more pieces and passed them around. The Indian girls were amazed; they spoke to each other in whispers, but didn't miss a beat in chewing the food. They beamed at Toby as he held his stomach and rolled his eyes.

The girls didn't miss a sound coming from the woods either; sometimes they turned their heads in unison at one noise, and then equally ignored another. Toby was impressed with their ability to think together in silence. He wondered if it was a talent that you could develop with another person, this type of nonverbal communication. He hoped it was, and he hoped he could learn to join in with them someday.

It was going to be a cloudy day, but the heat began to reach the sandbar. It was still just the first hour of full daylight, but Toby began to pace the shoreline hoping to see a sign of a barge coming downriver. *They should have been here yesterday!*, Toby thought. He circled towards the boat and took a quick look inside; Gina was still fast asleep. He saw the gleam of drool on her chin. Toby smiled and turned back to watch the river.

The girls were walking the shoreline about thirty feet downstream. They stepped silently from rock to rock. Toby stopped to watch them as they moved in a circle. They were closing in on something. Before he could figure out what the target was, Jaynee was on her knees in the water with a stranglehold on the victim. There was some struggle and Robin was in the water also. They pulled and tugged, getting soaked and muddy, but Jaynee finally had a grip on whatever it was and started to drag it to shore. Robin seemed to have the tail end and followed her sister.

By the time Toby jogged over to see what was going on, the girls had a three-foot river catfish pinned to the sandy beach. Toby offered to grab the head and hold it when Jaynee shook her head sternly! She loosened her grip slightly, and with her index finger pointed to the barb on the fish's jaw. It was a nasty looking thing! A spear from that barb would leave you with an extremely painful hand for days. With Jaynee's approval Toby picked up a rock and hit the fish; it took several whacks to do more than just stun the large fish. The commotion woke Gina and she sat watching from the boat. She smiled and looked like she'd had happy dreams.

With the same skill that the girls had used on the snakes, they had the fish cleaned, splayed, and ready for smoking. The dog was also very happy. He was now full of the fish's innards and sat licking himself. Gina came out from a visit behind the rock and approached the morning meal. With a mocking pout, she said, "It looks like I've been replaced." The girls smiled at her and received her praises without understanding a word.

The girls smoked the fish over the fire and the dog slept off to the side. Toby watched upstream with a growing sense of dread.

◊ ◊ ◊

# 51

## ~appear and disappear~

It was midday and there was still no sign of the barge. Ella was a day late and Gina was starting to share Toby's concerns. "We could wait until dusk and row upstream to the Landin'," Gina remarked.

"Ella told us to wait here. She said they'd be along," Toby replied. "I think we should follow her directions. I know it's been a day, but maybe they had some other things they had to do. Or maybe Ernie isn't as strong as he felt before!"

"Do you think Stefan will be with them?"

Toby shook his head and shrugged.

"Well, we should do something, don't you think?"

"Not yet," Toby answered. "I think that Ella will do just as she said. When they're loaded and ready, they'll be here." Toby took Gina's hand and squeezed it. "Gina, *nobody* is more eager than me to head downstream. I miss my mum and sisters." He turned and sat on the boat's seat. Gina joined him, with her back to the river.

"Toby, I've been wondering, about the girls. I mean, they're *great* out here! We're more of a burden to *them*! They could find food under a rock! But, what's going to happen to them if we take them to Pittsburgh?"

Toby gave her a long look before he responded. "Well, I guess that's something we shoulda talked about before we traded for them!" Toby sounded a little angry, but softened his tone when he saw the hurt look on Gina's face. "I think my mum will make room for everybody, but *we'll* have to make our own way and earn our keep somehow." Toby's eyes shifted to the river upstream.

"I never said she wouldn't…. It's just that, look at the girls. They don't speak English and they're too young to be on their own. We wouldn't be allowed to keep them, as we don't have anything and we're too young ourselves."

Toby nodded in agreement to everything she said. Finally, he said, "We should ask Ella and Ernie about it. I think they'll know what would be the best thing to do."

"Well Toby, I won't leave them," Gina said as though stating a fact. "I mean that *we* shouldn't leave them."

"I agree. That's why I want to ask Ernie and…."

"Toby what if they don't come?"

Toby smiled and looked past Gina. "Then somebody else is running their barges!"

Gina jerked her head around to look over her shoulder and saw the three barges that Toby had been watching all along.

"You!" She stood and swatted at his shoulder. Another miss! She used her hand to shade her eyes from the sun and looked at the people on the barges. Ella waved. Gina returned the wave and scanned the barges for Ernie. "Toby, where's Ernie?"

"I can't see him," he said.

When Toby turned and looked for the girls, they were gone! The dog had also disappeared, but the fish smoked quietly on the wooden rack. Gina realized that the girls were missing and quickly walked to the woods and called their names. She waited and called several more times. There was no answer.

The barges pulled closer and dropped anchors. As the men tied the crafts together, the barges moved back and forth in the water like a large serpent. Toby rowed the boat out and met with them as Gina paced back and forth calling the girls' names.     As Toby rowed Ella back to the shore he said, "I think there's a language problem!" Ella furrowed her brow and waited for an explanation.

Gina turned and came to the boat. "Toby! They're gone!"

He stepped from the boat and whistled into the woods.

Gina told Ella the story of the Indian girls and watched as Toby paced back and forth, calling the girls.

◊ ◊ ◊

# 52

~river musings~

Toby turned from the wood line and looked around. In the sand he saw small footprints leading to the rear of the two rocks. He followed them and crouched down behind the rocks. The two girls were there with the dog.

Jaynee and Robin looked at Toby with fear in their eyes. He curled a finger at them, beckoning them to step out from behind the rock. When they didn't obey, he repeated the gesture. He saw more fear in their eyes. He was puzzled, but getting impatient: It was time for them to listen to him!

This time he motioned to a spot beside him with pointed determination. Jaynee rose slowly and moved forward. Robin followed her, tears sliding down her face. The dog had quit wagging its tail and followed them.

The girls lagged behind Toby as he approached Gina and Ella. When he looked at Ella's face he saw her glaring sternly at the Indians. Gina asked Ella what was going on.

"Oh, you've got yourselves a pair there!" Ella spoke without taking her eyes off the girls or her hands off her hips.

"What are you saying?" Gina asked with astonishment.

"They're a pair! Got Ernie and me for some pelts, cheese, tobacco, and whiskey!"

"What?" Toby asked.

Gina stared at Ella, who kept her eyes on the guilty pair.

"You two need to understand. These people only steal! They came around—with an old man, and that cur dog. Helped out with some work at the shack, seemed like they were good people, but as I was working with the girls, the old man helped himself to things in the cabin."

Robin started to pee, making a wet spot in the sand. She held Jaynee's hand in a white-knuckled grip. Jaynee was visibly shaking, as well.

Gina interrupted Ella. "That terrible ol' man treated them like dogs—no!—worse! They've been catching snakes, skinning them, and—AND treating the hides! They just caught a big fish this morning and they even smoked it! We'd still be hungry if they hadn't caught us food!" Gina went to Robin and hugged her.

Toby nodded to Ella, and said, "They are a pretty helpful pair."

"Well, look to your belongings an' see what's missing," Ella said.

Toby checked the front of the boat and then looked across the campsite. His eyes surveyed the entire area and his expression changed. "Gina, the snake skins are gone. And so's the mountain lion skin," Toby finally said with disappointment.

Gina turned Jaynee around to face her. The girl kept her eyes to the ground, as did her little sister. Toby and Gina were crushed.

"Toby, take the boat out to the second barge and bring in the man named Pete," Ella said.

In the seven minutes it took Toby to get Pete, none of the women or girls moved. Toby and Pete strode up behind the group. Without turning, Ella said, "Pete, tell these two little thieves that I'm going to give them to you and the others for fun, if they don't return the goods they stole."

Pete spoke several Indian phrases. There was nothing in the cadence of the language that sounded similar to an English sentence. But Pete clearly relayed the message; the girls' faces twisted into looks of anguish. Ella raised an arm and pointed to the woods. Jaynee turned and whistled to the trees. After several minutes the old man appeared, carrying the pelt and skins.

Ella understood that Toby and Gina felt the same betrayal she herself had felt. She spoke tenderly to Gina. "You have to understand it: They simply don't have the same sense of trade. The old man has taught them to steal and they don't know better. He will take all he can from them, too, using them and giving back nothing. It's probably the way he was treated," Ella said, looking between Toby and Gina. "It's just a continuation of their cheating bad habits. Don't you see? They'll always disappoint you, and it's only 'cause they were taught to." She put her hands on Toby's and Gina's shoulders and said in a firmer voice: "Don't get me wrong. It's not all Indians. It's just this bunch."

Gina refused to abandon her faith in the girls, but she was furious with Yeah-no. She went to the old man, took the pelt and snake skins, and carried them to the boat. Then she took the whip from the boat and walked to face the Indian man. He stood frozen, his eyes glued to the leather snake that Gina held. Without a word, Gina shook the whip, raised her arm, and lashed out.

Yeah-no yelped and covered his face, expecting another lash. Gina obliged him and struck twice more! He whimpered and backed up one step at a time. Gina's anger wasn't abated; she turned and put her face inches from Jaynee's. The girl looked at her without emotion; she would take anything Gina served, but Gina was looking for a sign of remorse. It took a long moment, but the girl finally dropped to one knee. Robin followed suit, and they didn't move.

"Ella, I won't abandon them. I won't! They're just what *he's* taught them to be. I can teach them another way. I know I can!" Gina looked at Ella and then to Toby. He refused to be the first one to answer her and gave her a skeptical look instead. He didn't want to make a decision yet, but wanted Ella to convince Gina that she was wrong.

Ella spoke hesitantly. "I believe you will, Gina. But...don't you think it's going to be just a bit difficult for you and Toby?"

Gina's eyes slid to Toby and he looked at her long and hard. "Ella's right," he said. "It's hard to hear, but it's a hard truth. We'll have to watch every move they make, at least for awhile. Do you really want to make that part of your duties? Part of our life?"

Gina listened to the two people she trusted most in her life and knew that they wouldn't lie to her. But that didn't change her mind about the girls. "I won't leave them with that pig! I can't. I'll stay here and go with them before I leave them with *him*. Toby, it's like what I had to do on the farm. No girls should have to live that way! They'll be *my* problem—I promise! And I won't hesitate to use the whip!" She flashed it before the two kneeling children and Robin whimpered.

They finally agreed to take the girls with them. Pete said one final thing to Jaynee and Robin in their own language. It sounded like a harsh admonishment, and the girls nodded in agreement. Both of them had tears streaming down their faces.

They gathered their belongings and put everybody in the boat. Toby pulled hard at the oars and finally asked Pete what he'd said to the girls.

"I tol' them that they owed their lives to you both," he said as Toby turned the rowboat against the barge and Pete tied it off.

The girls huddled together tightly on the second barge as Toby and Gina walked around. They stopped to pet Bea, who now seemed calm about being on the boat and happy to see them. Ella and Pete told them what to do as they helped with the barges' progress downstream.

Toby was steering the rudder of the second barge and was instructed to keep it centered on the back of the lead barge that Pete was steering. Ella commanded the last barge, keeping it directly behind Toby's.

The centers of the barges were stacked shoulder-high with goods such as barrels of whiskey, sacks of grains, large bales of dyed wool, bundles of hickory wheel spokes, and wooden handles for things like shovels, hammers, and picks. Bea stood near the front of the barge on a short tether, penned in by the bales of wool. Gina stood by Bea and occasionally shot stern looks at the huddled girls. Toby thought about how he wouldn't want to be on the receiving end of one of those looks.

After the first hour, Toby had Gina bring him a small barrel to sit on. He was soon leaning over the rudder, half-asleep. It was warm, and the sun's rays magnified his drowsiness. Whenever he nodded off, Gina came up behind him and playfully kicked the barrel and laughed when he jumped. He couldn't reach her, but he swung behind his back, making wide backhanded swats in the air. She smiled at him with a proud look.

She shifted her eyes to the girls. She and Toby had decided to let them "suffer" for awhile by making them sit in silence. Toby considered stealing a personal affront, but in the frontier it could mean life or death. He thought again of Jerry's story about thieves' ears being cut off, and the girls needed to learn that stealing was wrong—and dangerous!

As they drifted down the river, Toby spent some time thinking about what he might have to face when he got back to Pittsburgh. Would people believe the truth about the whipping of the other boy? Would Toby be whipped as punishment? He thought of his sunburned back and cringed at the thought of the whip striking it. Toby's mind drifted back over the past few weeks. How long had he been traveling now? Was it five or six weeks? So many things had happened! And compared to some of them, a beating wouldn't be all that bad.

But what if they decided to jail him? Who would take care of his mother and sisters? And Gina? And now Jaynee and Robin! That was a lot of women to take care of!

The river's main flow was slow and it took the rest of the day's light to get to West Monterey. There was a long, slow bend in the river and then another one curving to the left. It was just dusk as they made the last curve. Toby could make out several buildings on the multi-tiered ground of the riverbank. There was one large building that was painted the same dull red color of the warehouse back at the Landing.

When Toby looked over the barge's load to Pete, he saw him working the front rudder hard to guide his barge towards the side of the river. A stone pier jutted out about sixteen feet into the water. The top of the pier was even with the deck of the barges. Toby concentrated and made what he thought were the right pulls on the rudder and smoothly followed Pete in. They were about a hundred yards out. Toby looked back to Ella and watched her grim face as she deftly worked her end of the wooden "snake" towards shore.

Toby began to wonder how they were going to stop. He glanced quickly from Ella to Pete while minding his steering. Pete was closing in and the dock was only thirty yards away! Toby was standing now and pushed away the barrel because it blocked his footing. Gina grabbed the barrel out of his way and also began to wonder how they'd stop. "Better get to Bea," Toby said without looking at her.

Gina stepped around the girls and held Bea's head. Jaynee and Robin peered around the load at the shoreline. There was a fire built on the shore. As Toby got closer he could see a woman standing behind the fire. He looked closer. NO! The woman was tied to a pole directly behind the fire!

◊ ◊ ◊

# 53

## ~frozen in time~

Toby saw Pete looking at the woman, too. He looked back at Ella and saw her turning the barge away from the shore and holding an anchor on a chain. With one more look to the shoreline, she tossed the anchor. Toby felt the barge line tighten first from her barge to his, and then from his barge to Pete's. Pete was now the dangling end of the three barges. At the last moment, Pete pulled hard on the fore rudder and swung the first barge away from the shoreline. He picked up his anchor and was about to toss it when there was a rifle shot!

Toby ducked. Gina screamed and went to the girls; they crawled behind a barrel and were safe—for the moment! Ella knelt down and peered at the darkened shore. Toby looked back to Pete and saw him still holding the anchor and slowly tipping over the side of the barge into the water.

"Toby!" It was Ella's voice. "Under the oilskin in front of you, there's a rifle—use it!" Toby crawled on his hands and knees, threw back the oilskin, and found the rifle. *What the hell do I know about guns?,* Toby thought. *I've never fired one in my life!*

Gina was the next to speak: "Toby, just cock the hammer, aim, then fire!"

He followed her directions, but when he aimed, he realized that the target was nowhere in sight. He closely watched the shadows and looked for any movement. He searched the area just outside of the fire's light. He turned his head to where Pete had been and tried to remember where in his peripheral vision he had seen the flash. He pointed the gun to that area.

Toby could just see Ella's form. She aimed a rifle at the same spot. "Who are you? What do you WANT?" Ella demanded in a harsh voice. Toby waited for a response, waiting to close his sights on a target. Again Ella yelled: "What do you want? Eula! Can you hear me?"

The woman tied to the stake lifted her head and nodded without saying a word.

Toby tried to watch the front barge and keep an eye out for a target at the same time. He saw Bea swing in a short circle, stepping in a nervous dance. "Easy, Bea," Toby said in as calm a voice as he could muster.

"The GIRL! And the gold!" The reply came from the darkness as Toby was looking at Bea. He missed the opportunity to fine-tune his aim on the location of the shooter.

"What!?!" Ella's voice rang out again. Toby was about to tell her what the man had said when he realized she was baiting him

"The GIRL!" the voice replied.

"LUKE?" Ella shouted. "What the hell do you think you're doin'!?!"

"Send Gina in, with the gold, and we'll leave the rest of you alone! Or we'll sit here and practice shootin'. Whaddya think? A shot through one of them whiskey barrels? That should give you a good fire to see by."

Toby thought he could pinpoint the source of the voice. *You slimy bastard!*, he thought. He looked at Gina, who seemed angry and frightened.He noticed Jaynee staring at him. Jaynee gave Toby an up-nod of her head. Her hands, which had been hugging Gina and Robin, fell to her sides. Toby wondered what that was about when Jaynee whispered something to Robin, rolled to the side of the barge, and slipped into the water. Toby was shocked and puzzled at her behavior. Gina called to Jaynee, but she was gone. Gina hugged Robin and kept looking back and forth from the shore to Toby.

Eula was heaving her chest and fighting to get loose. The fire crackled and rose higher. Toby realized why Eula was struggling—she was close enough to the fire to be burned!

"Maybe you need ANOTHER lesson!" said another man's voice. It was Lucca.

"DAMN IT!" Toby said out loud. He looked at Gina. Her eyes were huge with terror.

Toby looked back at Bea. Her ears perked up and she swished her tail, still doing a nervous dance. Bea was looking directly back at Toby when the musket ball hit her behind the jawbone. Without blinking, the mule's knees buckled and she dropped straight to the deck of the barge.

Toby screamed, "I'LL KILL YOU! BOTH OF YOU!" Tears filled his eyes, and something he hadn't felt since he whipped the thief in Pittsburgh welled up in his chest. Toby nestled the heavy barrel of the gun into one of the feed sacks and waited to fire. He squinted hard to force out the tears.

All at once Gina stood and held her hands out to her sides. "I'll come! Leave the rest of them alone!" Before Toby could say anything to her, she stepped around the bales and barrels to the shore side of the barge.

"Gina, get back!" Ella shouted. "Get down! They'll kill you!"

"No, they just want their slave back." Gina stood without moving.

At that moment, little Robin darted to the same side of the barge and stood beside Gina.

"Look Luke, we get two for one!" Lucca said. Ella fired a shot at the source of the sound. There was a groan and the sound of someone falling to the ground.

"Pa!" Luke called. "Pa!"

Little Robin did something that no one expected. With one fluid movement she pulled the leather tunic up over her head, dropped it to the ground, and stood naked facing the dock area! She wiggled her naked little body in a sort of dance.

Ella was reloading her rifle and looking into the darkness.

"She's next to die!" Luke screamed. Toby fired his rifle in the direction of the threat.

There was a garbled noise, like the sound of someone trying to scream with a mouthful of water. Then everything went quiet.

The barge passengers saw Jaynee step into the firelight. Her hands and arms were covered with blood and she held a knife that dripped fresh blood. She went to Eula and cut her loose before collapsing to the ground. Eula gathered up the Indian girl and staggered to carry her away from the fire.

Toby saw Gina reach down to her thigh and grope through the dress's fabric; all she felt was the empty knife sheath. She was astonished when she realized that Jaynee had stolen her knife before she dove into the water. Gina looked down at Robin and helped the little girl put her tunic back on.

Toby ran past them and fell to his knees in the large pool of blood next to Bea. He lifted the mule's heavy head, only to find Bea's gentle eyes frozen in time.

◊ ◊ ◊

# 54

## ~a vacuum and a badge~

Toby sat in numb silence; his pants were soaked in the mule's blood. He was only slightly aware of things going on around him. He stroked Bea's head and looked into her lifeless eyes. How many times had those eyes looked to him during the past month? The firelight lit up her lifeless gaze, making her look even sadder.

He continued to stroke Bea's head. *It wasn't right!*, Toby thought. A month ago, he was a just boy living safely in his parent's home, teasing his sisters, playing games with his buddies, and waiting for his father to come home from work. Now, his father was dead and Toby had horsewhipped another boy, traveled through the wilderness, gotten lost, gone hungry, survived poisonous snakes, been almost drowned, killed a man, nearly been killed by a mountain cat, and hid from the sheriff's men. All of that and spent time in a woman's arms. And now he'd lost Bea!

He felt Gina's hand touch his shoulder, but he didn't turn. He looked into the glassy eyes of the mule and wanted to cry, but he couldn't. Except for the ache in his gut, he simply felt alone and empty, even though Gina stood behind him and the others were nearby.

He heard a commotion from the front barge and realized that Ella had swum to it and helped put Pete back on board. Then he heard Ernie's voice. *Where had he come from?* Toby turned his head and saw little Robin looking at Bea's lifeless form. She was crying and looked so sad. When she saw Toby looking at her she turned and dove into the river, and then swum to the shore and her sister. He heard another splash and dumbly watched as Ella swam to see what condition Eula and Jaynee were in. Toby's head began to clear some as he realized that he should do something. He paused and shook his head. He wanted rid of it all! *Why had he ended up here like this?* It was as if a large vacuum had brought him to this very moment.

Gina squatted beside him, trying to avoid the blood and trying to get him to say something. Toby pulled away from her touch and ignored her. He continued to stroke Bea's head. The barges were moved closer to the shore and tied off. Gina stepped onto the stone landing. Only then did Toby stir again. He sat and watched the others around the fire, tending to their wounds and sorting out the events. He realized that he had nothing to add to the circle of people at the fire. And he didn't want to abandon Bea.

He sat with her the entire night. The others left him to his grief. Toby watched the stars appear and then finally disappear as the morning light came. He was aware of Gina approaching him twice during the night. He was grateful for her concern, but didn't speak to her.

By morning, his legs were locked in position and it took him some time to lift Bea's stiffened head and neck from his lap. When he made it to his feet, he leaned against the wool bales. It took him awhile to stop looking at the mule's lifeless body and focus on other things around him.

The others were still inside the warehouse and nothing was moving. He walked to the stone dock and then up a grade to the fire. He pushed at some of the unburned wood with the toe of his boot. Sparks flew and hot coals, buried under the ashes, came to life. He stooped and pushed half a dozen pieces of wood into the coals. The fire crackled and began to restore its flames.

He stayed by the fire, warming up and drying out from the early morning fog. He looked at his pants and boots; they were caked with dried blood and dirt, all mixed together in a kind of reddish-brown mud. He didn't want to touch them or clean off the muck. He wanted to wear them forever as a kind of badge or reminder.

Gina and Ella appeared at the doorway of the warehouse and walked to the privy. Toby still didn't feel like talking to anyone, but he knew that things would go on and that he would need to be a part of them. Ella waved to him on her way back, but didn't speak. She went back inside the warehouse, but Gina walked directly to Toby. She smiled tentatively and warmed herself at the fire. The silence hung over them until Toby asked her, "Everybody inside alright?"

Gina nodded. "We were more concerned about you...."

Toby shrugged and stared into the fire.

"If you want to—to change pants, I'll rinse those out, uh, in the river," Gina offered.

He nodded in resignation. He had to wash off the past and start fresh. Gina went to the barge and returned to the fireside with a clean pair of pants. "These were Hattie's husband's," she said. "She gave them to me—to us, before we left." Toby pulled the pocketknife from his pants and handed it to her to hold. Then he pulled off his boots and his pants. Gina took them and walked to the river.

He was dressed again when Jaynee and Robin came out and stood near him in silence. They warmed themselves at the fire, and each made a trip to the woods to answer the call of nature. Jaynee looked up at him and waited for him to look at her. He felt it and looked into her dark brown eyes. He held out an arm and she nearly danced into the embrace. Robin ducked around his other side and nestled up under his other arm. He smiled at each and kissed them on their heads.

Gina returned and hung the pants over the post that Eula had been tied to last night. She smiled at the three of them and started to say something when the others filed out of the warehouse.

◊ ◊ ◊

# 55

~new river folk~

Pete and Ernie walked to the fireside. Pete had a bandage on his head and told Toby that it was from faking his death the night before. He said that he fell into the river on purpose, but hit his head on the anchor in the process. "But it's better'n bein' shot!" Pete said. Toby admitted that he'd been fooled and smiled at the clever stunt.

Pete continued the story: "Then Ernie slipped off the barge to save me. He was keeping quiet to slip up behind those two on shore. I was a goner if'n he'd not put me back onto the barge. I was going to try to get to Eula and cut her loose. But that little one there did a fine job!" He poked Jaynee's stomach and gave her a broad smile. "And, of course, THIS one, too!" He stooped to Robin and held her around the waist. She grinned from ear to ear.

Ernie squatted down and held out his hand to Jaynee. When she tentatively took it, he gave her a handshake and then kissed her hand. He did the same to Robin. "Pete, tell them that they were brave women. And I think Toby should give each one of them a single-claw necklace to prove it."

When the girls heard this, Robin squealed and clapped her hands. It was a big deal for them to wear a claw! Such an honor was usually reserved for the bravest hunters only. Jaynee and Robin were crying happy tears when Gina approached and said, "What's this? You men making my girls cry?"

Ernie filled her in on the awards and Ella called out from the warehouse: "FOOD!"

Toby entered the warehouse for the first time and realized that Pete and Eula shared the back of it as their home. Ernie laughingly called them "the Southern Office of the Channel Cat Trading Company." Over breakfast, Toby learned many things that the others had already discussed.

"To Toby and Gina—and you two little ones!" Ernie said, toasting them with his cup of hot tea. "We'd like you to join us. We decided that you bunch would make terrific river folk! Ella and I have finally put together enough money to buy us boats! Real river boats with steam engines! And then we can come upriver all year long and haul goods *both* ways!" Ernie, Ella, Eula, and Pete all beamed at the "kids" and waited for their response.

Gina was as stunned as Toby was. A dozen thoughts raced through his head in a few seconds: His home was in Pittsburgh! His mother and sisters had to be taken care of...he had to return the cart...and maybe have to pay for losing Bea! But he knew one thing instantly: He couldn't go back and work in a shop after all that he'd gone through! All *they'd* gone through! *And life on the river!*, he thought. He wouldn't have to worry about Gina and the girls, because they'd be on a boat—with him! He looked to Gina and saw how happy she looked at Ernie's offer.

"O'course, if you don't want the job...." Ernie added, winking at Ella. He sipped his tea and waited for one of them to answer.

Toby spoke as he gazed into his cup. "There's some things I have to think about—to make sure of—before I could give you my true—"

Gina interrupted. "*I'll* take it! Count me and the girls in. If this dunderhead doesn't want to share it, he loses!" Gina gave Toby a backhanded swat on the arm (this one connected) and smiled.

The Indian girls looked wide-eyed at Toby, thinking he would strike the woman back for her disrespect. When he started laughing, Robin backhanded her sister's arm, gave a one nod of her head, and put her elbows on the table. She had no idea what was going on, but she knew how to make people laugh.

After breakfast, they laid Bea to rest in the river's bottom. Ernie explained to Toby that "she will always be a part of the river this way." Toby liked that idea. Then the men dug two graves for Luke and Lucca. Toby wanted no part of it. He said that he cared less for those murderous bastards than he did for some of the fish that the girls had caught and cooked.

At the midday meal they decided that this first river trip was early enough in the year that they could probably make four to six round-trips before the fall season. "Maybe more if we're lucky," Ernie said.

They talked about making arrangements to have wood or coal available along the river to power the steam engines. Ernie and Pete discussed the downriver towns that could be used for staging this. They wanted to find people to be traders for them. The traders would also set up trading posts and sell items that the barges hauled north from Pittsburgh.

The men helped to load the barges with the heavy items, but that only took an hour. They spent the rest of the afternoon sitting under a tree, planning the details of the trip, all the while watching the women load everything else.

"O'course, you know we've got to run all these plans by the women and make sure they approve, don'tcha?!" Ernie laughingly told Pete and Toby. Pete nodded his understanding at the statement, but Toby seemed to miss the point.

"Toby, you'll be seeing your mum and sisters in two days!" Ernie said. Toby's heart leapt in his chest, the idea of a hot pie and his own warm bed made him shiver.

Later on, Pete was standing near the open warehouse door, smoking on his pipe and looking at lightning to the north. "You might be seeing your mum a bit sooner than two days, Toby, if that storm drops a lot of rain upriver!" Toby and Ernie went to the door and felt the rush of cool air moving in from the advancing storm. Lightning danced and flashed in the night sky, brightly lighting up the horizon towards the Landing.

Ernie watched one particularly bright flash and began tapping his foot. When he heard the thunder, he stopped. "I count eight," he said to Pete.

"Nine...closer to ten." Pete replied. "That puts her 'bove Foxburg."

"And that better put us past Brady's Bend by dawn," Ernie said. "ELLA! Get the women packed up and on board. Pete, fill up the lanterns and get 'em hung. I'm gonna close up shop."

In half an hour they were all on the barges, with Ella and Ernie on the first, Toby, Gina, and the girls in the middle barge, and Pete and Eula trailing in the third. Toby wondered what it was going to be like on the trip south to Pittsburgh. The air suddenly got colder and the wind blew directly into their faces. Toby put on the heavy coat he'd had since the beginning of the trip, and felt again for the gold coins sewn in the collar. He hoped to be able to give them to his mother and sisters....

"Keep astern of us Toby, we don't want to end up jack-knifed on rocks!" Ella called out. After that he couldn't hear her; the rain arrived in a solid curtain as fat rain drops slammed onto him and the contents of the barge.

Gina had rigged the cart with the oilskin cover again, and it provided cover for her and the girls. Toby sat on a barrel, minding the rudder and feeling the rain soak into his clothes. He could no longer see the front barge or the lights of the last one, just pitch black rain. He wondered how Ernie could find his way ahead. All Toby could do was watch the direction of the line tied to the bow of his barge, and hold his head to allow the rain to run off the brim of his hat –away from his line of vision.

Toby had hoped that the trip home was going to be easier, but now, he wasn't so sure.

*Still,* he thought, *it'll make a good story to tell to somebody—someday…*

◊ ◊ ◊

This ends Toby's first adventure. If you would like to read more about the further adventures of Toby and the gang, go to www.babygrapebooks.com to order the sequels to this story. You simply won't believe them!

◊ ◊ ◊

# Acknowledgements

I think that there are always more people involved in writing a novel than the author can remember. Also, I doubt that anyone could remember all the people who contributed a smile, a gesture, or a word that unwittingly becomes part of a character's makeup. To those people I can only say thank you through the story here.

For those who went before us and lived through the hardships similar to events in this story, I thank with humble respect.

And to the friends, relatives, and avid readers that indulged me through this endeavor, I give my eternal thanks. (I am using first names only for privacy issues.) Thank you to: Vickie, who read each chapter as it was created and offered support all along; Rhonda (for the five stars); Patty (and her encouragement); John (for his early editing); Ron, Penny, and Cori for the time out of their lives to read such a rough draft and offer suggestions. I would also like to thank Sierra for her help with computer problems and file storage and Adam for his technical help, as well.

Professionally, I give my sincere gratitude to: Jennifer McGuiggan from The Word Cellar (www.thewordcellar.com) for her professional editing and proofreading; and to Emily Zuzack for the great artwork she provided for this book and has agreed to provide in the coming sequels. Lastly, I want to thank the people at Media Post Inc. (www.mediapostinc.com) for their great work in creating the animated Baby Grape website: www.babygrapebooks.com.

◊ ◊ ◊

# Author's Bio

Thom Rogers lives in Western Pennsylvania with his dog Annie. In addition to his many other interests, he spends a lot of his time putting together ideas for Toby and the gang's next adventure.

# Artist's Bio

Emily Zuzack grew up in Western Pennsylvania where she spent most of her childhood daydreaming and imagining through pencils and paper. She eventually used her penchant for mental meandering to obtain a Drawing Degree from Edinboro University of Pennsylvania, and hopes to illustrate many more books. You can reach Emily at: emzuzack@gmail.com

Printed in the United States
203196BV00007B/202-231/P